The
Track

GARY LEE VINCENT

Burning Bulb
PUBLISHING

The Track
By **Gary Lee Vincent**

Burning Bulb Publishing
P.O. Box 4721
Bridgeport, WV 26330-4721
United States of America
www.BurningBulbPublishing.com

First Edition.

Paperback Edition ISBN: 978-1-964172-38-5

Dedicated to
my daughter, Amber.

PART ONE:
THE FALL

CHAPTER 1

Thompson Middle School stood on Johnson Avenue in Bridgeport, West Virginia. The Middle School was actually one of a set of three: the Thompson Elementary School stood opposite it across the road, while the similarly-named High School was right next door.

The schools were exactly what a passerby would expect them to be, beehives of academic learning where the young were processed by the old to become upstanding young adult members of society.

That was the aim anyway. As in all ventures that involved humans, there were bound to be both successes and failures, some more glaring than others.

But for the most part, the trinity of Thompson schools did their best to fulfill their academic mission.

Of course, the same couldn't always be said about the students who arrived there every morning to have their heads stuffed with wisdom, and departed each afternoon with their heads supposedly containing that freshly-imparted knowledge.

But children being what they were, there were always going to be kid-made disasters occurring.

CHAPTER 2

Wednesday Morning

"Okay, honey, have a nice day at school," David Harris told his daughter Jess as he dropped her off at Thompson Middle School that morning.

"Okay, Dad."

12-year-old Jessica 'Jess' Harris undid her seatbelt and then leaned over and kissed him on the cheek. But she did it self-consciously, and only because she knew her father expected her to.

Kissing one's parents on the cheek was something *kids* did, for heaven's sake. Most mornings, Jess cringed while performing the daily ritual, but this morning no one was watching her. The drop-off /pickup loop was filled with cars that were each dropping off their own load of boisterous offspring, the parents giving said offspring last-minute instructions to behave themselves.

No one had noticed Jess's hurried peck on her father's cheek. At least she hoped no one had.

The throbbing of the car engine gave Jess a sense of urgency. She felt like things were waiting to be done, and fun was waiting to be had, like every second longer that she spent here in her dad's car was one second longer that she wouldn't be with her friends.

Besides, Daddy would be available at home when she got back there.

"Okay, hon, off you go!" David said with a grin.

After taking a quick inventory to ensure she hadn't left anything behind in the car, Jess opened the car door and got out. She shut the door, turned, and waved back at her father.

"Bye, Dad!"

"Okay, see you in the afternoon."

And then David Harris set the car in motion and drove off.

Jess didn't immediately turn and hurry onto the school campus. Caught amidst a throng of excited youngsters, who surged past her in waves, she watched her father's car depart until two other cars cut off her view of it, and then she turned her attention to the nearby buildings. This morning, due to the high volume of cars in the drop-off/pickup loop that ran past the school, her father had dropped her off about fifty yards from the school entrance, which meant she was standing just a short distance from the entrance to the adjacent high school.

Jess stared enviously at the high school students as they made their way onto their own campus.

Soon, very soon, that'll be me for sure.

Watching the throngs of older boys and girls as they grouped up and laughed their way into the high school, Jess felt herself gripped by the urge to suddenly be older. To her young mind, high school was where it was at. While middle school wasn't exactly bad, the proximity of Thompson High had her constantly aware that she was barely two-thirds of the way through her grade-school education.

Feeling a returning sense of urgency to join the rush of those hurrying to be educated, she turned away from the high school and giggled in the direction of the elementary school opposite.

At least, I'm no longer in elementary. I'm a big girl now.

That gave Jess a feeling of satisfaction and she began walking towards the entrance to the campus, looking around for familiar 7th-grade faces from her own class as she did so.

She saw her friend Tommy Bradley get off a school bus and hurry onto the campus. And then Jess also saw her best friend Mimi Richards getting out of her mom's car.

Jess quickened her steps, and was just in time to wave good morning to Mrs. Richards as she pulled away from the curb.

And then she and Mimi were stepping onto the campus together, and Jess felt like her day had properly begun. There was nothing like your friends to make you feel good about yourself.

"Hey, I found this really cool fashion app," Mimi began telling her enthusiastically, as they went.

"Yeah?" Jess laughed. Because her mother worked in a clothing store, Mimi was obsessed with all things fashionable.

"Yeah, it's really cool," Mimi explained. "Once you sign up, you get your own cool mannikin and you can name her what you like and then dress her up, and if you do a good job at choosing her clothes, you earn points and get better dresses and . . ."

Jess caught the fire of her bestie's enthusiasm and laughed. "Tell me about it during lunchtime," she said and then pointed forward at the school entrance where a portly man sternly surveyed all the young arrivals. "Mr. Hess is watching us. "We'd better hurry to class."

And so, hurry to class they did.

CHAPTER 3

The morning passed in a whirl of mathematics and social sciences and bemused 7th grade faces as they attempted to soak up the basic theory of those concepts that held the human world together.

Jess had a brain for science subjects, but the stuff about government and economics seemed too nebulous to understand.

She grasped the basic ideas easily enough. However, the problem was that too much of the end product of the social sciences—the social upheavals and assassinations, and the way the economic market fluctuated, seemed to depend on human misbehavior.

While Ms. Tomlinson gazed angrily at everyone over the tops of her spectacles and explained why the cost of eggs had risen so high during the Biden administration, Jess sneaked a look across the classroom at Mimi, who looked as confused as everyone in class, a point that was made when Tommy Bradley raised his hand and after being given permission to speak, solemnly said:

"But, Ms. Tomlinson, last week you taught us that the prices of things on the supermarket shelves are determined by supply and demand."

"Yes, that's right," Ms. Tomlinson agreed. "Go on."

Tommy nodded and went on: "So, if eggs cost too much, it has to be because there's a shortage of eggs and there are a lot of people who want eggs."

"Not exactly, but . . ."

Ms. Tomlinson paused to properly formulate her reply, which gave young Tommy Bradley the opportunity to finish presenting his question: "So, Ms., if there's a shortage of eggs, that has to be because there's a shortage of chickens to lay them. Why doesn't the government just stop people from eating so many eggs, so that we'll have more chickens next time around to lay enough eggs for everyone to eat? Or why not raise chickens that lay twice as many eggs?"

While the teacher looked confused by Tommy's reasoning, the boy's question was greeted by nods from all of his young counterparts, Jess included.

It seemed perfectly logical to her that if one needed more eggs, you didn't eat so many, so you had more chickens to lay more eggs for you.

And Jess was just as confused as everyone else in social sciences by Ms. Tomlinson's 15-minute attempt to explain why creating a drop in American egg prices required more than simply doubling the number of American chickens, or hiring Olympic-grade chickens for the job of egg production.

And so it was that the morning passed and lunchtime came.

CHAPTER 4

"I think adults lie a lot," Mary Lindsey, who was also in Jess's class, told Jess and Mimi after school while the trio of them were waiting to go home.

Like several other kids, their trio was seated on one of the two concrete tree enclosures that stood in front of the school building.

"Huh?" Jess said, surprised by the comment.

"What I mean is—" Mary began to explain, but was then interrupted by Mimi saying: "Okay, guys, my mom's here. Gotta go."

"Okay, see you tomorrow," Jess said and watched as Mimi ran across to her mother's blue car, which was just pulling up alongside the campus.

After waving at Mimi's mom and watching them drive away, Jess glanced at her cellphone to see what time it was. She absently wondered when her father would get here to pick her up too. Most days, it was her dad who picked her up, her mom generally being too busy and often too far away to make the afternoon school run.

As for her friend Mary Lindsey, Mary lived just down the road, but she always dutifully waited for her older brother to walk over from the high school next door so that they could walk home together.

After her fleeting check of the time, Jess returned her attention to Mary, who'd apparently been patiently waiting for this to happen.

"I said, I think adults lie a lot," Mary said. Take, for instance, what Ms. Tomlinson told us about the price of eggs this morning. Everyone knows that's wrong. If eggs are expensive because there's a shortage of them, what you need is more chickens to lay them, not that the president is causing any of it."

Jess scratched her scalp. "Yes, I think so too—"

9

"I think adults lie when they don't know what to say, like when we're having a pop quiz. They just make up something that sounds sensible." As if infected by her friend's gesture, Mary scratched her head too. "My mom and dad lie all of the time, and then they punish me when I copy them."

Jess was surprised by this information. "My parents never lie," she told Mary.

This information, in turn, amazed young Mary Lindsey. "They don't?"

Jess shook her head. "Never, that I know of. We go to church regularly, and the preacher always tells us that lying is a bad thing, so no one in our house lies."

"I don't know," Mary said, with a puzzled look on her face. "According to my dad, preachers are the biggest liars of them all." Now, Mary looked really confused. "My dad drinks all the time and he's always fighting with my mom over something and cussing at me and my brother too, and yet he never goes to church, because according to him, he says Christians are dupes and that the preachers are only after the congregation's money, and they'll tell any lie they can to get it."

Both 12-year-old girls mused on this for a while, equally confused.

"Hey, girls!"

Jess snapped out of her confusion and smiled at Barry Lindsey. Just like it did each time she saw him, she felt her young heart beat faster.

Though pubescent, Jess was still too young to understand how meeting Barry Lindsey made her feel.

Barry grinned at Jess and his sister.

"Hey, I see that you're hanging out with the cutest of your friends again."

"Hi, Barry," Jess said and felt herself blushing.

She couldn't help it. Even young as he was, Mary's brother had the air of the quintessential bad boy about him. Jess knew that meeting him affected her in a way that she found uncomfortable, not unpleasant, but just uneasy, because at her age she had no experience in male-female relationships.

She could read in his eyes that he liked her. Maybe he even liked her the way that her father liked her mother.

And of course, Barry was older than she was, and was already in high school. That was a separate attraction, as it made Jess feel older herself.

So, as not to seem too much of a child to him, she cocked her hip and made as sexy a pose as her mind could come up with, which with her diminutive chest also thrust out, would have looked corny to a watching adult, but which, to teenagers whose main idea of romance were PG action movies and romantic comedies, worked just right.

To her satisfaction, Barry's eyes brightened up, like he'd just really noticed her for the first time.

"Wow, Jess, you're really filling out," he said. Then he nodded at his sister. "C'mon, let's go—you know how cranky Mom gets whenever we're late." Then he grinned at Jess. "See you around sometime. Hopefully soon."

Jess nodded demurely back at him and lowered her eyes. With all of the older high school girls around him, she didn't expect Barry Lindsey to ask her out or anything, but she liked the fact that he'd taken notice of her.

If I was older, maybe . . .

Barry and Mary walked off just as Jess noticed her father pulling up to get her.

Still grinning with satisfaction, she walked over to get into her dad's car.

By the time Jess Harris had arrived back at home, all thoughts of Barry Lindsey and of her juvenile attempts to impress him had disappeared from her mind.

But little did Jess Harris know that by attracting Barry Lindsey's attention to herself, she'd just made the biggest mistake of her young life.

CHAPTER 5

Home was where the heart was. Home was different from school.

"Hey, honey, gimme a hand with getting the groceries in," her father told her as they got out of the car.

Jess did so, and after they'd carried everything into the house, David did what he usually did, which was to hand his daughter her mother's shopping checklist.

"Okay, kiddo, you know the drill."

He watched Jess roll her eyes just like her mother did in similar situations.

The 'drill' in question involved Jess matching the groceries that he'd just purchased with his wife's shopping list to ensure he'd not forgotten anything during the supermarket run he'd made before picking up Jess from school.

David got himself a can of Coke from the fridge, leaned against the kitchen counter while opening it up, and watched Jess sorting stuff while he quenched his thirst.

Jess had her mother's dark hair, but she'd gotten both her height and her athletic build from her father. Face-wise, David thought each parent's genes had scored fifty-fifty.

Not sure if that's a bad or a good thing, David mused. *We'll have to wait a few years and see what the young men of her generation think of her looks.*

Observing the serious expression on the girl's face as she picked out each object and matched it against the checklist, David felt an intense paternal satisfaction.

Yep, the kid turned out alright. Willow and I have done a pretty decent job of raising her. She's kind and obedient and . . .

Then he felt some thrill of fear when he realized that technically Jess wasn't a teenager yet and those parent-dreaded years now loomed large on the horizon, but then he calmed himself.

I don't think she's gonna change that much. Well, I hope that she doesn't. I like this calm and well-behaved version of her.

He finished his drink and tapped the can on the kitchen counter to get Jess's attention.

She finished checking off something on the list and shot him a look.

"Honey, remember to text your mother to buy the items I forgot on her way back home."

"Okay, Dad," Jess told him.

"Yeah, and fix yourself a sandwich to eat. There's lots of lunch meat in those grocery bags."

Jess raised two packs of lunch meat and waved them at him. "Found them." Then she looked mock-serious. "But you forgot the ketchup again. Mom's gonna be mad at you."

Now it was David's time to roll his eyes.

But then he laughed and headed to the back of the house and his office.

***

49-year-old David Harris had recently retired from his NASA engineering job during a recent buyout of higher-grade professionals. This happened every so often, usually after an audit or an executive order, as a way to lower the agency's personnel budget while providing an opportunity to onboard a younger workforce at lower wages.

At the moment, he was working from home and attempting to start up a new consulting business.

David's wife, Willow, was 52 years old and worked as a real estate agent, and at any point in the day could be just about anywhere in the county.

This meant that of Jess's parents, David was the one with the more flexible schedule, and so he was normally the one who both took Jess to school and fetched her back again, though sometimes (meaning on those days when she had no early appointments to show a house to a client), Willow did the morning school run.

It was arguably possible for Jess to walk home from school in the company of some of her friends.

"It'll toughen her up," Willow had told David the one and only time that they'd discussed it. "She has to start realizing that daddy and mommy don't need to do everything for her."

But David was against it. "There's too many damn predators out there," he'd firmly replied his wife. "And, no matter what some irresponsible movies would have us believe, in the real world, a 12-year-old is no match for an adult."

To David's relief, Willow had gracefully conceded that point.

CHAPTER 6

After fixing herself a sandwich with plenty of everything, Jess went to her room to watch TV. Her room was on the second floor, at the front of the house.

Lurking at the back of her mind was the need to do her homework before her mother got back home and got on her case about the importance of academics in today's world, but she decided to enjoy herself a little first.

So, she watched some YouTube television. It was all teen stuff, but between movies, she happened to click on a high school track meet and watched that, too, for a while.

Jess didn't mind sports, but her mom seemed to think they were largely a waste of time.

"Sure, you get famous running," Willow Harris would say. "But who pays your rent afterwards?"

And yet, Jess felt entranced by the look of concentration on the runners' faces.

And also, there was something almost machine-like about the way their bodies moved. The repetitive motion of the runners' limbs seemed hypnotic, poetry in motion in the literal sense.

Young as she was, it struck Jess that in their unique world, in the world of athletic competition, there was no room for mistakes, no margin of error, no leeway that could be allowed. There was something fascinating about that—being an athlete seemed to require an almost mathematical control of oneself, as if the human body was being stripped down to an engine.

And then there was the expression on the winner's face.

But that was, of course, also countered by the expression on the losers' faces.

On one hand, you had someone who was too exhilarated to feel their exhaustion, while on the other hand, you had a group of individuals who seemed to be worn out. Not worn out by the physical effort they'd put into the race, but instead by the psychic drain they must feel because they'd lost, as if by winning the race, the victor's prize was to suck energy from them all.

The races ended, and Jess clicked on a Katy Perry music video.

It now occurred to her to get her homework done fast because, in keeping with her dad's instructions, she'd texted her mom, telling her to buy Heinz ketchup and some hamburger buns on her way home. Her mom replied that she'd be home early today.

And so, possessed by the sort of subliminal dread that was the sole preserve of tweens with overachieving mothers and who'd left their academic tasks unfinished, Jess got out her schoolbooks and began working.

CHAPTER 7

The next day was one of those increasingly rare days when Willow Harris dropped Jess off at school.

Jess rode beside her mother in silence. It wasn't that she was scared to speak to her mom, but that this morning, her mom seemed to have a lot on her mind.

From past experience, Jess knew that when her mother was like this, it was best for her to keep quiet. If she asked any questions now, for instance, her mom was certain to give her 'yes' and 'no' answers with no further explanation or even reply at all.

Jess had also noticed that while driving, her mother seemed to pay a lot more attention to the road than her father did.

But this didn't mean that she was a better driver; she was simply a more nervous driver. Jess could see this clearly. Her mother drove like she disliked driving.

Jess contented herself with playing a word game on her phone. This proved to be a wise move because barely a moment after she'd begun doing so, they stopped at a red light, which gave her mother the opportunity to look at her.

"What's that you're doing, young lady?" came the expected question.

"I'm playing 'Spelling Bee Superstar,' " Jess replied.

Her mother nodded approvingly. "Now that's a great game for a young girl."

They were unable to continue their conversation because the red light turned green, and Willow Harris once more riveted her attention on the pavement ahead.

Once they were at school, Jess got out of the car. She made no attempt to kiss her mom's cheek first.

She stepped onto the curb, into the sea of similarly-arrived 11-, 12- and 13-year-olds, and waved back at her mom through the passenger side window.

Her mother wasn't emotionally expressive like her father was. Indeed, Jess found the difference between them puzzling. While her father was more relaxed and laid-back, her mother was always pushing, pushing, pushing.

Her mother always seemed to have a goal in mind. Her mother always had something she felt she needed to do.

"Now you be good, honey," Willow Harris said. "Don't go upsetting your teachers with any nonsense."

"Yes, Mom," Jess obediently agreed.

And then, her mother turned her focus back to the steering wheel and the road ahead and put the car back in Drive.

As she watched her mother drive off, Jess couldn't stop smiling.

It's like Mom has already forgotten she brought me to school. I wonder what's on her mind today?

"Hello, Jess!" an unfamiliar male voice called out behind her.

She turned around to see who it was and was surprised to see Barry Lindsey walking towards her from the entrance to the middle school. A look behind him showed his sister Mary turning into the campus, so they'd clearly just arrived at the school together.

"Hello, Barry," Jess said shyly once he reached her. Since their meeting yesterday, she'd managed to forget about him. But now that he was here with her again, she felt butterflies fluttering in her belly. Once more, it was an uncomfortable, but not unpleasant feeling.

"You're looking beautiful today, Jess," Barry told her.

She couldn't reply, except to say: "I'd better hurry and catch up with Mary, so I'm not late for first period."

"Sure, sure," Barry agreed with a grin. "But, hey, gimme your phone number first, then we can chat later."

18

Before Jess could think about it, Barry had his cellphone out of his pocket, and she was dictating her phone number to him.

"Okay, see you after school," he told her. "And if not, I'll be certain to text you later."

Then, just like her mom, Barry was gone too. Jess stood watching him until he met up with two of his friends and they walked into the high school together.

Standing there on the curb like that, looking the other way while her fellow students streamed past towards the school entrance, Jess had a sudden impression that by giving Barry her cellphone number, she'd just gone against the grain of common sense, but she decided she could manage it.

I'll be fine, so long as Mom doesn't find out, she thought.

With that in mind, she hurried towards school. On the far side of the campus entrance, Mimi Richards was just getting out of her mother's car.

Jess was impatient to share what had just transpired between her and Barry with her best friend.

***

"I think he wants to be your boyfriend," Mimi told her as they hurried to class.

"I don't know if I like him *that* much," Jess told Mimi. "And we're too young, aren't we?"

"I don't know that we're too young," Mimi told her, her face creasing up while she thought about it. "My brother Tom is fifteen and his girlfriend is thirteen, and she's over at our house a lot. And her parents know about it and don't mind, though they did come over to our house once to meet my mom and dad." Mimi shrugged. "Terri is just one year older than both of us. When's *your* next birthday?"

"In six months."

"Maybe you guys should wait then, since he's – what, fifteen or sixteen – and you're twelve. But texting one another should be okay."

Jess sighed. "As long as Mom doesn't read them, I think Dad would be okay with me having a boyfriend—but Mom would kill me. All she wants for me to do is study, study, study."

"Hmmm," Mimi agreed as they turned into class.

CHAPTER 8

That night, Jess went to bed early. Or at least she told her mom and dad that that's what she intended to do.

But once in her room, and with the lights off, she waited impatiently to see if Barry Lindsey would indeed text her.

And then, at about 10 p.m. he did:

'Hi, beautiful,' the text read.

That's me he's referring to!

'Hello, handsome,' she replied.

It took a while before he replied back.

'So. Didn't c u after school.'

'Dad came early. Bed now, time 4 zzz.'

'Still awake, pop in bad mood.'

Jess admitted this was very exciting.

'Y bad mood?'

'Drunk & pulled over by cops 2nite.'

'Pulled over? What's that?'

'Means they say u drank 2 much.'

And so on and so on the conversation went.

Until finally, long after her parents had gone to bed, Barry finally signed off with: 'Kiss kiss.'

Even though Jess had greatly enjoyed the conversation, she didn't feel bold enough to 'Kiss Kiss' Barry back. Instead, she told him: 'c u 2moro.'

Then she fell asleep and had pleasant dreams.

***

Of course, the next day at school, Jess told Mimi everything. This included showing her their texted conversation.

"Oh, so he does like you!" Mimi said excitedly as they ate their lunches. "That's great."

"Yes," Jess agreed. "But it's also very complicated. I'm not even sure if I want him as a boyfriend."

"What's complicated about it?" Mimi asked her, her face taking on a slightly vexed expression. "He's cute. He likes you, and you like him back."

"I don't know that I like him back. And I'm worried about what my parents will think if they find out."

"They won't find out if you delete his texts."

Jess agreed that that was true and was possibly the best course of action.

"And 'kiss kiss' him back tonight," Mimi finally advised.

"I don't think that's a good idea," Jess protested.

"It's just a text message. It's what my brother and his girlfriend always do. Okay, sometimes they kiss for real, but most times they're just texting themselves like they've nothing better to do."

Jess, who had no brothers or sisters of her own, finally agreed that replying to Barry's 'Kiss, Kiss' with one of her own was a harmless course of action.

The two girls finished their lunches and then spent the rest of their lunchtime playing with different fashion apps on their cellphones.

CHAPTER 9

That Sunday morning, Jess went to church with her parents.

"Why do we change churches so much?" she asked them when she discovered that that Sunday they were apparently headed for a new church they'd never attended before. "We're always going to different places."

"It's because we can't decide if we're Catholics or Pentecostals," her mother replied with a laugh that suggested she wasn't amused.

Jess looked at her father. "Is what Mom says true, Dad?"

"Well, sort of," her father replied after making the right turn the GPS had just told him to.

"I don't understand," Jess said.

Her mother looked up from her cellphone and said, "It's easy to understand, young lady. I was raised a Catholic by my parents, while David was raised a Protestant. So now that we're married, we need to find a place that we both enjoy attending."

"And you haven't found any in all this while?"

The idea that they'd been searching for a suitable church for so long—at least since she'd been born, which made it twelve long years—really surprised her.

Her father laughed at the question, "We only search from time to time. And sometimes we revisit the same places."

"Okay," Jess said a little dubiously. "So, Dad, if you're Protestant and Mom is Catholic, what am I?"

"Whatever denomination you choose to be, hon," her father replied. "Just grow up to be a well-behaved young Christian woman, and your mother and I will be very proud of you, no matter what church you worship God in."

***

The church they finally arrived at was the Blessed Hope Baptist Church. The building was large and imposing and clearly very old, a fact that impressed on Jess how young she was, so that like all young people, she felt a great pressure to grow older as fast as she could. However, she also realized that doing such a thing was as impossible as mentally willing flowers or animals to change their natural colors.

Once they'd gotten down from their car, an usher met them and after some discussion with Jess's parents, led Jess away to the youth section of the building, where she was soon left in the company of a group of kids of her own age. She thought she recognized one of the boys at the back of the room from her school.

A young woman was teaching this youth class.

"And so, kids," the young lady resumed once Jess was seated, "We must always remember that God, our heavenly father, expects us to always do good and not evil, to bless and not curse, to heal others and not hurt them . . ."

Jess listened attentively. She liked the idea of God. She liked the idea of having a super-parent who oversaw her own parents and called them 'children,' someone to whom she could report them if necessary.

But my parents are very nice to me, so I don't report them to God at all.

But it was a nice buffer to have anyway; that knowledge that if her mom and dad did misbehave, she had a heavenly court to take them to.

***

"So how did you like it?" her father asked her afterwards, while they were driving home again.

"It was very nice until we began singing choruses," Jess replied honestly. "Almost none of the kids in my Sunday School class can sing."

After laughing over this, her father asked her mother: "What do *you* think, honey? Give it another try, or keep looking?"

Her mother seemed to debate the pros and cons in her mind for a while. At least to Jess, it looked like she was thinking seriously.

"I'm not sure if I like the preacher," Willow Harris finally said.

"What didn't you like about him?" her father asked.

"Oh, you know, same old thing. Maybe it's just me and my Catholic upbringing, but to this day, I still find it hard to understand why Protestant preachers talk so much about the church needing money."

Her father glanced away from the steering wheel and laughed. "But, honey, from what the old guy said, they really do need to raise some money, and fast at that. Hey, baby, are you sure you're not just sore 'cos the preacher wasn't talking about Mary mother of God and the saints?"

Willow Harris flung her hands up in a gesture that Jess could tell was mere dramatic exaggeration. "Oh, alright then, darling, let's go back there again, and we'll see if I change my mind."

As the car sped to home sweet home, Jess wondered what her parents would think if they knew that in Barry's latest texts to her, he'd been talking about how much he liked her 'sweet breasts.'

CHAPTER 10

"He actually texted you that?" Mimi asked in shock the next day after school, when she and Jess were once again waiting to be picked up. "He said he likes your . . ."

Jess nodded and showed her last night's WhatsApp chat in which Barry Lindsey had eulogized the shape of her breasts.

"Wow!" Mimi said after reading them. "He really likes them."

Jess shook her head. "I'm confused about this. So, I googled it. The internet says it's a nice thing for a woman's lover to say to her."

Mimi shook her head. "My mom warned me that that's what old perverts say to little girls before hurting them."

"But, Barry is almost our own age," Jess protested. "He isn't an old pervert."

Mimi made a thinking face. "And, teens—we're not teens yet—teens have sex too."

"You mean the Sex Ed classes?"

"What else?"

"Sooo, what do I do?" Jess asked in anguish. "I'm confused."

"Hush," Mimi told her. "Here comes Barry now."

"Oh, my God, what do I do?" Jess said.

Then she managed to turn around, and there Barry was. He looked as tall and cute as she remembered him, and suddenly, it didn't actually matter what he'd texted her. The texts were all just flirting anyway, and now that she'd shown them to Mimi, she intended to delete the entire WhatsApp chat once she got home.

"Hi Jess," Barry said in a soft voice with his eyes never leaving hers.

"Hi, Barry," Mimi replied when Jess didn't. Then she grabbed her bag and added, "Oops, my mom's here. See you guys tomorrow."

Jess didn't even realize that she'd left them.

"What did you mean by what you wrote to me?" Jess asked Barry.

He looked around furtively, gestured at the other kids seated nearby, and then whispered: "We can't talk about that here. Too many folks about. We need to find a place where we can talk alone."

"Alone?" Jess asked. She half wanted him to explain, and half wanted him either to vanish into thin air, or her father to drive in then to pick her up, so she'd not have to talk to him anymore. "But I've not agreed to be your girlfriend yet."

"That's what we need to talk about," Barry told her.

Jess's attempt to reply to him was thwarted by Mary Lindsey hurrying down the school steps towards them.

"I'm hungry," Mary told her brother after grabbing hold of his arm. "I could eat a horse and its rider in one go."

"I'll text or *call* you later," Barry whispered to Jess before Mary dragged him away. "And we can fix a place to meet up and talk properly."

Then they were walking away, and Jess was left with her muddled-up thoughts and emotions.

***

"You're quite silent this afternoon," her father remarked on the drive home. "Are you alright, honey?"

Jess made a pretense of grabbing her belly. "I think my period is about to start, Daddy," she lied.

Her mind, however, was awhirl with the strange possibilities of what tonight's discussion with Barry might result in.

CHAPTER 11

'I need 2 speak 2 u,' Barry wrote. 'Let's meet under the bleachers.'

'I don't wannna cut class. Mom will kill me. Dad will help.'

'don't be a scaredy cat. Mom can't kno. Nvr tell parents what ur doin.'

'My parents ALWAYS find out bout stuff.'

'No 1 will kno. Ltz mit up.'

'when.'

'U chuz.'

'I dunno. Yeh, I know. Thursday.'

'2 far off. I wanna kiss U, kiss ur sweet breasts.'

'Not 2 far. Mimi has 2 go 2 d dentist on Thurs, so no 1 will notice.'

'OK. Thurs then.'

'What time?'

'Break time in Jamieson Stadium. Under d bleachers.'

'I dunno. Dark & lotsa bugs'

'Don't b a scaredy cat.'

'I hate bugs.'

'I'll protect u.'

'kiss kiss.'

'kiss kiss u 2.'

After they broke off their chat, Jess did some thinking.

I'm gonna get into trouble if I do this. But if I don't do it, Barry is gonna call me a scaredy-cat.

Her young body was thrilled with excitement and worry. It was a long time before she finally fell asleep.

CHAPTER 12

The days of the week came and went. Monday, Tuesday, Wednesday.

Classes, classes, and more classes.

And every night, more and more texts arrived that stirred Jess's mind to an excessive degree.

The texts became explicit to a degree that would have alarmed an adult, but Jess missed the danger signals. As far as she knew, Barry Lindsey was just a kid like herself, only a few years older than she was.

Mimi's only response on seeing them was to say: "Wow! he wrote you *that!*"

Part of the problem with Mimi was that once or twice her brother's girlfriend had shown her some of their own romantic texts (which were themselves a bit risqué), and so she assumed such conversation was normal.

And so, with no one able to advise them for the better, the two girls piloted one of them towards disaster.

As for Jess, she now found it hard to concentrate in class.

Maybe Barry was right and I really should've agreed to meet up earlier, she reasoned after realizing that she'd not heard a word of what Ms. Tomlinson had said about the difference between Socialist and Capitalist financial theory.

But it had to be Thursday when Mimi wouldn't be at school. Something in Jess's mind didn't want Mimi or anyone else to know about this.

Mimi will tell me not to go. She'll try to stop me from meeting Barry in the stadium. And also, Mimi is very poor at keeping secrets. Everyone will know where I went. I think Mimi is already telling people that I'm dating Barry, which is a lie!

And so, with no one the wiser as to her plans for Thursday, that day rolled over into the next.

CHAPTER 13

That Thursday, Jess felt an intense thrill as she walked towards the Shane Jamieson stadium during lunchtime.

This was really the first time that she'd done something as risky as meet up with a boy on her own. It made her feel older.

Jamieson Stadium served all three Thompson schools, though it was closest to the high school and farthest from the middle school.

It had a sports field, racetrack, and an endless series of bleachers—so many bleachers, in fact, that when Jess arrived and found the gap in the chain-link fence that students used to access the place during off-hours, she was confused as to which one Barry would be at.

And besides, she was quick to realize that she and Barry wouldn't be the only ones taking advantage of the bleachers' seclusion. A short distance farther off, she noticed a boy and a girl, both of them apparently high-schoolers, slipping into the shade beneath another set of bleachers.

Interestingly, it was the girl who was pulling the boy after her.

Jess felt both excited and repulsed. She'd heard stories of students slipping off the campus to make out here, but hadn't witnessed it before.

"Kiss, kiss," she heard a now familiar voice whisper to her.

She spun around and found herself face to face with Barry.

"You scared me," she reproved him, punching him on the chest when he pulled her towards himself.

Then he was holding her tight and it felt nice, very nice in fact. Much nicer than when either her dad or her mom hugged her.

"Someone will see us," she protested halfheartedly, and pulled away from him.

"It don't matter if they do," he told her. "We're too far off for anyone to really tell who it is."

Jess looked back at the high school and agreed that what Barry said was true. No one looking from the school buildings could possibly identify them. Even without the kids' playground in the way, from that distance, it would be impossible to single out exactly who was standing over by the stadium.

Barry was carrying a plastic bag and now pulled two cans of Pepsi out of it, and passed one over to her. "So, did Mimi go to the dentist today like she said?"

Jess nodded. "Yeah, she did. She called me last night to say how frightened she was. But her toothache was really bad now."

Barry nodded and opened up his soft drink, and indicated that she would do the same.

They stood like that for a while, staring around the area behind the bleachers. Cars passed by the stadium, but the signs hung up on the chain-link fence—two of them ironically advertising dentists—both prevented them from seeing who was driving past and kept those motorists from seeing them.

Once or twice, Jess's eyes went towards the building on the edge of the stadium, where the stadium's locker rooms were. "I heard that people go in there to kiss and do other stuff," she told Barry. "Is it true?"

"What kinda other stuff do you mean?"

"Adult stuff, like sex."

He nodded, a far-off look in his eyes. "Yep, it's true."

Jess looked at her wristwatch. "Break time is over," she said.

"Let's get under this bleacher, so that no one can see us."

They slipped down into the shadows of anonymity. Of course, it wasn't completely dark down here, as the gaps in the tiered seating let in rays of sunlight, but once they'd moved in deep enough and ducked behind the bleacher struts, they were practically invisible from the outside.

"So, what do you wanna talk about?" Jess asked. "We could just talk after school."

But Barry was already bringing his lips close to hers to kiss her. He gripped her shoulders.

"Stop!" she gasped and pushed him away.

He stopped, but held onto her. "What's the matter?" he asked.

She could see his smile on his face, and all of a sudden, it no longer reassured her. Now, it seemed to mock her.

"You said we need to *talk*. I'm not your girlfriend."

Barry laughed. "We are talking," he said and resumed trying to kiss her.

"Let me go!" she squealed in protest.

But his lips were already on hers. And after he'd kissed her forcibly for a short while, she relaxed and kissed him back.

"See, that's not so bad, is it?" he asked with a grin after they'd separated.

"Not really," she agreed, wiping her mouth. "But I wasn't expecting you to do that. You said we were going to discuss if I would be your girlfriend or not. That's all."

He'd moved so that the rays of light coming between the bleacher seats illuminated his face clearly.

Jess didn't like the look in his eyes now. They reminded her of the creepy people in movies, the ones who abducted young people and did horrible things to them.

"I think I should be going back," she said worriedly.

She began getting to her knees so she could crawl out to where she could stand freely, but he pushed her back down.

"Not yet; we've more to discuss," he said. Then he leaned forward and placed his hands on her chest. "C'mon, show me those sweet breasts of yours!"

The feeling of his hands on her chest gave her instant gooseflesh, and not in a good way. All of a sudden, she knew that she didn't want this to go any further.

She realized that she'd made a huge mistake by coming here to be alone with Barry. She should have told Mimi she was coming here with him.

"No, stop!" she protested and once more tried to get up again.

But this time, he shoved her roughly to the ground and then forcefully slipped his hands up under her top.

She attempted to scream, but his mouth was on hers again. She felt powerless and miserable. His hands were on her flesh and she couldn't move and then . . .

And then it got much worse. Jess felt him pushing down her pants and parting her legs and then . . .

And then he was hurting her, really hurting her down there, and she wanted to scream, but his mouth was still pressed roughly on hers, muffling her expression of her terror and agony.

Jess's defilement seemed to last forever. But thankfully, she passed out before it ended.

CHAPTER 14

Jess came out of her faint to see Barry buckling up his belt. Once that was done, he knelt down over her and said:

"Hey, you better not tell anyone about this, or I'll . . ."

Leaving the threat hanging in the air, he turned, ducked out from beneath the bleachers, and hurried away across the road and back towards the high school.

Down on her back in the grass, Jess watched him leave. She still couldn't wrap her mind around what had just happened to her.

Yes, her private parts hurt like fire was burning her down there. But worse than the physical pain was the emotional pain.

She was suddenly plagued by an agony of the soul that she couldn't describe.

Lying there under the stadium bleacher with tears beading up in her eyes, Jess Harris had the crystal-clear knowledge that something priceless had just been stolen from her.

Something I'll never get back.

Unfortunately for Jess (and this seemed to make it worse), she felt that she was too young to fully appreciate what had happened to her.

Yes, she knew that she'd just been raped, and she knew that she felt horribly violated, but she also suspected that she'd only properly appreciate the damage to her psyche when she was older.

At the moment, she was plagued by feelings of desolation that she didn't even have words for.

Oh my God, no! were the first coherent thoughts that entered her mind. Everything else was a jumble of hurt emotions.

She felt anger and shame. Mostly shame.

She was unaware how long she sat there nursing her pain, suffering her inexpressible agony.

Then suddenly, Jess heard voices nearby. Alarmed by her partial nakedness, she ducked as deep into cover as she could and stared out of the dimness in fright.

But it wasn't Barry coming back. It was the boy and girl whom she'd earlier noticed further along the bleachers, departing now.

"Do I see you tomorrow then?" she heard the girl ask him.

She didn't hear the boy's reply, but the fact that they were leaving the bleachers reminded her that she needed to leave here, too.

So, Jess quickly brushed off the dirt the best she could and pulled her pants up. Then she picked up her cellphone and crawled out into daylight.

Once she was standing upright again, she realized that school had just been dismissed for the day. Ahead of her, the high school students were spilling out of their building.

She walked in a daze, walking past the seniors without seeing most of them.

Her young mind was fighting to process a fresh dilemma.

I've been raped! But who do I tell?

Jess's heart pounded with the fear that her parents — especially her mother — would find out what she'd done.

She couldn't shake the feeling of guilt that if she hadn't gone off with Barry, none of this would have happened to her.

And she felt that her mom would blame *her* for what had happened. Maybe her dad would realize that she'd not wanted something like this to happen, but her mother would express her disappointment loudly.

So, I can't tell Mom and Dad! How about the teachers?

But of course, if she told the teachers what Barry had done to her, then the teachers would tell her parents, and that was the same thing.

Hey, I'll tell Mimi. Mimi will understand that it wasn't my fault. I didn't want Barry to rape me!

But here, too, there was a big problem. Mimi wouldn't keep Jess's ordeal to herself. Mimi had a tendency to get melodramatic

35

sometimes, and it was certain that try hard as Mimi might to keep her mouth shut, in a few days' time the rumor of Jess's rape would circulate in their school, which would lead to the teacher's finding out what had happened to her, and which would lead to her parents finding out.

And then Mom'll kill me! And afterwards, Dad will ground me for life.

And so, with this mindset, by the time Jess Harris had arrived back in school and was retrieving her school bag from her locker, she'd realized that all of a sudden, she was all alone in the world, with a terrible secret that she had to keep all to herself.

"Still period pains, daddy," she lied miserably to her father while he drove her home.

She was worried that he might detect traces of her fall from grace on her face. But to her relief, he looked at her like he believed her. "Hmm. If those continue, you're gonna need to visit your pediatrician…or gynecologist," her father replied.

"No need to, daddy," Jess quickly replied. "I'll be fine by tomorrow. I promise."

But she knew she was lying. She was sure she'd never be fine again.

CHAPTER 15

When they returned home, David Harris served them some baked rigatoni he had prepared earlier. Jess sat in the dining room with him, chewing her food but not tasting it.

"So, how was school today, honey?" he asked in his normal jovial tone of voice.

With tears threatening to spill from her eyes, she looked at him, but didn't reply.

She managed to hold back her tears. It was not that she didn't want to cry, but weeping would require an explanation, and she wasn't prepared to give him that explanation. She didn't understand how her life could rotate 180 degrees in a matter of ten minutes.

"Hey, are you sure you're okay?" her dad asked after a while.

She looked at his concerned face and wished she could pour out her pain into his heart. But just as she was about to speak, her worry and shame about his reaction intervened, and she nodded glumly.

Her fear paralyzed her tongue. She was certain that if her father knew what had happened to her, he'd think she'd done it intentionally to shame him.

So, she just nodded and continued picking at her pasta.

"My tummy still aches," she told him. "I'll be fine after I take some Motrin."

After that, she felt her father's eyes on her for a while, and sensed that he wanted to question her further, but eventually he seemed to accept that she was telling the truth about having period pains.

She ate most of her meal without even tasting its normally rich flavor.

After her father left the dining room and shut himself into his office, she fled upstairs.

Now, safe again in her own space, she identified one source of her discomfort.

I'm filthy, filthy, filthy.

She stripped off her clothes and flung them away from her. Then she hurried into the bathroom and showered. She washed herself for a very long time.

When she came out of the bathroom, she fell into her bed and began weeping.

Jess wept most of that afternoon. She only stopped weeping when she once more remembered that her tears would give her dreadful secret away.

After a while, she picked up her cellphone and sent Barry a text.

'Why did u hurt me like that? I thought you liked me.'

She waited for his reply all day long, but none came until evening, when her mother returned home, and she had to keep up the charade that her belly hurt her and not her soul.

CHAPTER 16

The next day Jess once more had the good fortune to be dropped off at school by her mom.

She considered this fortunate because, with the way that Willow Harris concentrated on the road while driving and her general preoccupied state of mind in the mornings, there was no chance of them having any conversation about her glum mood.

Things went seemingly as they always did.

Willow dropped Jess off at school and drove off.

As she usually did, for a few seconds, Jess stood watching her mother leave. But then her mother made a turn that took her past the stadium, and yesterday's painful memories piled on Jess's heart again, and now tears came to her eyes.

In a state of panic, she turned around and stared down the street to see if Mary and Barry were approaching. But no, the coast was clear. Either the Lindsey siblings had already arrived, or they were still a distance from the school.

Jess had no idea what she'd do if she saw Barry this morning. Would she start screaming or faint or would she attack him with whatever weapon she found handy?

Keeping her head down, she hurried onto campus and walked towards the school building.

"Hey, Jess, wait up!" she heard Mimi calling behind her.

She slowed down a little, and soon Mimi joined her.

"How was it at the dentist?" she asked Mimi.

"Nasty, really nasty," Mimi told her laughing. "I almost bit the nurse!"

Jess laughed at that. The image of her bestie attempting to bite the dentist's assistant struck her as incredibly funny.

"Are you okay?" Mimi asked.

Jess nodded, but said nothing.

"Are you sure?"

"Yes, I'm fine!" she snapped back at Mimi, then seeing that Mimi was taken aback by the violence of her reaction, she forced a smile. "I'm okay."

"Ahh, I get it," Mimi said, an understanding expression suddenly coming into her eyes. "Okay, did Barry annoy you?"

Hearing this, Jess almost let the cat out of the bag. But just in time, she remembered that Mimi would certainly spread the horrible news.

"He's nothing but a jerk," she spat with heartfelt vehemence. "He's a total jerk. I dunno what made me think we liked each other."

"Oh, so something did happen?" Mimi pressed on.

"I don't wanna talk about it."

"Barry broke your heart, didn't he?"

Jess almost laughed at that. And then she felt like strangling Mimi for being so dumb.

"I never cared for him that much anyway."

"Tell me what happened," Mimi insisted, as, part of a stream of 7th and 8th graders, they headed for their lockers.

"I don't wanna talk about it."

"C'mon."

"No. I'm not going to."

"Aw, Jess, tell me what happened. What did Barry say to you? Have you got the texts here? Lemme see 'em."

"There are no texts. I never want anything to do with him again. He's a jerk. Ask Mary if you wanna know what happened."

Mimi shook her head. "Uh uh, not Mary. She lies a lot. I don't believe anything she tells me."

In this vein of conversation, they arrived in class and the school day began.

Jess found it incredibly hard to concentrate in class. She'd looked forward to having something to do to take her mind off of what she was feeling, but every now and then her concentration was interrupted by a vision of Barry Lindsey atop her, what she could see of his face in the gloom beneath the bleacher contorted in animalistic lust.

This was largely brought on because her body hurt. She'd unwisely chosen to wear pants today also, and they chafed her badly down there.

And then she'd feel faint, like she was going to collapse on top of her desk, and then she'd notice old Mr. Fisher the mathematics teacher or Miss Leary who taught science, staring curiously at her.

I mustn't give myself away, she'd think and try to concentrate again. And she'd succeed until the next time.

She made it through to lunchtime and then fended off a fresh set of questions from Mimi.

Jess thought that she'd had it tough in the first half of the school day, but she felt even worse after lunch break was over. Finally, during the second-to-last period homeroom, she requested permission to go to the bathroom. Once there, she sat down and wept until she was certain the class was over.

Then she went back to the classroom and endured the last class.

After the final bell rang, while she and Mimi joined the stream of boys and girls hurrying away from the classrooms, Jess was suddenly gripped by a fresh horror.

What do I do if Barry is waiting for me outside the school?

The question made Jess faint, with the world threatening to spin around her and leave her trembling on the floor. Even though she was in the middle of a cluster of other tweens and there no chance of a repeat of yesterday's nightmare, she felt a massive terror settling on her.

She froze where she was.

Mimi, who was excitedly talking about attending a Renaissance fair with her parents that weekend, had gone several steps ahead of Jess before realizing she was talking to herself and then doubling back.

"What's the matter with you?" she asked Jess.

"I don't wanna see Barry," Jess told her.

Mimi nodded understandingly. "Okay, when we get to the front door, I'll look outside to see if Mary's there. If she's waiting, that means he'll be coming here. If Mary's gone, that means the coast is clear."

And so that's what they did. At the entrance to the building, Jess hung back while Mimi surveyed the landscape.

After she'd had a good look outside, Mimi turned around and gestured to Jess.

"Mary's gone. You can come out now."

Jess walked out. It suddenly struck her that she felt like a prisoner, like the criminals in movies must feel when the police were after them.

But I'm innocent—I'm the victim here! she thought.

And yet, she found the fact of her innocence almost impossible to believe.

The two girls walked out of the school premises together and then split off towards their separate rides.

"Hi, doll," Jess's dad told her when she'd climbed into the car beside him. He leaned over and ruffled her hair. "How was school today?"

"Horrible," she replied without thinking. "I wish I hadn't come. I wish I'd stayed at home."

She was so wrapped up in her own world of pain and confusion that she missed the worried look that came over her father's face when she said this.

Jess had other worries:

Was this how she was going to continue hiding from Barry Lindsey? Was she going to keep looking over her shoulder to see if he was stalking her? Would she forever be scared that he'd jump on her and sexually assault her again?

CHAPTER 17

David Harris was very worried by the overnight change that had occurred in his beloved daughter.

She hated school today. What on earth is going on? Jess has never said that before. She loves school, loves her teachers, and her friends.

When he stopped his car at a red light, he looked aside at Jess.

Damn, she looks sullen, really angry at the world.

Jess was slumped there in her seat, with her jacket wrapped tightly around her and looking like the weight of the world was on her shoulders.

What the hell? David asked himself.

"Hey, honey, is your belly still hurting?" he asked Jess after checking that the traffic light was still red. "Do you wanna go see the doctor?"

But she shook her head emphatically. David was shocked by how forcefully her refusal was, as if she were daring him to question it.

The fact that she'd not spoken since that first statement also bothered him a lot.

She looks just like every bratty, angry teen I've ever encountered, David thought with a sudden worried understanding. *Okay, so I've been expecting and dreading this change in her personality. But . . . but . . . how does such a change happen overnight?*

It never occurred to him that anything nasty could possibly have happened to his daughter at school. School, middle school at that, was a place where you dropped off a happy kid in the morning and picked up the same happy-but-a-little-exhausted kid in the afternoon. Middle school was a safe place, a protected safe zone in the otherwise crazy world. It was like an agreement had been reached by everyone that elementary and middle schools would be exempt from the world's craziness. Students with guns could murder their classmates in high school and university, but the lower echelons of the educational hierarchy, including kindergarten, were to be left alone.

So no, David Harris never suspected the horror that his little girl was currently experiencing.

He stared at Jess worriedly some more. But then, the insistent honking of the horn of the car behind him, knocked him out of his thoughts and back into the here and now.

Oops, the traffic light's been green for a while now.

Still bothered by his daughter's sullen attitude, David Harris took his foot off the car brake and let the vehicle roll on towards home.

CHAPTER 18

Back at home, Jess hurried up to her room, threw herself down on her bed and wept some more.

She felt under intense pressure and the pressure seemed to bubble up through her body till it reached her eyes and then it ran out of her.

She found it strange that as the aching in her body lessened, the hurt in her heart increased.

She wiped her tears dry, lay back in bed, and thought:

At least he didn't get me pregnant! I'm not pregnant!

She knew this because she was on birth-control pills.

Her periods had begun early, which wasn't exactly unusual, but then she'd begun having unusual pains in her belly. The gynecologist had traced the pains to ovarian cysts.

That diagnosis had led to Jess being placed on birth control pills to both regulate her periods and prevent the development of more cysts.

So, in that sense, she'd grown up early; still a child, but with some knowledge that her peers wouldn't have for a few more years.

Relieved that she didn't have an unwanted pregnancy to worry about, Jess dried her eyes and went downstairs.

Downstairs in the kitchen, her father was making dinner for both of them. Jess was greeted by a sizzling sound and the savory odor of frying meat, which meant that her father was frying burgers, the only food her mother said he could properly prepare.

And, even then, the burgers were often greasy. Eating them was a labor of love. Not like her mother's perfect burgers and crisp fries.

"Hi, honey," David greeted her. "You feelin' a little better now?"

She nodded back at him. She wanted to run over to him and wrap her arms around him and tell him that she'd been harmed by the nasty boy, but she just couldn't. And knowing that she'd never be able to tell him what had happened to her prevented her from telling him other things, all of the minutiae about her day which she'd always delighted to share with him once she was back from school.

She saw that he'd once more gotten that worried look on his face and forced a small smile. "I'm better, Daddy. I'm just feeling a bit exhausted."

He nodded understandingly and was maybe about to ask her a question, but then the smell of burning meat alerted him to the fact that their meal was burning.

This happened on a regular basis, and previously Jess would always laugh out loud each time her father attempted to salvage the food, but not today.

Today she felt as burnt as the food.

They ate.

All of a sudden, Jess realized that her parents were both a lot like the burgers and fries they prepared.

Daddy is soft and easygoing, and his burgers and fries are soft and soggy like he is, while Mom is herself as crisp and on-the-surface-perfect as the food she prepares. She's as stiff as lettuce or celery.

That moment of illumination passed and Jess shoveled the food into her mouth and afterwards washed up the dishes.

While she was drying her hands afterwards, her phone beeped. She wondered who the text message was from and discovered it had been sent by Barry.

Her heart beating madly, she ran upstairs to read what it said. Her father was lounging in the living room, and she didn't want him to see her reaction.

Once safe behind her bedroom door, Jess read the text message: 'Kiss kiss.'

She felt like screaming. Kiss, kiss? *Is that all he has to say?*

She considered not replying to Barry and didn't.

Instead, she got out her books and tried to study.

But after a while, her phone beeped again.

'Kiss kiss.'

Disgusted with both him and herself, Jess replied:

'U're a nasty person. U sed U loved me. Then U raped me!'

There was a short pause. Then:

'I didn't rp U. U wanted it 2.'

'No, I didn't want it. I told U 2 stp. Told u 2 stp.'

'U told me 2 do it 2 U. When U gals say stop U really mean do it.'
This was punctuated with a leering smiley face.

'Leave me alone or I'll tell my daddy what U did 2 me'

'Kiss kiss.'

LEAVE ME ALONE. I'LL TELL MY DADDY!

'daddy's girl.'

'I h8 u. I h8 u. I H8 U. I H8 U. I H8 U. I H8 U. I H8 U. I H8 U. I
H8 U. I H8 U. I H8 U. I H8 U. I H8 U. I H8 U. I H8 U. I H8 U. I H8
U. I H8 U. I H8 U. I H8 U. I H8 U. I H8 U. I H8 U. I H8 U. I H8 U.
I H8 U. I H8 U. I H8 U. I H8 U. I H8 U. I H8 U. I H8 U. I H8 U. I
H8 U. I H8 U. I H8 U. I H8 U. I H8 U. I H8 U. I H8 U. I H8 U. I H8
U. I H8 U. I H8 U. I H8 U. I H8 U. I H8 U. I H8 U. I H8 U. I H8 U.
I H8 U. I H8 U. I H8 U. I H8 U. I H8 U. I H8 U. I H8 U. I H8 U. I
H8 U. I H8 U. I H8 U. I H8 U. I H8 U. I H8 U. I H8 U. I H8 U.

After that, Barry seemed to get the message that Jess hated him and
wanted nothing more to do with him.

He didn't text her anymore. Not that day or ever again.

But of course, the damage had already been done.

***

After that horrible afternoon, Jess's days were spent in a state of
continual dread.

Barry Lindsey never came near her again, and yet, she kept looking
over her shoulder every now and again to see if he was nearby. It
became a reflex action; once she even heard the wind rustling her
window drapes and thought Barry was coming for her.

Jess slowly sank into depression.

CHAPTER 19

It was Sunday morning again, and Jess was on her way to church with her parents.

The day was bright and sunny, but she felt cloudy and heavy.

Where previously she'd always been enthusiastic to attend church services and mingle with the other kids there, now she was apathetic.

She wondered what God thought of her now. She didn't really understand the concept of sin properly—she viewed it the same way as offending her parents, but on a larger scale—but she was certain God must be very displeased with her.

And that made her feel even more alone in her suffering.

Her father drove into the church premises and parked between two cars on the west side of the parking lot. Then after unbuckling his seatbelt, he swiveled around and grinned brightly at her.

"Okay, honey, we're here!" David Harris told Jess. "Attempt two to see if Blessed Hope Baptist Church is the right church for the Harris clan."

Jess stared glumly back at him. "Yeah," she said with little interest.

Her father continued smiling at her, but her uninterested tone of voice angered her mother, who looked back also.

"What is wrong with you today?" Willow Harris demanded angrily.

"I don't feel like going to church," Jess said sullenly. "I just don't. I wanna go home."

"Well, young lady, you're not going home. We're here and . . ."

Willow was about to say more, but David stopped her with a hand on her arm. "Let her be, dear."

Willow looked back at her husband. "Well, she needs to straighten up. She's been like this all week."

David nodded understandingly at his wife and then at his daughter. "Okay, Jess, we're here at the church and we're attending the church service."

"I wanna go home."

On hearing that, David's smile soured a little. But he rallied: "Sorry, honey, but you're too young to decide on that. *We're* the ones who decide what you do and where you go on Sunday mornings. You've got the whole of the rest of the day to do whatever you want with yourself—"

"So long as you finish your schoolwork first," Willow interjected as she pushed the car's passenger door open. "Remember that, young lady—no work equals no playtime for you."

Jess stared defiantly at her father.

David shrugged back at her. "You heard your mother, honey. Now, let's all get out of the car and waltz onward like good Christian soldiers into the Blessed Hope Baptist Church."

Jess made a final attempt to stare him down. Her attempt ended when she sensed motion on her left. She turned to see what the shadow falling on her was, and realized it was her mother, standing by the car's rear window and staring pointedly in at her.

Her mother's eyes seemed to telescope in at her, to fold Jess into a littler version of herself.

Somehow Willow Harris's stare made Jess feel even smaller and more insignificant than she'd felt on leaving home. And if there was something that Jess knew about her mother, it was that Willow Harris had great reserves of stare-power, reserves which she used in varying degrees to make her husband comply with her desires.

Willow pulled the rear door open. "Alright, get out," she told Jess unsympathetically.

Jess conceded defeat; it was really bad being stared intently at like that.

After heaving out the most melodramatic sigh she could come up with, she got out of the family car and trudged along behind her parents until they handed her over to an usher, behind whom she then grumpily trudged along until she reached the youth section at the rear of the main building.

***

Today, the Harrises had arrived earlier for the service. This meant that Jess arrived while the junior youth class was singing praises to God.

The singing was backed by a band of three older teens, who were quite good on their instruments.

Little by little, Jess found herself being drawn into the music. She'd previously liked Iggy Azalea and Katy Perry and early Madonna videos. Since the attack, however, she'd hardly listened to any music. The happy songs didn't improve her mood, while the sad songs made her feel worse than she already did.

But this church music was nice. For a few minutes, she felt her problems lift off her shoulders. She felt like someone apart from herself.

But then the singing ended and the sermon began, and her depression returned.

Ms. Carter, the same young woman who'd taught the youngsters the last time, taught the class today also.

Ms. Carter had a high-pitched and quite strident voice that grated on Jess's nerves like lawnmower noise. Jess wondered how she'd just noticed that.

The result was that after about ten minutes of Ms. Carter's message on how David's victory over Goliath was an example for every young Christian—David himself being still a teenager when he slew the Philistine giant—Jess found her thoughts drifting.

She looked at the faces of the other boys and girls in the Sunday school class with her. All were either tweenaged like she was or in their early teens.

Most of the kids were enthralled by Ms. Carter's words, caught up in the past, as if in their minds they could actually see the young shepherd boy load up his sling with one of the stones he'd picked up and whirl his arm around while defying the deadly giant.

They had broad smiles and grins on their faces, and seemed as pleased as punch to be in church today.

But there were also a few children who looked tired and uninterested. And one or two who seemed downright depressed, like they had the worst life of any kid in the world.

One little girl seemed even sadder than Jess was.

Jess discovered that seeing these unhappy kids in church today made her feel better.

It's a true saying that misery loves company.

CHAPTER 20

"So, what do you think?" David Harris asked Jess and her mother while driving them back home.

The time now was just past noon and the weather was warm and everyone in their car felt sweaty.

"Honestly, darling, I dunno," Willow replied. "Today, I liked the service a little better than the last time we were here, but I'm still having a problem dealing with the amount of calls they make for donations for different causes." She paused, frowned and then added: "All of them worthy causes, of course. But personally, I'd like to hear more about God and less about money."

"The Bible says we can't serve both God and money," Jess said, without realizing why she'd said that. The words had just popped out, propelled by the pressure she felt.

Her father didn't reply, but instead concentrated on overtaking the truck ahead of them, which had slowed down at a turnoff.

"Yeah, that's true, dear," Willow said. "But not necessarily true in this case. God needs money too, you know."

"How can God need money?" Jess asked. "I thought he owns everything?"

Willow laughed. "No, I don't mean it that way, dear. What I mean is, God's *work* needs money. God is way up in heaven and they don't spend money there."

"Heaven's streets are paved with gold," David said. "God is one rich hombre indeed!"

Jess nodded, her interest already exhausted. "Okay, if you both say so."

Her mother gave her an odd look when she heard this, and then asked: "Jess, did something happen in church that you didn't like?"

Jess instantly shook her head and made a note to be more careful. "No, church was fine. The band was great. We all sang as badly as we did last time and then learned about David and Goliath."

"Okay, so what do you think about the church, Jess?" her father asked.

"I like it, daddy, but not as much as the last place that you and mom both disliked."

She watched as her parents gave each other a strange look and then burst out laughing.

"So, I guess that means we'll keep looking for our perfect family church," David said.

"We should keep attending here till you hear about another nice place," Willow told him. "This one's not bad, and it's also not too far from our house."

"They have some nice youth programs that you can attend," David called back to Jess. "You can get together with kids your own age and have fun."

"Okay," Jess nodded, but without much interest. About the only thing she remembered about the service was that she'd felt nice and uplifted during the singing, and then everything else had left her cold. It didn't seem worth the hassle.

"So would you like to attend the church youth group activities?" her mother asked.

"Yes, Mom, I'd like to," she replied.

And she noted that after she said this, her parents both seemed satisfied with her and didn't throw any more *irritating* questions her way.

So that seems to be the secret, she decided. All she needed to do was give her mother and father and everyone else the right answers, and everything would be fine.

No, everything would seem to be fine.

She'd still be hurting, but she'd be left alone to hurt in peace.

CHAPTER 21

"What do you think is wrong with her?" David asked Willow as they lay in bed that evening. "She's been acting really grumpy all day long."

"She's premenstrual," Willow replied. "She'll get out of it in a few days."

"Just that?" David said.

"*Just?*" Willow gave him a look of disbelief. "David, did you actually say 'just?' Sometimes I wish men go through periods too, just so you'd understand how they make us women feel. Then you wouldn't trivialize them."

David said, "Oh, I know how periods make *you* feel. You do your best to make me experience their lows with you."

She nudged him gently with her elbow and giggled.

"But what if it's something else?" David asked. "I'm thinking that maybe she's being bullied or something like that. Bullied kids tend to withdraw into a shell and become sullen."

Willow considered that and then shook her head. "Jess isn't the type to be targeted by bullies. We've seen how popular she is with the other kids in her class."

"So, what's the problem then?" He saw Willow's eyes narrow as she watched him. "Yes, yes, I know she's supposedly got PMS, but what if that's not it?"

Willow said, "Also, she could be having trouble with her studies."

David sighed. "You never let up on that, do you?"

"I can't help it that I'm neurotic about my child having the best education possible."

David wagged a finger in the air to indicate his disagreement with her. "Our daughter's a smart kid. She's never had trouble with her schoolwork before now, so why would it start now? So, no, I'll bet that that's not it."

"We could ask her teachers."

"We could, but I foresee that as being a waste of our time."

Willow sighed. "Okay, okay, you're right, honey, I don't really think it's any of those things either."

"So . . . what do you think is wrong with Jess? Unrequited love?"

Willow rolled her eyes. "At her age? Be serious, buster."

David laughed. "Yeah, yeah!"

Willow's facial expression now turned serious. "We've both been overlooking the obvious. You know, the baby elephant in the room?"

"What obvious?"

"Maybe it's finally arrived at our doorstep and we're refusing to see it."

"Honey stop talking in riddles. What's arrived on our doorstep?"

Willow Harris now burst out laughing. "You know, that phase in their child's developmental years that every parent dreads: the teenage rebellion phase."

David made a face, wrinkling up his forehead and squeezing his lips together like he'd just seen something supremely revolting. "Ugh, darling, please let it not be that. Anything but that."

Willow continued laughing and punched him in the chest.

David sighed. "You know, I've considered that too. But isn't she a little early for that? I mean, technically, Jess isn't even a teenager yet."

His wife shook her head. "Normally, yes, she'd be too young. But, remember, Jess went through puberty earlier than normal, so I guess it makes sense that she starts being a pain in the ass earlier than usual also."

David slipped an arm under Willow's neck and pulled her close to him. "Darling, hearing you put it that way—pain in the ass—terrifies me. You're making me dread what the next five or so years of our lives are gonna be like, if she turns home-terrorist on us."

Willow laughed some more. Then she leaned over and kissed him. "Hey, you wanna make love tonight?"

He shook his head at her and feigned horror. "And make another young terror? Hell no! I'm not sure how I'm gonna deal with Jess now that we suspect she's about to act up on us, and you're planning on planting a similar time bomb that'll detonate thirteen years in the future."

"What century are you living in, baby? The last one when I was still young? Honey, I'm *well past* menopause now. There's no more danger of you putting a bun in my oven."

David's eyes widened like he'd forgotten.

"Really?" he asked. "Nothing bad can come from our doing adult stuff now?"

They both burst out laughing. And when they finished laughing, they came together happily as husband and wife.

Neither of them even suspected the real nature of the human timebomb that lay ticking a few rooms away from them.

CHAPTER 22

And so, time rolled on in Jess's life.

Days became weeks and weeks became months. Jess's thirteenth birthday came and went. She finished 7th grade and moved to 8th grade.

Though she no longer enjoyed her studies as much as before, her intellectual ability ensured that she still maintained good grades; which was important to her as it meant her mother couldn't complain too much.

On the surface Jess seemed normal enough, just another teenage girl going through the usual difficulties of those years when hormones roved freely through a body and mind not yet fully equipped to cope with them. Her sullenness increased, and she became openly combative and argumentative with both her parents and peers. The sole reason she didn't argue too much with her teachers was because her mother would hear about it.

Her father was sympathetic enough. He'd apparently been a terror as a teen as well. But her mother told her to 'straighten up.' Willow Harris had been well-behaved all of her life and despite her mental understanding that this was a phase all people went through, she refused to tolerate too much of it in the house.

***

Once the physical hurt of being physically assaulted had faded, Jess's biggest problem now became the silence she'd also had forced on her.

Yes, being raped had been hell. But, being unable to tell anyone about it was a completely different sort of hell entirely.

Yes, feeling all alone in her hurting, was the horror after the actual horror. And it was a horror that looked like it would go on forever and ever.

Maybe this is the hell that I hear about in church, she once thought. *I sinned and now I'm in this hell.*

Unable to express her hurt and her fears and her worries to anyone, friend of foe, Jess felt like she was invisible, felt like she wasn't really there, and as such felt like she didn't really count as a person.

She began hating herself. This self-loathing crept up on her unawares so that afterwards, once she found herself entrapped inside of its negative web, she honestly couldn't tell when she'd begun hating herself. Jess just discovered that there were days on end when she felt like she was completely worthless.

Worthless: a horrifying summation of her life.

Depression, a vision of herself as a nobody spiraling down to nowhere.

Once she dreamt of herself falling, falling endlessly through space, only it wasn't really space as people described space. In Jess's dream space, the planets were the heads of people—her family and friends and her teachers and those kids she knew at church and each of these planet-heads were laughing at her, and when she asked them why they were mocking her, they all turned their faces away from her and began talking to each other like she wasn't there in outer space with them.

That night she'd woke up gasping for breath.

***

Jess's parents continued acting like she was simply going through her rebellious phase. They even told her so.

And Jess herself had lived her lie for so long that often she came close to believing her parents version of things herself.

CHAPTER 23

"You know, Jess, I think Tommy's gay," Mimi said.

"Huh?" Jess asked. It was after school again and she and Mimi were eating cookies and drinking Cokes while they waited for her dad and Mimi's mom. "Tommy?"

Tommy Bradley had already left for home, and so wasn't party to this conversation about his possibly deviant sexuality.

Mimi nodded emphatically. "He's just hiding it from everyone because he's afraid he'll be bullied if he comes out of the closet."

Jess nodded and fell as silent as before.

While neither teenager could be applauded (or blamed, depending on whom one asked) for their continuing association, Jess Harris and Mimi Richard's friendship was still as strong as ever.

Jess's new sullen outlook on life and withdrawal from most friendships hadn't turned off Mimi, like it had others, largely because Mimi herself was currently going through some changes of her own.

Having now noisily slipped fully into puberty herself, Mimi had made the rather unexpected decision to go goth. So now she came to class dressed all in black and with her face painted with so much makeup that Tommy Bradley once joked that she used up all of her dad's salary on her face each week.

(Tommy had himself transformed into a gangly, zit-infested youth who now wore glasses. He looked like bully-bait, but he'd also begun playing guitar, so everyone thought he was cool.)

Mimi's other transformation involved her putting on weight. As in, a *lot* of weight.

Once her hormones kicked in, Mimi had begun eating like mad. Indeed, Mimi ate so much now that Jess wondered if perhaps her best friend wasn't concealing some unvoiceable trauma of her own.

But no, according to Mimi, she was eating so much for a simple reason: "My mom's fat and my dad loves her to death. So I wanna get fat too so that I'll get my own share of his attention."

Her comment had been one of the few things that had made Jess laugh of recent.

"Do you really think Tommy is gay?" Jess asked Mimi.

As she asked the question, she swept her eyes nervously across the parking lot. After doing this twice, she wondered what she was looking for. But then she realized it wasn't *something*, but rather *someone* that her subconscious was attempting to locate.

But no, Barry Lindsey was nowhere to be found.

"Well, he does give all the signs that gay stereotypes do," Mimi had begun replying, but Jess broke in on her:

"What happened to Barry?" she asked.

"Your sleazy ex?" Mimi waved vaguely. "Oh, he's still alive. Mary said he told her to start meeting him at the high school after school instead of him meeting her here."

Hearing this, Jess heaved a sigh of relief. Barry's sister Mary Lindsey was one of those who'd dropped out of her circle of friends when her character had turned darker.

I doubt Mary has any idea why Barry won't come here anymore, she thought. *Works for me tho'.*

"Yeah, so Tommy really acts like he likes boys and not girls," Mimi went on. Then she fished in her pack of cookies for a fresh one, realized that she'd finished all of hers, and dipped her fingers into Jess's half-eaten pack instead.

"You'll hate being fat," Jess warned her. "All of the fat people I see on social media would rather be thin."

"My mom doesn't hate being fat," countered. "Why should I?"

"Wait and you'll see."

"My mom doesn't even want to do Ozempic. She says it's a government conspiracy to kill fat people."

"What's Ozempic?"

"Hey, your old man's here to pick you up. He's really cute. Give him a kiss for me, please."

Jess hadn't noticed her father pull up to the curb, but now she saw his car and waved at him.

"I don't kiss him anymore," she told Mimi sullenly.

Mimi seemed shocked by the info. "But you used to. It always used to make me so envious, you being able to kiss your daddy on the cheek like that. In my house, all the nice kisses are reserved for my mother. Then my baby sister gets the leftovers and so there's none left for me."

"Get over it, you're a big girl now."

"Apparently not *big* enough," Mimi retorted angrily and snatched Jess's pack of cookies from her hand.

Jess walked over and got into the car beside her father.

He smiled at her and she felt an intense sense of loss.

Yes, kissing her dad on the cheek had always embarrassed her, but now she missed it.

For his part, her father seemed to have accepted the fact that that morning ritual was over, steamrolled into pulp by the juggernaut called adolescence.

Jess went home, feeling that today had actually been one of her better days.

CHAPTER 24

While neither into the goth lifestyle or ideology herself, Jess's friendship with Mimi meant that she was soon associating with the other goth kids in Thompson Middle School.

There were about ten goth kids on the campus, with their leader being a tall boy called Jeffrey.

Though she hung out with the goths regularly, Jess was wary of them and particularly of Jeffrey, who had the sort of predatory vibe about him that she now associated with rapists.

Another problem with the goths was they tended to congregate near the bleachers, a location which had horrible associations for her.

However, she now regularly went and sat on the bleachers with the goths because Mimi was there with her.

So, they all sat there as one (usually when everyone else was in PE class, but sometimes during lunchtime too), a weird assembly of dark-clad teenagers and herself. They drank sodas and ate snacks and joked about how empty life was.

Jess got that last part. Her life really was empty.

"You're not really one of us," Jeffrey told her one day, after she'd been hanging out with them for about a month. "But we like you 'cos you're damaged goods."

"I'm not damaged goods," Jess protested a little angrily. She already felt low enough as it was, she didn't need to have the goths label her as something best discarded or sent back for refurbishment.

One of the goths, a very short girl with bright red hair named Meaner Tina, shook her head at Jess. "Don't get offended. He doesn't mean it like that. We're all damaged goods here."

"Everyone except me," Mimi called out from where she was stuffing her face with fries.

"Including you," Meaner Tina retorted. "No one eats as much as you do except if they have major daddy issues."

"Hey, I don't have daddy issues. I just want my fair share of his attention!"

The tiny redhead turned her attention back to Jess. "Take me, for instance. I'm really damaged. My dad caught my mom in bed with someone else and killed both of them. I walked in on him stabbing my mother to death." She shivered with the memory. "I don't think I'll ever forget that."

"That's horrible," Jess said, shivering herself. "What happened to your dad?"

Meaner Tina sighed. "He got like two hundred and fifty years in jail, so he's never getting out. And my mom's parents are dead, so I'm living with his father now, who acts like he blames *me* for what happened." She gestured upward with her hands. "So, I'm completely damaged. All I can do is let out the pain and hope I heal someday."

"We're all damaged," Jeffrey agreed. "I was in a car with my younger sister when a truck crashed into it. My sister was killed—bled to death all over me."

He fell silent.

"Nothing bad ever happened to me," another kid named Helix said. "But I keep having these horrible dreams where it's the end of the world and I'm being ground to paste by aliens, me and everyone else. And it's the same dream every night. It's driving me batshit crazy. I'm on so many meds that half of the time I can't see straight. But if I stop them, then I can't think straight either."

Helix looked exhausted, either by his dreams or by his waking life, Jess couldn't tell.

Jess was completely surprised by what she was hearing. She didn't understand what she was hearing and she didn't dare share her story with them, but apparently she wasn't the only person of her age that was suffering so much.

She looked at another girl. This was a girl named Shelly who was in her own 8th grade class.

"I'm suicidal," Shell (as the goths called her) said. "I don't know why I wanna kill myself all of the time, but I do. I've called the suicide prevention hotline like thirty times already." She laughed. "But now I'm on ATDs like Helix is—"

What are ATDs?" Jess asked.

"Antidepressants!" Mimi called out from where she was sitting.

Jess waved her acknowledgement at Mimi, and then looked back at Shell. "What were you saying?" she asked.

" 'Bout me being on ATDs?" Shell laughed. "Oh, they seem to be working. Nowadays I don't wanna kill myself so often. I just cut myself a lot more."

Jess eyes widened. "Cut yourself?"

Shell nodded. "Yeah, the wounds help me bleed out the pain." When Jess still looked confused, Shell peeled back the sleeves of her black cardigan and revealed that both of her arms had long scars on them.

"Can I touch them?" Jess asked her, with an enthralled look on her face.

"Sure, go ahead," Shell said. "These are old. I've got fresh ones on my thighs and my belly."

Jess traced her fingers along the lengthy scars on Shell's arms. Several of the scars crosslinked over each other, forming a web of healing skin.

"How do you do this? What does it do for you?" Jess asked in a stunned voice.

"You use a box-cutter or something that'll make a long but shallow cut," Jeffrey told her. You don't want to really injure yourself or cut yourself so deep you need to go to the ER. You just want to see yourself bleed."

"Bleeding is freeing," Shell told Jess with an ecstatic look on her face. "Once I cut myself, I imagine my pain flowing out of me in the blood. Afterwards I feel better for a few days and then when the suicide feeling comes back into me, I grab the box cutter or a razor blade and I purge myself all over again."

"I have to try this," Jess said. Somewhere inside of herself, she felt that this might just be the key that would set her free. They had two box cutters at home. She could easily snag one for her use without it being missed.

"What exactly is the darkness consuming you?" Jeffrey asked in his almost-baritone. "You've heard everyone else's stories, so you're not alone in your misery. You can tell us what the matter is."

Jess frowned and then sighed deeply. "My problem is that sometimes I feel completely worthless," she said. "I feel that I've no value to anyone. Not to myself, my parents, or even to you, my friends."

"That's just so sad," Shell said and then she began weeping.

"Nah, she's just hungry," Mimi told the goth kids. "Look at how thin Jess is. She needs to eat more often."

CHAPTER 25

That night, when her parents had gone to bed, Jess got out of bed and decided to put Shell's cutting technique to the test.

She'd already secreted one of her mother's box cutters under her pillow.

Now she turned on the reading lamp beside her bed. Then she pulled out the box cutter, slipped out a quarter inch of blade, and bared her arm.

She lined the knife up parallel to her arm and sliced into her skin.

Oh God! Jess felt like screaming. She'd never intentionally hurt herself before and this first time hurt like hell.

But then she saw the blood. Just a small line of blood trailed the cut, not even sufficient to be classified as a trickle. Definitely not enough to purge anything worthwhile out of her.

She took a deep breath and then cut herself again.

This time she dragged the box cutter blade along her arm for a longer distance. She felt the burning pain of the blade parting her skin.

And when she saw the blood, she also felt a feeling of satisfaction, a sense of accomplishment that she'd lacked for so long.

She cut herself once more, another long cut that really hurt her.

And then she felt something very strange. She realized that the pain she'd just inflicted on herself had conquered her inner hurt. All of a sudden, it seemed to her that the cloud of depression that had hung over her for so long had lifted.

Was the pain responsible or the blood? She didn't know, but she knew that she'd soon find out. After all she had a whole lot of body surface to experiment on and lots of days to experiment in. And she was certain that come tomorrow morning, her depression would be back to torment her again.

But for tonight, she felt a strange peace. She actually felt something other than loneliness and worthlessness.

Yes, she felt pain, but this was a kind of pain that she had control over, a pain that made her feel like she was back in control of her life, and was no longer spiraling down into a black hole, no longer a nobody traveling nowhere on the devil's rollercoaster.

***

And this was how Jess began self-harming herself.

She made sure to wear a long-sleeved shirt to school the next day so that her mother, who was dropping her off, wouldn't notice.

And then, at lunchtime, she cornered Shell and extracted from her as much information about the techniques and benefits of self-harming oneself as she could.

Shell gladly advised her.

Jess became a true self-harm devotee. Every night she'd sit up and cut lines into her body to take control of her life again.

She would relish her pain and see her terrors fleeing her in her blood and then go to sleep happy.

CHAPTER 26

Jess's 'pain cure' worked well for about a week or so.

But there was a crisis looming on her horizon.

As always, it was Mimi who first heard the damning news.

Once they had midmorning recess, Mimi pulled Jess aside and told her the story that was now buzzing on the school grapevine:

"Listen," Mimi whispered urgently. "Your ex is telling everyone what you're like in bed!"

"What?" Jess felt like the floor had just been yanked away from beneath her feet.

"It's true! It's true!" Mimi insisted. She was clearly worried, this made evident by the fact that for once she was eating anything. "Barry is lying to people how you and he had sex. He's saying you really suck at it too. Meaner Tina heard him bragging to someone about you and she texted me about it."

"But . . ." Jess said wide-eyed with shock. "But . . .?"

"What are you gonna do about it?" Mimi asked her breathlessly. "The story is spreading like a forest fire."

"I feel like killing myself."

"I would too."

"What exactly is Barry saying about me?" Jess asked Mimi in a trembling voice.

Mimi told her. Apparently, Barry Lindsey had been telling people the tale of how he'd raped her under the bleachers, but altering the truth and telling everyone that she'd been the one who'd practically raped him.

Hearing this, Jess felt devastated.

Just when I've got my life under some kind of control again, this has to happen to me!

***

"Listen, Jess, it's not that bad," Mimi said on seeing her start to cry. "All you've gotta do is tell everyone that he *tried* to rape you, but you got away from him. Once you say that, he'll be scared of the cops and back off, and he'll stop spreading nasty rumors about you."

Mimi was shocked when her advice made Jess break out in loud weeping.

She was even more shocked when Jess turned and ran off moaning, "It's not fair! Oh God, it's just not fair!"

CHAPTER 27

A few nights later, David and Willow Harris were watching television in the living room. The time was about 9 p.m. and as was normal nowadays, Jess had barricaded herself in her bedroom, and was doing whatever angsty teens did.

"How's our young terrorist-in-training?" David asked Willow.

"I wish you wouldn't call her that," Willow said with a bitter twist to her lips. "It's hard enough that she's doing the teenage angst thing twenty-four-seven now, but to imagine that she's gonna get worse is just . . ."

"Oh, she'll grow out of it."

"She's just started growing *into* it, and I already understand why some parents don't bother looking for their runaways. Some days, she's such a bundle of stress that I'm even wishing she'd run away herself."

David looked at her in mock horror. Then he laughed. "Hard day at the office, huh!"

She laughed too. "The craziest ever. You wouldn't believe what happened today."

David muted the sound on the TV and poised himself to listen.

"Two great deals fell through," Willow explained. "Well, one of the deals did; I'm still fingers crossed on the other one. The first was an old couple who I was showing a house over in West Milford. So, what happened was, we get there, and they love the place, but then while we're looking over the inside, the old man—well, he's about 65—he suddenly starts wheezing really bad. Apparently, he's asthmatic and they'd forgotten his inhaler at home. Long story short, we had to call for an ambulance to rush him to the hospital. When I called the wife this evening to enquire how he was doing, she tells me that her husband is in intensive care, and that she's mad at me for bringing them to a house with so many allergens in it. And now they don't want the house anymore. And they don't want us to help them find another one either."

"Wow," David said, pulling her close to him on the living room couch and stroking her long black hair soothingly. "Not your fault, baby. It couldn't be helped. "So, what happened in the other case."

Now Willow laughed. "Hahahaha! This one was almost the craziest thing I'd ever experienced. So, this Gen-Z couple comes in to sign their house papers. And then, right there in our office, they have a blow-up."

David pulled back a little so he could properly see Willow's face. "A blow-up?" he asked.

She nodded. Yes. Mr. and Mrs. Baker had a marital explosion of nuclear proportions. I was too busy checking that I had all of the necessary documents there on my table and wasn't looking at their faces at the time so I'm still not sure what set them both off, but all of a sudden, she slaps him twice and then he shoves her away, and then she picks up the stapler on my desk—you know that big antique one I use as a paperweight?—and she throws it at him."

"What?" David asked in surprise.

Willow nodded. "Yeah, she flings it at his head. But he's clearly practiced in this sort of thing, because he ducks out of the way almost before she launches her projectile through the air." Willow laughed. "The stapler just misses Harry Jones by a fraction of an inch, by which time Mr. Baker shoves Mrs. Baker away and she topples sideways out of her chair and then, while we're trying to restrain him from going over there and beating her up—he looks mad enough to pulverize her—she instead grabs the laptop off of my desk, folds it up and then throws it at her husband and the guys who are holding onto him. The two guys duck in time, but since they were holding onto Mr. Baker, he's got nowhere to run. The laptop hits him flush on the brow, and he goes down and doesn't get up again."

"That's crazy."

"And then, she runs over to him and starts weeping on him and telling him how she's sorry about it. Of course, he can't hear her 'cos he's out cold. He's got a long cut in his forehead, but he's still breathing." Willow really began laughing now. "And Mrs. Baker is still weeping madly and I get out my phone to call 911, but she tells me not to bother, that she'll drive him over to the ER herself. So, we carry him outside and put him in the passenger seat of their Nissan. And then, with tears running down her face, she comes back inside the office and asks me for the house papers. She says that she and her husband *love* the house and that they'll go over the papers in detail and sign them at home and then return them to me. I was as shocked as anyone else. So, I hand her the papers and she hurries out to her car and drives off with her husband. When I called her later, she said he has a concussion, but is otherwise okay, and that she'll bring in the signed papers for the purchase later in the week."

"Wow," David said. Some married couples are just crazy."

Willow laughed. "You know, talking about stuff really helps put it in perspective. While both of those two incidents were happening, it felt like the world was going crazy around me, but now that I'm telling you about them, it's different. I can see the funny side of things—in Mr. and Mrs. Bakers' case, I mean, and . . ." she paused and smiled at him. "But enough about my trials and tribulations. Honey, what was your day like? How far have you got with those consultancy proposals you emailed to Lockheed Martin?"

David frowned. "They're still stalling. I think they want me to lower my rates. But I'm not gonna do it. I know my worth. I know the market value of the services I'll be providing to them."

Willow nodded seriously. "Yes, I agree. Companies always try to lowball freelancers, and if you let—"

The doorbell rang then.

David glanced at the clock on the mantlepiece. The time was 9.15. "I wonder who's coming over this late?" He peered at his wife. "You got any idea?"

She shook her head, but then reconsidered: "Maybe old Mr. Gray wants to know if his package got mistakenly delivered to us like it did last time."

The doorbell rang again. This time, the person at the front door kept their finger on the buzzer for a long time, clearly so that those in the house would realize that he or she wasn't leaving until their business had been stated.

"I'll go see who it is and what they want," David said and got to his feet. Now he felt some irritation, because the person at the front door still had their hand on the buzzer.

While David walked to the front door, Willow got up and peered out of the living room windows. She didn't see anyone outside, but she did see a black and white SUV with a light bar atop it parked out in the street at the bottom of their driveway.

"I think it's the police," Willow told David as he stalked out of the living room.

CHAPTER 28

Yes, it was the police.

David Harris opened the door and was shocked to find a large Latino policeman with a sheriff's badge on his chest standing there.

David felt a momentary thrill of fear. Behind the man, down by the curb, his police cruiser stood looking as solid as a penitentiary.

"Good evening, sir," the officer greeted.

"Good evening, officer. What seems to be the matter?"

"I'm Deputy Sheriff Rodriguez," the officer introduced himself. "I need to talk to you and your wife, Mr. . . . ." he seemed to search his memory for the family name and then finished: "Mr. Harris."

"Sure, come on inside," David said. He was shocked by the officer's being at their home. Quickly, while leading the officer through into the living room, he ran his mind over the different possibilities that would prompt a visit from the police.

Is ma dead? Or sis? Or is it one of Willow's family?

He couldn't work it out and the uncertainty worried him even more.

One thing David Harris was sure of however: he knew that the police never visited you at home unless something was *very wrong* somewhere in your life.

But what can that be?

"Good evening, officer. What's the matter?" Willow asked the moment they walked into the living room.

"Please sit down, both of you," Deputy Rodriguez told them.

They did so, while he remained standing.

"Okay, so what is it?" Willow insisted. "Did someone die?"

Officer Rodriguez shook his head. "Thankfully, no. But I'm here to see if we can prevent that from happening."

"I don't follow you," David said, feeling the tension almost as a band wrapped around his chest and tightening.

"About . . ." Officer Rodriguez checked the time on his watch. "About fifteen minutes ago, our suicide prevention hotline center called us and told us they'd received a call from a teenaged girl who was thinking of killing herself. The young lady didn't give them her name, but we were able to trace the phone number to Mrs. Harris."

While saying this, he looked pointedly at Willow, and then pulled out a notepad. As he read the digits, Willow's eyes widened.

"That's the number I got for our daughter Jess," Willow said in a trembling voice. "Wha-wha-wha . . .?"

"Suicide?" David asked in a voice so low he could hardly hear it himself. "Jess called a suicide hotline?" He looked upstairs, like he could see through the ceiling into Jess's room and beyond that to heaven. "Oh, my God."

"Yes, thank God that she called them," Officer Rodriguez told the bewildered parents. "The responder talked her down, and she promised not to try it, but I was sent over here to check that she's alright and to notify you—her parents—of the situation."

Willow was now visibly trembling. "But why, why would she want to kill herself?"

Officer Rodriguez now looked visibly troubled. "There's no easy way to say this, so I'll just come right out with it."

David pulled Willow close to him and nodded. He was seized by the urge to run upstairs and check that Jess was okay, but apparently she was, so he steadied his nerves. "We're listening, man."

"Apparently, a few months ago, your daughter was attacked—sexually assaulted—by another student, a male student at the Thompson High School."

"What?" David shot up from his chair like a bullet. "What? Jess was raped? Raped at school?"

Officer Rodriguez nodded solemnly. "I'm afraid that's correct, sir. According to what your daughter told the suicide prevention hotline, since the sexual assault happened, she's been growing more and more depressed for months, because she didn't think you'd love her anymore if she told either of you, and . . ."

"But we love our daughter!" Willow had tears in her eyes now.

"I'm certain that you do," the deputy sheriff said. "So, she felt unloved and she said she recently began self-harming herself—"

"What do you mean, self-harming?" David asked.

"It's what some young girls do when they're very unhappy: they cut their arms with a knife or razor. It's a cry for help."

"Oh, my God. Is that why she's taken to wearing long-sleeved shirts and dresses all of a sudden? So we won't notice that she's been cutting herself?" Willow said this almost to herself. She looked miserably at the deputy. "I thought she'd taken to wearing long-armed clothes simply because the weather has been a little chilly."

Officer Rodriguez shook his head. "I'm afraid not, ma'am. Wrist and arm cutting is considered a cry for help by psychiatrists, but if the kids don't show their parents what's going on with them, how can their parents help them?"

"Hold on a minute, officer," David said. "Let me go upstairs and fetch Jess. And then she can tell us what happened herself." He shook his head. "I still can't believe that she was raped at school."

"Or that she never mentioned it to us afterwards," Willow added.

"I need to hear her say it to us herself," David said. "Until I hear the tale from her own lips I'm gonna feel like there's been some mistake."

He practically ran up the stairs.

Later he figured that Jess must've been waiting for him to come upstairs, because she opened the door immediately when he knocked on it.

He stood inside her room, staring sadly at her, and she too stared miserably back at him. He understood then that there was no real need to hear what she had to say, the truth of everything that Deputy Rodriguez had told him and Willow was right there in Jess's eyes for him to read.

"Oh, my poor, poor, baby!" David groaned, and suddenly tears filled his own eyes too.

And then he extended his hands forward to Jess and she walked tentatively into his embrace, and he hugged her tight.

"Oh, my poor poor, baby," he wept into her hair. "I'm so, so, so, sorry that something like that ever had to happen to you."

He felt her trembling against his chest, her small body full of tension. And then he realized that she was crying too.

"Oh, daddy, daddy, I'm so sorry," she gasped into his chest. "I wanted to tell you, but I was scared."

She continued weeping against him, loud sobs that quickly wet his shirt, but he sensed that, now that her secret was out in the open, her crisis had reached a turning point.

After they'd both wept for a while, David picked Jess up like she was a baby and carried her downstairs.

And then, while she sat on his lap, she told him, Willow, and Deputy Rodriguez everything that had happened to her on that fateful day six months ago when she'd gone to meet Barry Lindsey over at the Jamieson stadium bleachers.

CHAPTER 29

Deputy Rodriguez made certain to record Jess's statement on his cellphone.

David and Willow were both devastated by the revelations.

"How could this happen to her in school?" Willow asked in a shocked voice, once again speaking more to herself than to the two men. "Middle school is supposed to be a safe place for kids."

"Stuff like this happens a lot more than one can imagine," Deputy Rodriguez said. "A lot more. It doesn't get mentioned for lack of evidence."

David shook his head. Jess was still sitting on his lap. He held her tight and caressed her hair. She was trembling with emotion and he hoped it was the emotion of acceptance and not fear and dread.

"So, what is gonna happen now?" David asked the deputy.

Deputy Rodriguez wagged his cellphone at them. "Well, first of all, I'll play your daughter's testimony to the sheriff and we'll take it from there. I dunno what's gonna happen—and I don't wanna promise anything, sir, but we'll see . . ."

The deputy got to his feet and nodded to them both. "I guess I'll be leaving now. I'll see myself out."

The deputy left. David Harris realized that the lawman had left the family alone with a huge amount of pain. Pain that might never be erased.

David looked down at Jess, who sat motionless against him, though she was still trembling with emotion. He hugged her tight and looked at Willow.

Willow began weeping again. "How can this happen to her?" she asked angrily. "How in the world can something as horrible as this happen to our daughter?"

CHAPTER 30

Jess was surprised by how free she felt now that her secret was out in the open.

True, she still felt soiled and unclean, but now she no longer felt suicidal. She actually felt very embarrassed when she recalled making that call to the suicide helpline.

Was I really that . . . what's the word for it . . . yes, melodramatic?

Because even to her own mind, once she'd gotten her confession off of her chest, the pressure of being the sole owner of that knowledge had lifted.

So yes, in that sense, she felt things were better. At home now, both her father and her mother—whom she'd dreaded finding out— were bending over backwards to make her feel better.

"I'm fine," she occasionally protested angrily when her hormones acted up, but without much fire.

Overall though, Jess was shocked that she'd worried so long and so hard about losing her parents' love.

Her father, in particular, was now becoming so protective of her that it felt stifling.

Okay, so yes, she was a walking wounded person (an expression she'd heard a woman use on YouTube), but she was still an individual, and felt capable of looking after herself.

CHAPTER 31

At school though, not much had changed.

"We're lucky that no one really believes Barry slept with you," Mimi told Jess three days after the cop visited her parents. "So, you're in the clear."

Laden with books, both girls were walking through the school hallways.

"Barry is a real jerk," Jess replied angrily. "I wish he'd just drop dead so I never have to see him again."

Once more dreading Mimi's guaranteed overreaction to the info, Jess hadn't mentioned her aborted suicide plans to her. The longer this whole scenario played out, the easier it had become to pretend to Mimi that everything was peachy.

"So, did cutting yourself work?" Mimi asked her.

Mimi of course, was still eating her way through the day, except that she wasn't having much success at gaining weight anymore. Something about a hormone imbalance, according to her parents.

"A little," Jess replied. "But I'm giving it up. It hurts too much."

"Better not let Jeffrey and Shell hear you say that," Mimi cautioned as they made their way to the girls' restrooms. "They'll say you wimped out."

"I'll just avoid them. I'm not gonna have any fresh scars to show Shell now anyway. And . . ."

"And what?" Mimi asked.

"The real reason I gotta stop cutting is because my mom found out, and now she insists that I only wear short-sleeved clothes about the house so she can see my arms all the time. She even checks my belly and my legs. So, I'm done with that."

"That sucks," Mimi said with feeling. "I hate how parents are always getting into our stuff. They act like they own our lives." Mimi pulled out her cellphone. "Hey, I found this new app that lets you blend your photo-face with that of your fave movie actress. You can save the result for profile pix."

Mimi demonstrated the app to Jess for a while and then sent her the link to it.

CHAPTER 32

David Harris had never felt as frustrated before in his life as he did on that afternoon when he and Deputy Sheriff Rodriguez met with school principal Garrison and vice principal Shelly White.

The visit was unscheduled on David's part, as Deputy Rodriguez simply called him that morning and asked him to accompany him to Thompson Middle School to discuss how the investigations were coming along with the school principal.

That in itself sounded dodgy to David, who for the past week had wondered why nothing had so far happened.

He'd heard of no arrests and according to Jess, she'd twice seen Barry Lindsey on the middle school campus since then. He'd made no attempt to approach her, however, but nonetheless had given her some really nasty looks that frightened her immensely.

"Aren't you cops supposed to investigate this stuff on your own?" David asked Rodriguez while the deputy piloted the police SUV over to Thompson Middle School.

"We do," Deputy Rodriguez told him. "But it ain't as easy as it looks. That's why the sheriff asked me to take you with me today. So, you can hear for yourself what the school has to say 'bout this."

"I don't wanna hear what the school has to say," David protested. "I just want justice for Jess."

"Which is why we're here," Deputy Rodriguez told him and turned the police cruiser off the street and onto the school campus.

"I don't get it," David said as they disembarked from the SUV. "Shouldn't that punk Barry be in police custody? My daughter tells me he's still walking around free as the air."

Deputy Rodriguez gave David a pained look. "Sir, please just come with me to the principal's office. This ain't easy for me either."

Not knowing what to expect, but expecting it was going to suck, David followed the deputy into the school. While conversing with the man during their drive over, David had also been trying to get Willow on the phone. Not surprisingly, she was out of reach at the moment, maybe down in the southern part of Harrison County.

CHAPTER 33

"Listen, gentlemen," School principal Ron Garrison told both of his visitors after they'd seated themselves. "We'd like to help out here, but I don't see how we can."

David shook his head. "I don't understand."

"We're trying to keep this quiet and out of the news until we've confirmed we've got an actual case here," Deputy Rodriguez explained. "And so, we've had the school authorities make discreet inquiries and hold interviews with the students to confirm that your daughter actually *was* sexually assaulted."

"What?" David asked in confusion.

"Yes, Mr. Harris, sir. Sheriff says that's the right way to go. He thinks the school doesn't need adverse publicity if it's just a teen lover's quarrel." On seeing the anger that rose up in David's eyes at this comment, the deputy made the classic 'palms raised' gesture. "His words, sir. Not mine."

David belatedly remembered that the county sheriff's daughter was one of the teachers here, and his grandchildren also attended the high school.

Well, that figures, he thought.

Notwithstanding, he gave the principal an incredulous and aggrieved look.

Principal Ron Garrison sighed back at him. "The problem, sir, is that it hasn't just happened. I mean, the assault that your daughter alleges Barry Lindsey committed on her."

David was about to reply, but Vice Principal White shook her head at him. "No, hold on, please. It's like this, and I'm sure the deputy sheriff will agree with me: if your daughter Jessica had told someone—

anyone at all—what had happened to her right then, we'd have immediately contacted the law ourselves and they'd have performed a rape kit for her." Shelly White shook her head grimly. "If that had occurred, the police would have been able to establish not just that they'd had sexual intercourse, but also that it had been *forced* on her." She gave David a pointed look. "But the way it is, now . . . months later, there's absolutely no way in hell now that we can prove anything."

"It's her word against his," the school principal added. "She says he forced her; he says she didn't."

"Clearly, one of them is lying," the vice principal added. "The problem is, which of them do we believe?"

"My daughter would never lie about something like that!" David growled angrily.

Not for the first time since learning about Jess's ordeal, he wished that matters like this could be resolved by means as simple and direct as shooting the perpetrator.

Through his irate haze, David became aware that Principal Garrison was staring at him sympathetically.

Or was that pityingly?

"Listen, Mr. Harris," the principal said. "This is a difficult thing to discuss with a parent, but the problem is, that sometimes our children aren't exactly who we think they are. I've been a school principal for thirty years now, and your hair would curl to hear some of the things the children of law-abiding, God-fearing parents have gotten up to with their parents being none the wiser."

"But Jess is nothing like that," David protested. "She's not that sort of child at all." He raised his voice, not in anger, but rather to make them all believe him. "If Jess had been a rebellious child, I'd not be here now."

Deputy Sheriff Rodriguez laughed coldly, and addressed the principal. "Sir, you know I've already told you how I'm inclined to believe Mr. Harris. We've a recording of his daughter's call to the suicide helpline. It doesn't make for pleasant listening."

"I know, I know," the principal agreed. "The sheriff played it to me. But even that . . ."

"Once more, I think I need to cite that the problem in this case is the amount of time that has elapsed before the alleged incident came to light," the vice principal added.

David found that he was getting angry again.

That damn word 'alleged.' 'Alleged' because we can't prove it. Or . . . is it because we don't wanna prove it?

A scenario unfolded in David's mind. So far, there had been nothing about the attack on Jess in the news. Which was understandable, but David didn't understand how the school was making no attempt to expel, or even suspend Barry Lindsey from classes.

They're so scared for their reputation that the fight for justice takes a backseat.

"So, the kid is just gonna . . . I mean, nothing's gonna be done to him?" David stared at Deputy Sheriff Rodriguez in horror. "He's just gonna rape my daughter and go scot-free without even a slap on the wrists?"

"Please, calm down, sir," the deputy said. "This is a really complicated situation here. I agree with the school that Barry Lindsey can't be penalized in any way whatsoever unless we can lay provable charges against him. Which unfortunately, is proving almost impossible."

Deputy Rodriguez now shook his head at everyone in the room. "From where I stand, I'm willing to bet a thousand bucks that the kid is as guilty as charged. The apple never falls far from the tree, and I know his folks. His dad Billy Lindsey has had more brushes with the law than I can count. No-good trash is all the kid's dad is, and we regularly get called out to their place to stop him beating up his wife. So, I'm willing to bet the kid is just emulating his dad's bad behavior with women." Deputy Rodriguez sighed. "I'm just sorry, Mr. Harris, sir, that the damn kid had to pile up his crap on your front stoop, sir."

"No proof, no proof, they say," David said in a low disbelieving voice. "No proof."

"Okay, consider this, sir," Shelly White told David. "We tried to play up the suicidal angle with those students—friends of Barry—that we interviewed, but they all claim that Jess made that call to the suicide crisis line because she wanted to get Barry in trouble for dumping her."

"But that's complete nonsense!" David said.

"Please calm down, Mr. Harris" the principal said. "Barry's sister Mary says her brother told her the same thing."

"But the other kids? I mean Jess's friends?"

Shelly White shook her head sadly. "This is where it gets even more complicated. According to everyone we asked, your daughter's best friend is Mimi Richards. When we asked Mimi if Jess had told her anything about an assault, Mimi said no, but she'd figured out for herself that Jess was brokenhearted because Barry broke up with her."

"And suddenly it's public knowledge amongst the students that your daughter and Barry Lindsey had a relationship for a couple weeks," the principal added.

"So you see, Mr. Harris," Deputy Rodriguez said gently. "Our hands are tied. There is literally nothing we can do to that kid Barry unless he changes his story, or slips up in some way, or God forgive me for even thinking like this, attempts a similar stunt on another girl."

The deputy looked horrified at what he'd just suggested.

"Okay, I've got a question here," David told the principal. "Why is everything being kept so quiet? The kid hasn't even been charged. I know that there's an investigative technique where you arrest someone to put pressure on them, to see if they'll crack."

Once again, Deputy Rodriguez looked upset. "Principal Garrison asked the sheriff to keep things quiet because of the school's reputation," he explained.

"We don't want a situation where parents begin panicking and withdrawing their kids from here simply because of an unsubstantiated accusation," the principal confirmed, this time with notably less sympathy than he'd shown at the beginning of their discussion. "This middle school—or rather, I should say, this *group* of Thompson schools—has an excellent reputation in the state for academic integrity. It would be horrible to have that reputation tarnished by unsubstantiated accusations of rape."

"What about my daughter's reputation?" David asked in anger. He felt that he now understood what was going on here. Ron Garrison viewed Jess's accusation against Barry Lindsey as an attack against the school itself. And since he—Garrison—was the custodian of the school's history and traditions and of its perfect record, even the truth must be trampled down to maintain the illusion that all was well here.

David suddenly had the impression that Principal Garrison was secretly mocking him. His gray eyes seemed to say, *If you'd just kept better watch over your slut of a daughter, you'd not have this problem now.*

David felt something like white noise burning behind his eyes and had the feeling that he'd burst open if he couldn't hold someone accountable for what had happened to Jess.

"What about my daughter's reputation?" he asked again, in a miserable voice. "Doesn't that count for anything here?"

"Sir, we've been over this before," Shelly White replied in a concerned voice, as if she imagined he was about to have a nervous breakdown. "You'll have to accept that there's nothing at all we can do. We'd also like to see justice served here, but—"

"Yeah, I know, we ain't got no proof against the little rapist punk," David agreed sadly.

"*Alleged* rapist punk, sir," Deputy Rodriguez corrected him nervously. "You need to use the word 'alleged' whenever you refer to this incident, or else you could find yourself in court for slander. And I assure you, sir, that the kid's broke-ass dad needs the money he'd get from suing you."

"Yeah, yeah," David said. "*Alleged* rapist punk it is then." That bitterly stated, he got up to leave the principal's office.

David felt like throwing up as he walked back to Deputy Rodriguez's police car.

"I'm really sorry about this, sir," the deputy told him. "I can't imagine how you must be feeling, but you just heard for yourself that there's nothing we can do."

"I'm sorry too," David replied to the man. "I'm sorry for what our American education and legal system has become if a teenage victim can't get the justice that she deserves."

CHAPTER 34

"What're you doing this Saturday?" Jess asked Mimi that same afternoon, unaware that her father had earlier been to the school. "My mom and dad want me to go to the youth group meetings at our church, but I don't wanna go."

She and Mimi were sitting on one of the twin concrete tree enclosures in front of the school building.

Mimi gave her an inquisitive stare. "Why not? Some of them are fun."

"Not this one," Jess told her. I dunno what the problem is, but something's not right. If you aren't going out, I'll ask my dad to let me hang out with you instead."

Mimi got an 'interested' look on her face: "Ooh, are the youth leaders perverts?"

Jess almost laughed, and she shook her head. She liked how she could talk to Mimi like this, without the crushing weight of her trouble on her shoulders. Sure, she still did keep looking over her shoulder from time to time to see if anyone was stalking her, but even that worry didn't carry the same degree of terror that it had held for her yesterday.

Mimi still looked like she was eager to hear about 'perverted youth leaders.'

"No, not like that," Jess replied to her bestie's question. "They're not perverts. But I don't get it. We're supposed to be doin' church stuff, but last time I attended, we spent most of the afternoon watching a WVU football game on a large screen television. It was weird. We ate and drank and hung out with one another, and laughed, played board games and watched football and then we prayed to God and we all went home. There were other kids from our school there too."

"Really? Who?"

Jess tried to remember: "Larry Poole and his older sis Cheryl were there too. And Bobby Scott from 7th grade."

"That doesn't sound too bad," Mimi said. "I'd love to go out on weekends like that, but my parents aren't church goers, except if someone is being christened or someone dies or is getting married. It'd be great to not have Mom and Dad looking over my shoulder for some hours at least, or me not having to babysit my baby sister for a change. You know how Tom used to babysit both of us, but nowadays he's hardly ever home. And so, my mom is delighted that *I'm* now thirteen. It means she can go out with my dad whenever she likes. They don't have to pay a babysitter any longer." Mimi sighed. "Being a teenager really sucks."

Jess shook her head. "I like Christianity, but this meeting was very boring. Really boring. I wished I was at home watching TV instead." She shrugged at Mimi. "I told my dad I'd like to find another church, where I really feel *some* type of connection to God."

Mimi laughed and unpeeled a candy bar. "According to my parents, God doesn't really care about us, or else Earth would be a nicer place to live. I dunno if I believe them or not."

Mimi held the candy bar out to Jess. "Want some? I checked online; it's supposed to be very fattening."

Jess shook her head fiercely. "No, thanks!"

CHAPTER 35

David smiled at Jess as he dropped her off at school the next morning.

He still felt devastated after learning what she'd suffered at her school. He was angry at the school's unwillingness to do anything about it. He still couldn't get over how smoothly the cover-up had been arranged and even sold to him.

But as compensation, he also had the relief of knowing just how close to losing her he'd come.

Oh, my God! I can't get over how close it was. If she'd not called the suicide prevention hotline, but instead got in the bathtub and slit her wrists like she'd planned on doing? Oh, thank you, Jesus that I've still got my baby girl alive!

Jess grinned in at him. "Sorry, daddy, but I'm a big girl now. No more kisses on the cheek for you."

He laughed back. "I wouldn't dream of asking for one, hon. But of course, lots of hugs are still in order, aren't' they?"

She nodded. "Yes, daddy, hugs are still cool."

David nodded back at her. He'd begun hugging Jess every chance he got. His reasoning was to let her know that he wasn't disgusted with her or thought that she was unclean or any of those other misinterpretations that might occur to her.

It seemed to be working.

So, yes, several weeks later, Jess's eyes still bore some of that same haunted look that he and Willow had mistaken for teenage angst, and David could tell that behind her smile, she was still hurting, but he hoped that she'd heal. She was a strong girl; he knew this because of how long she'd kept her pain to herself without cracking from the strain of it.

He laughed. "Okay, honey, run along now and be a good kid. Don't go getting into fights and causing your teachers any grief."

"That's what mom always says," Jess said. "Okay, dad, see you in the afternoon."

He felt mixed emotions as he watched her walk away from him, mingling with the hustle and bustle of the other arriving students until he could no longer distinguish her from the rest of them.

So many young sheep who need a shepherd to guide them towards the green grass of adulthood, he thought with a cool smile after Jess had completely mingled in with the rest of her teen peers.

But then he frowned. *But some of those sheep are really wolves in disguise— doggone it! Wolves like that punk Barry Lindsey, who's harmed my little girl and yet gets to go free!*

What to do now? David didn't know. He and Willow had already discussed taking Jess to see a counselor who specialized in such cases. Willow liked the idea, but Jess was resistant to it. She said it had been hard enough talking about what happened to her with him and her mother, and later the school principal. How was she supposed to share her pain with someone she didn't know at all?

Jess said she just wanted to forget everything and let time heal her.

Well, we'll see if that works. If it does, fair enough; but if it doesn't, if I sense that Jess is having a relapse into her depression, then we'll have no choice but to send her to a shrink.

David took his foot off the car's brake and headed for home.

CHAPTER 36

Willow Harris was once more over in the town of West Milford, with Mr. and Mrs. Adams, the old man who'd suffered the fierce asthma attack, and his wife.

It had turned out that Mrs. Adams had simply been overwrought with passion because of her husband's health crisis. Once he was out of the hospital, he'd personally called Willow and asked her to meet them over at the house again, so they could finish looking it over.

This time Willow had first stopped at a pharmacy and bought an inhaler, which she took along with her, just in case. True, lightning wasn't supposed to strike twice in the same place, and she honestly didn't think the old couple would be so careless as to forget the husband's inhaler again, but accidents could happen.

However, this time everything went well. Mr. and Mrs. Adams finished inspecting the place and, right there on the spot, made the decision to buy the house.

Willow made an appointment with them to sign the necessary paperwork, and they all parted company on much better terms than they had the last time.

Driving back to her office, Willow felt in a good mood.

But then her thoughts turned to her daughter, and her mood soured.

What did one do in situations like this?

It's all well and good to offer advice to one's friends when one of their kids gets in a bad way, but what do you do when it's your own daughter who bites the poisoned apple? I don't know what to do! I didn't plan for this? This wasn't part of the script! God in heaven, what the hell have you just done to me?

Willow meant this last question literally.

Though not the most religious of persons, she was nonetheless a woman who believed implicitly in God and in Christ his son and who, if she didn't exactly go to church at all times, went often enough and acted on God's rules enough that she expected some sort of acknowledgement from the Almighty that her faith in him was reciprocated by his liking for her.

So, why Lord have you done this to me?

Although she loved her daughter with all of her heart, Willow Harris was having the devil's time of coping with the aftermath of Jess's sexual assault.

Indeed, in one sense, Willow was having a harder time coping with it than Jess herself was having, because Jess was in regression from what had happened to her, moving from her darkness into the light of a positive place, while Willow was in a state of progression, in which the consequences of her daughter's rape grew larger before her eyes with every passing day.

Willow herself understood that this was unreasonable thinking, but she couldn't help how she felt.

Her phone rang then where it lay on the passenger seat. She glanced over at it and saw that it was her husband.

After checking that the road was largely free of oncoming traffic, she clicked on the green button to answer the call.

"Hello, darling," she said. "Are you okay?"

"Hi, honey, how did the repeat showing go?"

"Wonderful. They've agreed to buy the house. I've just got to prepare the papers for their signature."

"That's great news. Listen, honey, I need you to do something for me. Can you make it over to Jess's school to pick her up?"

Before replying to him, Willow did some quick thinking. "Yeah, I think I can manage it," she said. "2:30, like usual?

"Yep," David replied. "Unless she has some student council after-school meeting I forgot to jot down."

"No problem. I'll call Jess and confirm when she needs me to pick her up. But what happened? Why can't you go?"

"I got a call from Lockheed Martin," David said. "They would like me to come in for a meeting at 2 p.m. to discuss the proposal."

"Oh, that's nice," Willow acknowledged, gripping the steering wheel extra tight as a large semi approached her in the opposing lane. "The fish are finally biting the bait."

He laughed. "I hope they will. Okay, honey, gotta go. Love ya. Hug Jess for me, okay?"

She laughed back, wondering where his sudden obsession with hugging their daughter came from. She would ask him about it later.

"Love you too," she told him, then returned her concentration fully to the road once he'd hung up.

***

Jess had no after-school activities today, and so dismissal time found Willow waiting for her.

She sat in her car and watched the students pour out of the school entrance.

They're like ants emerging from a hive.

Willow liked that similarity. Ants were very busy creatures. Indeed, the Bible advised people to learn from them because of how hardworking they were.

And the kids now spreading in every direction from the school entrance really give Willow the illusion of being brightly colored insects.

Some good, some bad, Willow thought sourly. *Some benign and some poisonous. Some of these young adults are butterflies and others are scorpions.*

Scorpions like that nasty boy who stung my little girl.

Unlike her husband, Willow was less surprised that Barry Lindsey would get away scot-free.

"It happens to women all the time," she'd told David. "There's no proof and then the woman's abuser is set free to abuse again. And women just have to put up with it."

97

David had had no reply. She could see how angry he was, but she knew that being as angry as he was was a waste of time.

What counts is action. Young women need to build their own lives independent of men.

She studied the emerging human sea of young faces; all of those young minds aglow with the possibilities that education opened up to them, those visions of what they could become in life, if they only dared dream big enough and put in the work to chase down those dreams.

But of course, one had to also take into consideration the snakes in paradise; the guilty corrupting the innocents; kids like Barry Lindsey; young fools with a genetic predisposition to personal failure who wrecked the dreams of others with their stupidity and evil.

Finally, Willow spotted Jess. She smiled as her daughter hurried out of school with the rest of the antlike youth.

Jess got into the car and strapped herself into her seat.

"So how was class today, darling?" her mother asked her.

"Oh, it was fine," Jess said in a noncommittal voice.

"You should be more serious about your studies," Willow told her as she joined the stream of cars that were departing the pickup loop.

"I am serious, mom," Jess said impatiently.

"Don't take that tone of voice with me, young lady," Willow said testily, without taking her eyes off of the road. "I'm telling you this for your own good. You're a woman, and a woman should have her own career and her own identity aside from men." She chanced a side glance at her daughter, saw that she looked angry and so added, "Later in life, you're gonna thank me for being so insistent on you studying your books."

"C'mon, mom, leave me alone," came the aggrieved teenaged reply, this one really the product of the rebellious soul that infected young humans between the ages of twelve and twenty. "Mom, I'm tired."

"I'm serious about this. You can't slack in your academic work."

Jess's response was to slump deep into her seat. "Don't worry," she grumbled. "I'm reading and I'll make good grades."

"It's very important that you do, young lady. Life can be . . ."

Then Willow gasped and stopped herself just in time. She had been about saying "Life can be cruel to woman who don't get good qualifications and have to depend on men for their livelihood."

Suddenly she felt like crying herself:

Life can be cruel? Cruel? What the hell is the matter with me? I was almost gonna put her down after everything she's suffered. Oh, dear God, you've gotta help me here.

To make up to Jess, she said. "Okay, dear, I'm sorry I lost my temper just now. I've been having a hard time at work."

She glanced aside at Jess again and added, "Okay, so I'll make it up to you. How 'bout if you and me go shopping for shoes? How does that sound?"

To her relief, Jess brightened up at the mention of shoes.

"You're serious?" she asked suspiciously.

"Yes, I'm serious," Willow replied.

"I can have any shoes I want?"

Willow laughed. "Yes, but if they're too expensive, your dad's gonna refund me the cost of them."

Jess giggled. "Okay! Okay, mom! Let's go!"

Well, bribing the child to be happy is better than nothing at all, Willow thought in some confusion, as she turned their car towards the Meadowbrook Mall shopping center.

It's most definitely better than her being angry all afternoon and thinking I don't care about her as much as her father does, when all I want is what's best for her, like he does.

CHAPTER 37

"Hey, daddy, stop! You're going the wrong way!"

Jess yelped this out because they'd just passed the turnoff to the Blessed Hope Baptist Church which the family had been attending for the past couple of months.

The church wasn't exactly Jess's favorite place, but even if it wasn't she had no idea where they were headed this morning.

Her mother laughed as the countryside rolled past their car.

"Relax, Jess, we aren't going to our old church today. Your father is taking us somewhere new."

"Oh? Where are we going, dad?"

David cleared his throat before replying. "I'm taking us to check out this new church I've heard a lot about online. It's called the Good Faith Assembly."

Good Faith Assembly? Jess mused on that for a while. She concluded that she might have heard the name mentioned before, or maybe seen an ad for the place on TV, or somewhere. Definitely not online though, as all she watched on the internet nowadays were romantic dramas.

"Best of all, they supposedly have a fantastic youth group there, one that you're almost guaranteed to love."

Jess sighed. Not that youth group nonsense again. She'd have thought her parents would have learnt their lesson from the last one she'd been part of.

"Dad, I don't wanna be part of any more youth groups," she protested. "I'm not interested in football!"

They'd been rolling through the approximate center of Bridgeport, which was largely deserted this early on Sunday morning. Jess stared out at the few people on the streets—a woman walking her dog, a couple riding bicycles, a woman pushing a stroller—and she desperately wished that she was older and that she had the power to stop this tyranny of being made to join youth groups.

I can't wait to be eighteen years old and an adult. If I can't have my way part of the time, then at least I can move out and not have to attend annoying church after annoying church.

"From what I hear of this youth group, they're different from the last one," Willow said. "They're very high energy."

"Mom, my energy level is high enough. You and daddy are always telling me to slow down!"

"Calm down, young lady, and listen," Willow said in a firm voice. "We've not even decided if we're going to be members of this church yet, so don't start throwing tantrums yet."

"Yeah, honey," her father told her as the family SUV rolled through the gates of the Good Faith Assembly compound and towards the parking lot, "You gotta save your tantrums for when they'll do you the most good, like your mom does with me."

Jess found that absurdly funny, though her mom clearly didn't.

PART TWO:
A NEW BEGINNING

CHAPTER 38

The Good Faith Assembly church was anything but what Jess had expected.

First of all, the service that she was attending was a combined one, with everybody—teens, parents, and old people—in the same hall.

She was ushered in along with her parents and shown into a pew alongside them. This both gave her the satisfaction of feeling grown up, but then reminded her that she was surrounded by adults and needed to keep the more raucous elements of her behavior in check.

You win some, you lose some.

The other thing that immediately struck Jess about the church was the energy she felt in the air. This had been apparent to her from the moment she stepped in through the double doors of the front entrance.

She could feel 'something' in the air in here, a weird sort of electric feeling that almost gave her gooseflesh, but in a very good way. And even more strange, after she'd sat on the pew beside her parents and had time to reflect on the odd 'buzz' that she felt, she could tell that whatever was in the air and was affecting her wasn't a physical thing. It was something else that she'd never experienced before.

It was both thrilling and scary.

The church was packed full of people. The hall or auditorium, which was circular in shape, had two levels, the ground floor where Jess's family were seated and an upper inner balcony that ran in a semicircle around the rear of the building. Up front, where normally a choir would be, was a band, complete with guitar, bass, keyboards and drums, along with the church deacons and the pastors.

Wow, this is a cool place, Jess thought, as the strange, unearthly sensation seemed to pass through her like fish swimming in water.

The family had arrived just as the singing was coming to its end. The music slowed and as the worship team led the congregation in a song about the glory of God, Jess felt like she could almost feel that stated glory coming down. She knew it was just her emotions, but she really did have that feeling as if God was here in the building right now.

The music ended. The congregation sang two contemporary worship songs, not traditional hymns like most of the other churches she had previously attended, and then pastor Bryan Howard got up to preach the sermon.

The pastor seemed to be about the same age as her parents and was tall with thinning hair, but he spoke with more vitality than her father did. He also had a pleasant sonorous voice.

"Now, listen, brothers and sisters," Bryan Howard said. "Why do we love God? Do we love God Almighty because of what we can get from him? Do we think of the good Lord on high as our spiritual ATM machine, someone who's there to pay our bills for us when we run out of money? Or do we love him because we're scared of him? I mean, do we love God—that's if we love him at all—because we think that if we don't love him, he'll wrap our new bimmer around a tree, or give us cancer, or won't let our kids grow up?"

The pastor paused and looked around the auditorium. "Oh no, folks. That is not the reason why we love our Lord God Almighty. That is not the reason why we love our Lord Jesus Christ. Holy brethren, now me tell you what the Bible says. Here in my Bible, in the book of First John, Chapter 4 and Verse 19, it reads: "We love him because he first loved us!" The pastor now left his lectern, danced along the stage, and then danced back to the lectern again.

Jess giggled. This was fun. She felt surprised by how much she was enjoying herself. This was fun like she'd never felt before in church.

She glanced cautiously at her parents, to see how they were taking the sermon, and maybe temper her own response to match theirs. But no, both her mother and her father were laughing too, as were most of the congregation around them.

Pastor Howard thumped his Bible hard, so that the noise reverberated through the hall.

"I dunno what your own Bible says, my brothers and my sisters," he went on, "but my Bible says that we love God—our heavenly father—because he first of all loved us. And now let me ask you all a question about this? What does the most popular verse ever in the Bible say?" Without waiting for a reply he said: "And the verse I'm referring to here, is John Chapter 3 Verse 16. Brothers and sisters, recite that verse along with me if you know it. On the count of three. One, two . . ."

"For God so loved the world that he gave his only begotten son, so that whosoever believeth in him should not perish, but have everlasting life!" the entire congregation thundered along with him.

Jess found herself reciting John 3:16 as loudly as everyone else around her, her father and mother inclusive. She stole another look at them. This time, her father caught her eye and grinned and gave her a thumbs up, as if to say, "This guy's good."

Pastor Howard preached on about the love of God for all men, and his message opened something up inside of Jess. She felt like the pastor's words were peeling away her layers of hurt; like she was an onion and even though her outer layers were bruised and dirty, she was all clean within, and she just needed to have those bad layers removed.

She sat there listening, almost in a daze, and then the message ended, seemingly too soon.

It's over, she realized in disappointment. She felt cheated; she felt like she'd just needed one more wash and she'd be clean, but that final bath of spiritual soap had been denied her.

Jess didn't know what was missing, but she felt sure something was. And just as surely as she knew something was missing, she suddenly had the certainty that here at the Good Faith Assembly church was where she would find that missing something.

CHAPTER 39

"So, what do you guys think about this place?" David asked after they'd gotten into their car. "Yay, or nay?"

"Yay!" Jess said immediately.

David and Willow looked at her in surprise. "You like it *that* much?" Willow asked her.

Not wanting to seem overeager, Jess shrugged. "I think so. This place—" she gestured out at the nearby church auditorium "—there's something different about it. Hey, daddy, I want to see what their youth group is like."

David nodded. She could see that he was pleased.

David looked at Willow. "And what is *your* verdict, sweetie pie?"

Willow 'hmphed' and 'hawed' for a bit, but then said, "Yeah, okay. You Protestants can't stop harping about how much money you need to build or buy stuff, but yes, let's hang around at this church for a few months and see if we fit in." Then she smiled at David. "I can tell that you already love this place."

David nodded. "Yeah, it kinda hits a sweet spot with me." He too gestured outside the SUV at the large church buildings. "I dunno what it is, but this place feels like home to me."

"So, we're coming back here, then?" Jess asked anxiously. She suddenly felt worried that that cleansing feeling she'd felt during the sermon might be denied her by her parents.

"Yes, dear, we'll be coming back here," Willow told her. "And you'll be able to check out their youth group. You're looking forward to that too, aren't you?"

"Yeah, sure, so long as they're better singers than at our last church," Jess agreed.

David and Willow laughed at that and David started up their car.

As they rolled their way back home, Jess considered that she'd won a small victory. She wasn't really interested in the church's youth group, but if that was the price for being allowed to visit the adult church, she viewed it as a small price to pay.

CHAPTER 40

When Jess got home after church that day, something altered in her.

Before she'd left for church that morning, she'd been in a passable frame of mind, and once in the church, she'd felt very good, better than she had in ages. But then, once she set foot at home again, she immediately felt her depression return.

The world around Jess had slowly but steadily been growing bright again since her discovery that, rather than her parents being against her because of what had happened, they were firmly on her side.

But now, all of a sudden, the world seemed dark and unwelcoming again. She felt paralyzed, like she had no value, and the entire world was against her.

Her father noticed the cloudy look on her face, but didn't say anything. He was used to her unpredictable mood swings. Some days, his little girl would seem as right as rain, almost as bright as she used to be, and the next day, she'd be completely miserable again.

It hurt him no end, and each time she had these regressions in her attitude, he felt himself more and more in favor of taking her to a therapist before it was too late to help her.

Jess frowned all the way through that day.

The next day, Monday, she felt just as bad. She went and sat with Mimi and the goths and wallowed with them in how the misery of the world was something that couldn't be helped. She watched Shell draw the blade of a switchblade along her right arm from elbow to wrist, opening her skin up like an envelope. Jess found herself entranced by the red line of blood that the shallow cut produced. She was almost fascinated enough to attempt cutting herself again.

The only reason why Jess didn't do it was because her mother no longer allowed her to wear long-sleeved clothes around the house.

But the darkness remained in her mind and simmered behind her eyes, seemingly building up to an explosion again.

CHAPTER 41

Noticing Jess's dark mood, David did some emergency online research and found that the Good Faith Assembly's youth group met on Wednesday evenings and on Saturday afternoons.

David Harris recalled how Jess had looked on Sunday morning and hoped that placing her once more in the same environment might have the same soothing effect on her again.

And so, three days later, Jess again found herself at the Good Faith Assembly church, sitting in the main auditorium along with about a hundred other young people. Unlike on Sunday, a large arch banner had been erected that said "WELCOME TO ASPIRE YOUTH" and the young people all walked under it as they entered the space.

Once more, she was struck on arrival here by the feeling that there was an energy in the atmosphere here that was lacking in the outside world. She'd arrived in a gloomy frame of mind, unwilling to come, but knowing that she really had no choice in the matter because her father insisted on it.

But once she stepped into the church building, no, once she'd gotten out of his car in the parking lot, whatever presence existed in the air over this place hit her like rainfall, and her blues vanished, more or less like they were participants in a magic trick.

Jess had no words for it, but once more her young mind could tell that it wasn't anything creepy.

Today's main focus was youth Bible study. After a joint time of praise and worship, the youth group split up into three.

There were three youth group pastors; one for the 12-to-15-year-olds, one for the 16-and-17-year-olds and one for everyone 18 years old and older.

A young woman named Rosemary Hodder was in charge of Jess's class, which comprised about 30 boys and girls. Rosemary Hodder was in her mid-twenties and was tall and fat. She had a very jolly demeanor that automatically set Jess at ease.

"Alright, boys and girls, welcome to today's meeting. Now, first of all, just like we always do, let's have a word of prayer and welcome our heavenly father into our midst." She pointed to a boy in the front row. "Cody, you pray for us."

Cody got to his feet and mumbled out a prayer. Jess didn't hear most of it, but she said 'amen' when everyone else did.

"Okay, now that we've welcomed God into our midst," Rosemary Hodder said, "let's get down to business."

Then her eyes lighted on Jess and she smiled at her and gestured to her. "I see we have a new member in our midst today. Come forward, dear, and introduce yourself."

Feeling very awkward, Jess walked forward and then waved shyly at the class.

"Hello, everyone. My name is Jessica Harris, but everyone calls me Jess. I'm thirteen years old and I'm a student at Thompson Middle School."

Sister Hodder beamed at her. "You're welcome here, Jessica, I mean 'Jess.' Isn't she welcome, boys and girls?"

On this gentle prompting there was a groundswell of hand waves and grins, along with several of the closest kids getting up and walking over to shake hands with Jess and several of them also hugging her.

Jess was impressed by how nice everyone was. She had no sense of not being welcome here.

"Welcome, Jess," everyone present said in one way or another. Their voices weren't loud, though, because of the other meetings being held in the church at the same time. In addition to the youth group meetings, Jess noticed at least two adult meetings being held simultaneously up on the balcony tiers.

"You can go back to your seat, Jess," Sister Hodder told her.

Jess walked back to her seat on the pews. She felt a little bit embarrassed with everyone's eyes on her, but once she was seated, the kids returned their focus to Ms. Hodder.

"Now, kids, as you all know, this month Pastor Howard has us all studying the love of God towards mankind," the youth leader said. "You know that the vision of our church—the Good Faith Assembly—is heavily biased towards evangelism, towards spreading the word about our savior Jesus to the unsaved. And to properly spread the Gospel to the lost, we need to understand God's love for the unsaved . . ."

Since introducing herself to everyone, Jess had been processing the environment she found herself in.

At least we're not watching football games here!

She paid close attention to Ms. Hodder's words. Slowly, she felt like she understood how, because God loved sinners so much, Christians were in turn expected to love those who were outside of the Body of Christ.

"I'll give you my personal testimony," Rosemary Hodder said after a few more minutes of explaining that God's ultimate plan for mankind was that everyone should be born again so they would make it to heaven. "I've shared my story here in the past, and some of you would've heard it. But for those of you that haven't, including our new member Jess, listen up."

Ms. Hodder smiled at them all. "Now, for those of you who are new here, I wasn't always this fleshy."

Jess was among those who disbelieved this. Rosemary Hodder looked as robust and solid as a pillar. She was everything that Jess's bestie Mimi Richards desired to be.

"Oh no, I wasn't," the youth teacher went on. "See, when I was fifteen years old, I got into using drugs." She nodded at their bemused faces. "Yes, I did. And I wasn't just smoking pot either. I was a hardcore junkie."

Jess found this hard to believe. She'd seen videos of junkies both on TV and on the web, and they looked nothing like this woman did.

"Oh, yes. I was so addicted to heroin that I'd do anything to get a fix. By the time I was sixteen, my weight was down to eighty pounds."

That really got Jess's attention.

Jess was now sure that Rosemary Hodder was lying.

I weigh more than that!

But she discovered that Rosemary Hodder was telling the truth. An idling television had been elevated on a stand behind her, and she now gestured to the boy seated next to it. "Play the video clip, Tony."

Tony fiddled with the TV remote and the floral screen saver dissolved away and Jess and the others found themselves watching a low-resolution video of two teenage girls walking along a street. Then the camera moved in to focus on their faces.

Jess gasped in fright. The teenage girl on the left was clearly Rosemary Hodder. But what a mess she was! Her hair was unkempt and her clothes were rags and her face . . . her face was thin and bony and her eyes were sunken pits and . . . well, she was so scrawny that Jess's mind couldn't really find the words to describe how she felt while watching the video.

"Damn, she looks like a zombie!" the boy next to Jess said in horror.

"Yeah," the girl in front of the kid agreed. "Like she ain't had breakfast or lunch or dinner for two months."

"Surprised?" Rosemary Hodder laughed at the shocked expressions on her young congregation's faces. "Don't be. In that vid I'm about average weight for a junkie. It's 'cos doing smack kills your appetite for food."

She gestured at her face in the video, where she was smiling, deep in animated conversation with whoever was filming she and her companion, although the audio had been muted.

"Don't worry about the lack of sound," she told the teens. "It's muted 'cos we're swearing a lot. God doesn't want you hearing that. Also, we weren't discussing anything spiritually edifying. We were wondering where we could cop some dope."

She gestured at Tony. "O.K., that's enough."

Tony stopped the video but left the video player app open, with Rose Hodder's teen face in focus on the screen.

"So yes, kids, that was me," the youth pastor told them. "I was as far away from God as it was possible to be without physically going to hell. Believe me, there was nothing, and I mean literally *nothing*, short of actual murder, that I didn't do to earn my next fix. In short, for me the needle was God."

Now that the image on the screen was focused on just Rosemary Hodder's emaciated face, Jess found herself zoning in on it. Something about the woman's bony visage mesmerized her. Rose Hodder's junkie expression struck Jess as being disturbingly familiar, though she didn't know why that was.

Rosemary Hodder grinned. "But then it pleased God to send some of his children, youth workers from this same church, to preach to me out there on the streets, and those youth workers told me the truth about God's love, and God gave me the grace to listen to them and to accept his message of Jesus's sacrifice on the cross at Calvary. I got born again that same day. And so here I am today before you all, a completely new creature." She laughed loudly. "Okay, yeah, I'll admit that I've put on a little more weight than I intended to. But just looking at me in this video, you all gotta admit I had a lot of catching up to do. So maybe I overshot the mark a bit."

Everyone laughed at that statement, including Jess, who'd just made a stunning association:

Her eyes in that video! They look like mine when I used to stare in the mirror. She's smiling, but behind her smile there's emptiness and hopelessness. She looks desperate; like what the goths describe as 'damaged goods!'

Rosemary Hodder continued her message about how God's love was incomparable to any other love, be that the love of parents or relatives, friends or lovers, husband or wife. God Almighty's LOVE apparently trumped them all.

"And this deep agape love that our heavenly father showers on us has the aim that the whole world should know similarly of his love and be born again just like we are . . ."

Jess listened with a glowing hope in her heart. She had to talk to Ms. Hodder about this. Because, just like the others present, Jess could see that the difference between the drug-addicted teenage Rose Hodder and this older version was like night and day.

I want what she's got! Jess thought. What worked for her might just work for me, too!

The Bible study ended. After the three youth groups joined up again at the front of the church auditorium for a time of worship and prayer, the youth service ended for that day.

Jess checked the time on her watch. Her father would be here soon to pick her up. But in the meantime, she got up and hurried toward the front of the church to speak to Rosemary.

"Oh, hello again, Jess," the youth pastor greeted her brightly. "What can I do for you?"

"I want to know how to be born again, Ms. Hodder," Jess told her urgently. "I really need what you've got."

CHAPTER 42

David arrived at the Good Faith Assembly church to pick up Jess a little behind schedule. By then, most of the attendees for the youth group meeting had dispersed.

As he drove into the church premises, lots of cars were driving off, and several groups of older kids were exiting the front gate and walking home along the sidewalks.

David parked his car. Then he got out of it and looked around for Jess. After realizing that she wasn't outside of the church auditorium, he headed into the building.

Inside the church, David was again struck by the same strange sense of peace that he'd felt on his first visit here.

Once more, David felt like he'd come home. He'd been raised as a Methodist and this was an Assemblies of God church, but both shared a similar ambience.

He looked around the church hall until he spotted Jess.

She was sitting at the front of the church, praying with a young woman.

David nodded at the sight. Then he took a seat on one of the rear pews and waited till Jess and the woman were done praying.

While doing so, David did some praying of his own:

"Dear, God," he prayed silently, "please help my daughter Jess break out of the darkness that's been holding her captive for this past year. I know all things are possible for you, and so please help her. I'm not saying I've been the most responsible of your children, so maybe don't do it 'cos of me, but do it just because of her, as she's so young and innocent and doesn't deserve any of the troubles and problems she's been saddled with. In Jesus's name, amen."

David lifted up his face and sighed.

I dunno when last I said a prayer this honest, he thought glumly. *When I do remember to pray, it's always about something concerning work or whatever . . .*

By now, Jess and the woman had finished praying.

David watched them turn around, and he waved at them. Jess noticed him waving and pointed him out to the woman. And then the two of them began walking down the nave of the church towards him.

He got up and headed for them, so that they met up at about the middle area of the hall.

Both Jess and the woman were smiling, which David was very pleased about. It seemed to him like God was already answering his just-concluded prayer.

"Hello, I'm Rosemary Hodder," the woman with Jess greeted him. "I'm your daughter's youth group pastor."

David shook her hand. "Pleased to meet you, Ms. Hodder."

David was surprised when Jess leapt forward and hugged him. "Hey, daddy, guess what happened to me?" she asked when she pulled away. Then before he could guess, she grinned and said: "I just got born again."

Born again?

He stared at her in surprise. "Born again?" he asked.

"Yes, daddy, I'm *saved!* I'm a child of God, and I'm going to heaven when I die." She looked at Rosemary. "That's right, isn't it?"

Her youth pastor nodded. "Yes, it is, dear. The Bible says, *'If anyone is in Christ, he is a new creation. The old things have passed away; behold, all things have become new.'"*

"Yeah!" Jess said and punched the air. "Oh yes! I'm a new person now!"

David was surprised at how delighted she was.

Yes, God really is answering my prayer. But . . . before I'd even asked him for what I wanted?

"Thank you so much," he told Rosemary Hodder. "I think this is exactly what she's been needing all this time."

"Oh, I give God all the glory," Ms. Hodder told him. "After I prayed the prayer of salvation with Jess, she hinted to me that she's been going through a really rough time in her life over the past year."

David sighed. " 'Rough time' doesn't even begin to describe it." He looked down at Jess's beaming face and said a silent 'thank you' to God.

"But, praise be to God, those dark days are over now," Rosemary Hodder said. She gave David a slightly nervous look. "She'll keep attending our church, won't she? I'd like to personally follow her up and see that she gets the right spiritual teaching to ensure she grows in the faith."

"There's no need to worry about that," David replied with a smile and a laugh. "Our whole family will be here each Sunday from now on."

"Yes, we will," Jess said excitedly.

CHAPTER 43

"She got 'born again?' " Willow asked David later that night, when they were about to go to bed. "Why isn't simple Christianity enough for you Protestants?"

"Oh, baby, don't view it like that. You saw how happy she is? Didn't you?"

Willow was sitting on the edge of their bed, searching inside her nightstand for a comb. She turned from her task and sighed at David. "You don't seem to get it, honey. Jess is simply in another of her 'up' phases. I'm starting to think she really should see a shrink. You know, the longer we let this lag, the more damage we may be doing her."

David who was already lying in bed, although propped up against the headboard with his back supported on a pillow, nodded, his own enthusiasm for Jess's new devotion to God suddenly tempered by his wife's lackluster response.

"You're right, of course," he agreed. "I'm myself worried that 'the higher the high, the lower the low,' as they say." He raised a finger at the ceiling. "But . . . let's give our baby girl a week or two, and see how this works out. If she crashes back to misery, I'll book the appointment with the psychiatrist myself. I promise."

"Fair enough," Willow agreed. She gave up looking for the comb she wanted, got into bed, and snuggled up beside David.

CHAPTER 44

The next day, Jess borrowed her mother's crucifix necklace and wore it to school.

She still felt enthused by her Christian 'conversion' as she viewed it, even though she'd been a 'Christian' for as long as she remembered.

But this being 'born again' stuff is different!

That much was certain. The biggest change that Jess felt now that she was 'born again' was that the huge emotional weight that she'd been struggling under ever since Barry had sexually assaulted her was gone for good.

Jess couldn't even find the smallest trace of it remaining.

Yes, Jesus really has cleansed me of my sins!

She felt free as a bird and as light as the air. The salvation wasn't just a head knowledge belief; it was a *conviction*. She felt a deep, deep purity and an intense joy that nothing could dull, not even when she saw Nicole Harper, another 8th grade girl, though not in her own class, giving her nasty looks. In fact, Nicole's trio of girl friends were also giving Jess nasty looks as she walked past them.

Jess, who'd never spoken to Nicole outside of class projects, simply figured that she must be having period pains or boy trouble.

I hope Nicole isn't being stalked by some creepy boy.

For the first time in ages, Jess really concentrated on her studies. Even Ms. Tomlinson's weird explanations of how the human moneysphere worked made lots of sense to her.

During lunch break, Jess and Mimi made their way over to the stadium to hang out with the goths.

"That's a nice cross you've got on," Meaner Tina told Jess. "Where'd you find it?"

"It belongs to my mom."

Meaner Tina leaned over and picked the cross off of Jess's chest. "I always feel sorry for Jesus, dying the way he did and no one ever seems to appreciate it."

"That's just how life is," Jeffrey Dean said, leaning over from where he sat to stare at Jess's cross also. "It's mean and nasty."

"He's wearing a crown of thorns," someone said.

"I feel like *I'm* wearing a crown of thorns," someone else said.

Then Jess felt her happiness bubbling over inside of her, and couldn't restrain from asking: "Hey, guys, guess what happened to me yesterday?"

"What happened to you yesterday?" Mimi asked. "I've been meaning to ask you all day. You seem very happy today."

"I went to church and got saved," Jess said, speaking all in a rush. "They have this cool youth group and they were talking about how God's love is for everyone and I prayed along with the pastor and now I'm saved. I feel great."

Mimi had been in the process of unwrapping a candy bar, but now she paused and stared incredulously at Jess. "Saved, like 'born again' saved?"

Jess nodded happily. "And now I feel great. I don't feel miserable anymore."

"I think she's high," Shell told the others. "If being happy was that simple I'd have gone to church ages ago."

Jeffrey stared intently at Jess's face for a while, then shook his head.

"She's still damaged goods, but in a good way," he told the others. "I think God superglued her pieces together again, but he didn't find all of them, that's why she's so hyper."

Jess didn't understand what he meant, but that explanation seemed to settle things for the goths.

She sat there with them feeling fantastic, while everyone around her wallowed in gothic misery, and while Mandy and Black Jane (who both had bulimia) argued over the right way to purge themselves after stuffing themselves with food.

CHAPTER 45

Over the course of the following two weeks, Jess became more involved in the services and activities at the Good Faith Assembly church.

David was pleasantly surprised when, that Saturday morning at breakfast, Jess asked him to take her to the church for that afternoon's youth group meeting.

"You're really serious about this, aren't you?" he asked Jess.

She nodded enthusiastically. "Yes, I am. I can't explain how much of a difference being born again has made to me."

David was aware that Willow was scrutinizing their exchange. He waited for her objection, but she didn't say anything.

So off to church Jess went that afternoon, to immerse herself more deeply in the word of God.

CHAPTER 46

Jess's integration into the life and activities of the Good Faith Assembly church was very swift.

Soon, under the spiritual guidance of Rosemary Hodder, she became recognized as one of the most on-fire young members of the youth group.

Because of her own journey to salvation, Jess had a deep interest in saving other hurting youth.

With her father David's full permission and her mother's grudging acceptance of the situation, Jess began accompanying the Aspire Youth group on evangelical outreaches.

"Come on," David urged Willow, "you can't argue that is good for her."

"Hell yeah, I can," was Willow's unimpressed retort.

David had to laugh at that. "Gimme a break! If she'd been at home, she'd have been watching TV anyway, or over at Mimi's house."

This last was a factor, because Mimi's family had recently moved closer to Jess's part of town.

Willow Harris originally had reservations about her daughter's friendship with Mimi Richards because Mimi's mother, Tracy, didn't seem proactive enough about life, but now Willow had no idea why her own daughter continued hanging out with a young adult who seemed to spend her entire weekly allowance on white face paint and black lipstick.

At least Jess isn't that bad yet, was Willow's main comfort to herself.

CHAPTER 47

"Hey, guys, wait for me!" Jess shouted after Tommy and Mimi the following Wednesday morning, running her way through the press of arriving students to catch up with her friends.

The pair paused by the entrance of the main school building to wait for her.

Jess joined them, breathing hard from the exertion, and they walked in together.

"So, guys, what's new?" Jess asked them as they made their way along the school hallways with the other kids.

"Nothing much," Tommy replied. "I got to playing Dragonball and haven't yet done my American History homework, so I'm gonna be in for it if Mr. Baines asks for the papers."

"You should just use ChatGPT," Mimi told him. "That stuff is killer. It's like a best friend with brains."

Tommy laughed. "Maybe I'll check it out."

"My mom would fry me like an egg if I used AI to do my homework," Jess said. "She's so hard on me about studies. I wish I had brothers and sisters, so she'd stop getting on my case all of the time."

"I've got brothers and sisters," Tommy replied, "and I don't think it makes that much difference. My mom is always yelling at my older sister to pay less attention to guys and spend more time studying."

"Boys are so cute," Mimi said with deep feeling.

Jess now realized that something was different about Mimi this morning. "Hey, why aren't you eating something?" she teased. "Are you scared the cute guys won't like you if you're too fat?"

Tommy laughed at that, and they both listened to hear Mimi's reply.

Mimi waved it off. "No, no it ain't that. I just heard that we're having sports tryouts this week and next and I'm thinking to join our running team. So, I've decided my dad can keep my mom to himself. I don't wanna be fat anymore."

"Which sports are they trying out for?" Jess asked, feeling an unusual stirring of interest.

"Track and field mainly. The time trials for those are being held tomorrow afternoon after the final bell."

"Jimmy and Davey want to start running too," Tommy said. "But I don't see much point in it. I'm already in the school band, and I wanna join the chess club."

They were in the hallway leading to their class, and the original sea of students they'd been part of had now trimmed down to a mere stream. But still, Mimi whispered her next statement to Tommy: "Hey, boy! The more I know you, the more I think you're gay."

Tommy blushed. "Hey, don't say that! You'll get me bullied!"

"Why do you think I'm whispering?" Mimi asked him. "I don't want you falling out of the closet and hurting yourself."

"But I'm not *in* any closet!" Tommy groaned in exasperation.

Mimi laughed. "Haha! That's what all gay people say till the fall out of it."

"I wanna do the track and field tryouts too," Jess said. Then she grinned. "Hey, let's all go. It should be fun."

Tommy, desperate for anything to distract Mimi from commenting about his supposed sexuality, thought about it. "Okay," he finally said. "I'll ask my dad to come pick me up later than usual tomorrow."

"Cool," Jess said. "I'll talk to my dad as well."

***

While eating lunch, Jess googled 'track and field tryouts.'

The general opinion was that they weren't too hard. Apparently, you simply turned up and ran like mad to impress the coaches, who'd be timing your speed on the track. Some sources even said that all you had to do to be on a middle school track and field team was to show up regularly for practices.

Okay, now I've gotta ask Dad to let me attend tomorrow's tryouts. Dad is gonna say 'yes,' but Mom is gonna say 'no' and tell me I should be home studying instead.

She prayed. "Lord God, please help me here. I really do want to do these track and field tryouts. Please, Jesus, help me get permission to be there, in the name of Jesus. Amen."

After praying this, she felt peace and decided that God had heard her.

Then, during a break between periods, Jess did some thinking:

She realized that she wasn't even certain why, all of a sudden, she had made up her mind to attempt running.

Maybe it was because she'd spent the past year running from herself? Running from Barry? Running from those memories that threatened her sanity, threatened to make her kill herself?

She examined the scars on her arms and then fingered the heavy cross hanging on her chest.

If I'm that good at running from my past, she thought, *let's see how I'll fare in real life.*

CHAPTER 48

To Jess's delight, her father immediately agreed to let her stay after school for the track and field tryouts.

"I don't think this is the right time for that," her mother objected, like Jess had known she would.

"Oh, what harm can it do, baby?" her father countered her mother. "It's just for a couple hours tomorrow afternoon. I'll pick her up after I—no, no, I'm free Thursday afternoon, I'll go watch her try out." Then, her father grinned at her mother. "Why don't you come along too? This might be fun."

"Oh yes, come along, Mommy," Jess pleaded desperately. "I really want to do this!"

But Willow Harris shook her head. "I'd like to, but I can't. I'm showing a house to a couple at that time tomorrow."

David nodded his understanding to her, and then looked back at Jess. "Looks like it's just you and me, kiddo."

CHAPTER 49

The next day after school, Jess and Mimi both arrived at the Jamieson stadium, both dressed up sporty and raring to go. Mimi was for once devoid of makeup.

"I'm going on inside," Mimi told Jess at the stadium entrance. "I don't wanna miss anything."

Jess nodded and gestured across at the stadium parking lot. "Okay, I'll come inside once my dad gets here."

Bubbling with sporting enthusiasm, Mimi ran off. Jess stood there waiting. She'd left Tommy Bradley also waiting for his mom back at school. Tommy said his mom wasn't really into sports, but his two younger sisters wanted to watch him run.

Jess's father arrived and parked his car and got out and looked around.

After he'd alighted from his car, David Harris noticed a few friends of his who'd also come to watch their kids and hailed them.

While Jess waited for him to get through saying hello to his friends, she looked ahead at the bleachers that framed the Thompson stadium.

Seeing the bleachers instantly flooded her with sad memories. She felt like a clamp was squeezing her heart and now questioned the wisdom of coming here, of all places.

Oh, help me Jesus, she prayed silently. *I really want to do these tryouts.*

And just as suddenly as the hurt and pressure had come on her, she felt as if God had heard her prayer. She felt relief and peace surge through her.

Thank you, Lord, she prayed.

"Okay, honey, let's go in," her father told her.

After saying hello to her dad's friends also, she walked into the stadium with him.

Wow, I didn't think there would be this many of us, she thought as she and her dad walked around the bleachers and she saw just how many hopefuls had come for the tryouts. *Making varsity is gonna be harder than I thought!*

'Varsity' or first team was Jess's ultimate goal. However, seeing how many teenagers were here to compete for the same slots, made Jess rethink her strategy.

Junior varsity might be okay too, then I can work my way up. Wait up! I don't know if I'm really interested in this!

The parents, kids, and head coach Mike Simpson and his assistant coaches were gathered down by the track near the middle section of the bleachers on this side of the stadium.

Once the coaches noticed Jess's arriving contingent, they waved them over to join the others.

They reached the crowd just as Coach Simpson was starting his talk. Coach Simpson was in his fifties, but still pulsing with vitality; wiry and muscular in his track suit. He actually looked healthier than most of the parents in attendance, all of whom were younger than him.

"So, welcome, ladies and gentlemen, boys and girls," the coach told them. "I'm glad you can all come out here today for our tryouts. Since you're already here, I don't think I need to give you my pep talk 'bout how great track and field is, and what benefits it has. . . ."

Jess looked around for Mimi. She located Mimi on the far side of the crowd. She also noticed her goth friend Jeffrey Dean sitting on a bleacher and looking angry.

Jess laughed at the look on Jeffrey's face. He turned, saw her looking his way, and rolled his eyes.

Jess returned her attention to the coach's speech.

". . . So you're all very welcome," Coach Simpson was saying. "Now we're gonna time you all for a variety of distances. The times are to see which of you run fastest, and which of you have staying power." He laughed. "And, girls, you've got to run all the distances too." Then he added, in an aside to the parents: "Trust me, moms and dads, girls will be girls. Left to themselves, your daughters are all gonna want to only run the 100 meters 'cos it's the shortest distance we got."

The parents laughed at that, and several young girls grinned like they'd been caught with their hands in the cookie jar, and the coach went on:

"Now, while we're calling this meeting our 'time trials,' y'all gotta keep in mind that today isn't entirely about running." He turned and gestured out at the sports field, to illustrate his point. "If you look out there, you'll see we're set up for all kinds of sports. "Some of you boys and girls can't run to save your lives, you're even slower than tortoises, but you'll be great at other events. The tall ones amongst you may be good at the high jump and the hurdles, which is a completely different running game from regular running. And others of you will do well in events like the shot put or discus. Our aim here is to build a team, a cohesive team where no one will be left out. So, don't feel bad if you don't make the cut for the sprints and the coaches send you over to attempt some jumping."

Coach Simpson laughed. "Okay, now I think that's enough ranting on my part." He waved his stopwatch and clipboard at everyone. "Let's git down to business. And kids, please remember, you're here to give your best. Okay, all of you kids form up in two lines—one line each for boys and girls—and give your names, classes, and ages to coaches Dennison and Rodriguez, so we don't credit your time to someone else."

After pointing out the male and female coaches that he'd just referred to, Coach Simpson turned and walked off to discuss something with two other coaches.

Those parents present gave their children last-minute advice and then retreated to make themselves comfortable on the bleachers.

"You'd better get in line," David Harris told Jess.

"Okay, see you, daddy." Jess hurried off and joined the line facing assistant coach Lita Rodriguez.

The rest of the late afternoon and evening passed in a lot of running.

First Jess and the others did warm up exercises, stretches and things like that. Then, their names were called and they hurried off to do their best in each time trial.

The first race was the 100 meters sprint. On the other side of the stadium, a temporary arrangement of lines had been sprayed on the track so that the 200 meters trials could be held simultaneously over there.

Jess was in the second race here and fourth race over there.

Before they ran, Coach Rodriguez gave them last minute instructions: "Now remember, girls, you need to stay inside your own lane. If you run outside of your lane that's an automatic disqualification. Also, if you go before the starter pistol, that's a disqualification also. So don't jump the gun. Literally don't jump the gun."

Jess and the other girls, all arranged in a line across the track, nodded.

"Okay, get ready. On your mark!"

Jess felt her heart racing, from excitement not exertion, as she knelt down at the starting line for that first time.

She closed her eyes, said a silent prayer for God's help, and then opened her eyes again and stared ahead at the finish line. Her entire world felt like it suddenly shrunk down to that point ahead of her, that white line painted across the red track.

"Get set . . . !"

The starter pistol went and Jess went with it. She ran like all of hell was after her. She didn't look either right or left, she just kept her eyes focused on the goal.

At first, she could see the other girls out of the corner of her eyes, but all of a sudden she seemed to be running alone.

And then she crossed the finish line and tried her best to slow down. Finally, she did, and then she turned around to look back to where she'd begun from.

"Wow, you're fast," the black girl who'd been on her right said. "Where did you learn to run so fast?"

The other girls were also looking at her in amazement.

"I dunno," Jess replied honestly. "I've never tried it before. I was just scared of finishing in last place with my dad watching."

But she looked over at the bleachers and saw that her dad was applauding her and that Coach Simpson also had a smile on his face.

That was when Jess realized that she'd won the race.

I won? I actually won?

Apparently, she'd gone so fast out of the blocks that none of the other girls could catch up to her. By the time she'd crossed the finish line, there was at least ten meters of space between her and the girl who'd come in second.

Maybe I can do this after all, she thought in amazement.

She ran over and hugged her father.

***

Now that Jess had gotten over her initial nerves, she found the rest of the races easier to run.

She ran the girls' 200 meters in good time too. Though she didn't win that one, she came in third place.

Then she went over to sit by Jeffrey, who'd just come in fourth in the boys' 400 meters. The goth boy looked really odd to her now that he wasn't decked up in black and silver clothes.

"I hate sports," he told her grumpily. "They're my idea of a complete waste of time."

"So, why are you trying out then?" Jess asked him.

Jeffrey nodded over at the bleachers. "That's my dad over there, the big man with blonde hair who's calling on his phone. Dad was a superstar athlete in high school. He wants me to be like him."

Jess nodded. "My dad's the one over there behind Coach Rodriguez. "He doesn't push me to do anything I don't want to."

Jeffrey nodded. "Good for you." Then he pointed. "Hey, look, Mimi's about to run her 200-meter trial."

Jess and Jeffrey were seated on the bleachers, near the starting point for the hundred meters. With the way the temporary 200-meter track was set up, this meant that they were a few meters away from where that race would end.

Because the 200-meter race would end near the starting point for the 100-meter race, the next 100-meter race was staggered with it, so the participants in the former race didn't crash into those for the latter.

This was Mimi's first race. By the time Jeffrey had pointed her out, she was already standing by the blocks.

"On your marks, get set . . .!"

And then they were off, with both Jess and Jeffrey up and cheering for Mimi.

And she ran quite well too. Keeping her own for about half of the race distance. But then something really weird happened. Just as Mimi was coming around the turn in the track, a small dog belonging to one of the watching parents jerked its leash from its owner's hand and ran onto the track. The dog ran right behind the girl on Mimi's right and right into her path.

Mimi, who was in the third lane, instinctively ducked to her left to avoid running into the dog, but this unfortunately made her crash into the girl in the second lane and the two of them went to ground together, which a few moments later, was followed by the girl in the first lane falling over them.

While the three overturned girls lay on the track hurting and feeling confused, the dog that had caused their accident had long since set off running after the three girls still in the race. With the crowd cheering the dog on, it almost caught up with the winner before she crossed the finish line.

The stadium exploded in amusement. Jeffrey and Jess looked at each other in confusion.

He shrugged at her. "I don't think Mimi's gonna be a huge fan of dogs from now on."

"Me either," Jess agreed.

Mimi finally salvaged her dignity and walked over to them, while girls and boys made jokes as she went by.

"I'm having second thoughts about this," she told Jess and Jeffrey. "Coach Rodriguez says I can try the 200 again after getting some rest, but I'm so bruised now I don't wanna run anymore today."

"Hey, there's Tommy!" Jess said, pointing down at the far end of the track. "I didn't see him arrive."

"My dad's waving at me," Jeffrey told the two girls. "I'm gonna go see what he wants."

Jeffrey walked off and Tommy walked towards them.

"Sorry I'm late," he said. "My mom came to watch me run too, but then my kid sisters both insisted that I first accompany them to buy candy." He pointed out his mother and the two young girls in question seated up on the bleachers.

"Oh, that's fine," Mimi said. "I'm grateful that you missed all the fun and excitement."

"Huh?" Tommy looked confused. "What's she talking about?"

Mimi cringed. "Please don't tell him," she begged Jess, and then added. "Haha, Tommy! Jess is our new star runner!"

"That was a fluke," Jess said.

Then Jess saw that one of the girls she'd run the 100-meter with was searching the bleachers for someone.

The girl finally locked eyes with Jess and gestured for her to come over while lifting up four fingers. "I think I'm up for the 400-meter," Jess told her friends, getting to her feet.

***

Jess's 400-meter run was also very good. Once again, she zoned out into herself as she stared at the track, and once the starter pistol rang out, she ran like hell was after her.

She was running in the second lane and because of the way the runners were staggered in the 400-meter, this meant that like it or not, try or not, she could see the runners in the outer lanes seemingly ahead of her, though in actuality, considering the actual distance covered, they might actually be behind her.

She'd experienced a similar spatial dislocation during the 200 meters, but for a shorter period, as everyone soon converged on the homestretch.

But in this case, Jess had the sense that she was being left behind, so she ran even faster than she had before. Not being experienced in interpreting the relative distances between the runners, she focused on putting them all behind her.

Then two things happened simultaneously.

Jess suddenly became aware that the stadium was cheering, and a verse from the Bible leapt into her mind.

The verse was Philippians 4:13: *for I can do all things through Christ who strengthens me.*

Filled with a sudden peace and a feeling like she'd gotten a miraculous second wind from outer space, Jess gave the race her all.

And then, suddenly, it was over.

And Jess, completely exhausted by her unfamiliar exertion, discovered that she'd won again. Once more by a good distance.

I won? How?

While the crowd cheered and cheered, she hugged two or three of the other teenage runners, waved to her father, and then collapsed to the ground in exhaustion, breathing hard and looking up at the sky.

Once she'd gotten her wind back, Jess got back up to her feet and walked over to the coaches to find out what her time was.

"Yeah, kid, you make the grade," Coach Simpson told her happily. "Varsity for sure, once we train you a bit."

Hearing that, Jess felt like she was walking on air.

She left the coach, and ran over to her father.

"I did it, dad, I did it!" she yelped excitedly.

"I knew you'd make the team," her father told her, while embracing her warmly.

Jess had rarely felt better in her life than she did today.

CHAPTER 50

Jess's feeling of euphoria lasted all through that evening.

"She left all of those other girls behind like they were her shadows," her father told her mother. "You needed to have been there to see it."

"That's wonderful," her mother said. "Let's hope she blows the wheels off of the competition in her studies also."

Jess saw her father give her mother a really sharp look after this response, but he didn't say anything harsh to her, though Jess sensed that he was disappointed with what she'd said. However, after a few minutes, his face resumed its delighted expression.

Jess had dinner with her parents and afterwards went upstairs to her room. She had a shower and then lay in bed dreaming of what she'd accomplished.

After daydreaming for a while, Jess decided to look through the messages on her cellphone.

She had lots of congratulatory texts from friends of hers who'd heard of how great she'd been on the track:

'Wow, U got wings 4 feet,' one girl had written.

"If u kpt going like ud be in Mexico 2moro," a boy had written.

Someone had also posted the video of Mimi's racetrack encounter with the dog to YouTube. Jess clicked through to that and almost died laughing when she watched it again. The video perfectly recorded the confusion on the faces of Mimi and the other two hapless teens.

The comments were hilarious also.

'I've heard of dog attacks, but this is crazy!'

'Who let the dog out? Woof, woof, woof, woof.'

'Just a lesson that it's a dog-eat-dog world, girls!'

Jess was still reading comments when several WhatsApp notifications came in a group.

These messages were all from unfamiliar phone numbers, but thinking that they were yet more friendly congratulations, Jess clicked to read the one at the top and was instantly shocked by its content:

'U need 2 run faster than that 2 escape ur drty reputation, btch,' the text read.

Confused, Jess clicked on another.

'Hey, slut, do u cum that fast when u run wt Barry?'

On reading this, Jess immediately dropped her phone on the floor as if it was poisoned. Then she sat on the edge of her bed staring down at it. She began trembling, and a riot of confused thoughts started up inside her head.

What? Who would say a thing like that to me! Why would they say that to me!

After a while, she calmed down a little and began feeling a little foolish staring at her cellphone down there on the floor. If her mom or dad knocked now, what could she tell them if her phone was on the floor and like it was doing, was still beeping up fresh notifications?

So, Jess retrieved the cellphone. And even though her emotions were troubled now and she was certain that reading more of these anonymous messages would hurt her a lot, she felt compelled to read them, she felt like she needed to know exactly what they said about her.

So she swiped the screen on, and continued reading.

'SLUtttttt! DIRTY SKANK!' two of the other texts read.

'Congrats, btch!! U're not D fastest Draw in d west, but u're D fastest whore in West V!'

Jess stared at this last text for longer than she had at the others, then she dropped her phone on the bed and burst out crying.

"Oh God," she wept aloud, beating on the bed with her little fists, her body trembling like a leaf in a high wind, "Why has this started again?"

Suddenly she felt oh, so alone. Like she was the only young girl in the world and everyone else hated her.

Her first thought was to run downstairs and show these hurtful texts to her parents, but suddenly she was struck by the unreasoning dread that they wouldn't understand, that they might believe that she'd once more done something to cause this persecution.

Jess's emotional crash because of these harassing text messages felt like a complete inversion of her previous high. As reflective as if one had turned a smile upside down.

She found it impossible to understand how she could feel both on top of the world and down in the depths of despair on one and the same day.

She collapsed on her bed and beat against it with her fists, with tears streaming from her eyes and despair pouring into her heart.

She wept and wept and finally fell asleep weeping.

CHAPTER 51

By the next morning, Jess felt better and a lot more composed.

After praying to God to help her overcome the bad feelings that kept threatening to come back into her life, Jess decided to put the incident of the texts behind her.

After all, she'd heard the saying: Sticks and stones may break my bones, but words can never hurt me.

At school, she showed the bullying texts to Mimi.

"Who do you think sent these to me?" she asked Mimi.

Mimi, who still wasn't overeating, but was today once more obscured beneath thick layers of gothic makeup, shook her head. "I'm not sure, but I think it's gotta be Nicole."

"Huh?" Jess asked. "But why?" Now that Mimi mentioned it, Jess suddenly remembered the mean looks that Nicole Harper and her friends Leah, Emma, and Rachel had given her a few days ago.

So, did that mean she'd misinterpreted their stares?

"But why?" she asked Mimi again.

Before replying, Mimi looked around conspiratorially and then pulled Jess aside near the student lockers.

"From what I hear," Mimi told Jess in low tones, "Nicole is desperate to be Barry's girlfriend. She really loves him, but Barry is giving her the cold shoulder. So, Nicole is jealous of you, 'cos you used to be Barry's girlfriend."

"I'm tired of this," Jess said, tugging on Mimi's arm. "Let's go find Nicole and the other girls and clear this up."

But she and Mimi then engaged in a tug-of-war. "No, no, no," Mimi said, still whispering loudly, while holding Jess firmly in place where she was. Actually, Mimi was whispering louder than if she had been speaking normally.

"Why not?" Jess asked angrily, her whole body a bundle of tense frustration as she struggled to get free of Mimi's grip and go looking for Nicole Harper. "I've not done anything to Nicole. Why is she picking on me?"

"Just wait," Mimi insisted. "Wait until I make sure it's Nicole." Mimi let go of Jess and spread her hands emphatically. "What if you accuse her and she denies it? You'll look very foolish."

Jess agreed that she was right. She calmed down and agreed to let Mimi confirm her suspicions.

And later that day, when Jess walked past Nicole Harper and her friends, she gave no sign that she'd noticed them, even though she was very aware that the four girls were talking about her.

CHAPTER 52

The next day, Saturday, Jess's father took her out shopping to get her several sets of running clothes and proper running shoes.

She got home, tried everything on for her mother to see also, and then, bubbling with excitement, waited for the weekend to end and Monday to arrive.

She was so excited that she largely forgot about the previous day's insulting text messages. And, when she did remember them, she waved them off. She'd not gotten any further texts from those unfamiliar numbers. She texted Mimi to see if Mimi had found out anything about who'd sent her the texts.

Mimi replied that she'd not yet confirmed if Nicole and the other girls were responsible or not, but she was working on it.

Of course, as night approached Jess became apprehensive that the bullies might text her again, but as Saturday drew to a close, she was able to relax.

So no, bad texts on Saturday, and none on Sunday either.

CHAPTER 53

Monday arrived, and Jess began training with the track team.

Practice would be held four days a week, after school, at the Shane Jamieson stadium; for one-and-a-half to two hours each day.

This meant that her father rescheduled his pickup times to early evening.

"I never imagined one had to train so much," her mother told her. "When will you find time to study if you're doing so much running?"

"I'll do my studies once I get home," Jess replied with a grin. "Don't worry mom, I got this."

***

After school was dismissed for the day, Jess and Mimi hurried over to the stadium to join the other kids.

Once the kids assembled for practice, Jess did a double-take. There were almost as many kids present in the stadium this afternoon as there had been for the tryouts, though on her way over to the stadium, Jess had noticed some kids going home like normal.

Those boys and girls had clearly decided they weren't at all athletic and quit on their own, because Jess didn't recall anyone being trimmed out by the coaches last week.

Of course, there were still several kids present who didn't want to be around, but whose parents had insisted they do track and field, if only to get them out of the house for a few additional hours each day, possibly because of their high nuisance value at home. Then there were others who couldn't quit sports training because their parents insisted that they needed the discipline of competition.

The hapless goth leader Jeffrey Dean seemed to belong to the second category of conscientious objectors, while Mimi Richards clearly fit into the first category.

"I don't know what I'm gonna do," Jeffrey grumbled to Jess. "My dad insists that I gotta be a jock."

"My mom just wants me out of our house," Mimi told them both. "I dunno what it is with her now, but she never talks calmly to me anymore. She always yells about something to me. I think she's pregnant again, and she's not happy about it."

"How can you be sure?" Jess asked.

"She's getting fatter," Mimi replied. "Just like she did for my baby sister Bonnie." Mimi laughed in wicked delight. "It's not just me she yells at now. She yells at dad, too."

"Okay, kids, gather round," one of the coaches called out.

***

And so, the day's training ritual began. As part of a very rowdy group, Jess learned about warm-ups.

First, they did stretches and then form drills.

The form drills—'A' skips and 'B' skips and 'Knee ups' were funny at first, and Jess almost overbalanced during the straight-leg runs. But, little by little, she gained an understanding of exactly how to position herself and memorized exactly how to do each exercise correctly.

Then everyone did short sprints—fifty or so meters—a few times.

"You're not competing now, just working to get your blood flowing and your muscles relaxed and ready for the real workout to come," the coaches advised their noisy charges.

Jess ran with that in mind, and after these warmup sprints were concluded, she sat on the bleachers with the other kids while Coach Simpson gave everyone a lecture on teamwork.

"Now, kids, at this junior level, track and field competition is all about points. And no single person on a team makes up all of those points; the team wins as a result of a shared effort. So, there's no space for big egos."

"What's a big ego?" Jess heard a girl whisper behind her.

"Thinking the cake belongs to you alone 'cos it's your birthday," Mimi replied to her, triggering a stream of hushed laughs.

"So, while some of you are either better or worse than others and we can't use all of you for every track meet, you gotta bear in mind that even when you do compete for the school, you're just one teenaged gear of a big machine, and the team is that machine." The coach laughed. "True, the machine may not function right if you ain't doing your part, but without the machine working, you alone won't be doing anything at all. Do you kids all get that?"

There was some laughter as Jess and the others nodded.

"Now, here's how we're gonna organize everyone . . ."

Once Coach Simpson had explained how the training would proceed, the boys and girls split up and headed off with their assigned coaches.

Jess worked hard. She focused on what the girls' coaches told her to do and ran as hard as she could. Now that those girls on the track and field team who'd not been around during the tryouts were back, she discovered that she wasn't as fast as she'd imagined, just faster than her untrained peers, but the coaches still said she'd run varsity if she worked hard at it.

And so, Jess knuckled down and trained really hard.

CHAPTER 54

That week passed fast, almost as fast as Jess was running on the track.

Each morning her father dropped her off at school, and once classes ended, she hurried over to the stadium and got busy with the other student athletes.

On Tuesday night, Jess received another slew of nasty texts.

'Oh, how fast d slut runs!'

'Dirty dirty btch,' and such like.

After reading these texts, Jess felt really bad and felt like crying again, but then she told herself that she was stronger than that. She wouldn't cry about this, nor would she tell her parents about it either.

She did, however, screenshot the texts and sent them to Mimi.

'This must stop!' She wrote. 'Dnt nd this nonsense along wt bks & running.'

'Stl wrkn on it,'' Mimi texted back. 'We'll sn fnd out who's doin it.'

A few more texts came in. Jess deleted them without reading them, blocked the sender's numbers and went to sleep.

Nothing happened on Wednesday, but more bad texts came in on Thursday. Once Jess saw that the numbers weren't from her contacts list, she deleted the messages unread, and blocked the senders' numbers again.

Something bothered her though: how were the senders finding new phone numbers to insult her from? Because even though Jess couldn't recall the original numbers that had sent her obscene texts, she knew that once she blocked a number on her cellphone, she couldn't receive texts from that same number again. Which meant these follow-up insults were coming from different phones. Jess knew that as a young teenager, you needed your parents to get you a phone. And she didn't think parents had time to waste bullying teens on their daughters' behalf.

Sure, Jess had heard of burner phones—untraceable temporary phones that expired after a set period. But, in this case too, she felt that the same restrictions would apply: no shop was going to sell burner phones to kids, and no parents were going to buy burner phones for their kids in the first place, let alone phones to bully other kids from.

She found out the answer to her question on Friday afternoon.

On Friday there was no track and field practice. After the final school bell, Jess and Mimi were sitting out front with Mitch and Alice, two of the goth kids, all of them waiting for parental pickup, when Tommy Bradley joined them.

"Hey, what's going on?" Tommy asked Jess after setting down his backpack. "Last night, I got a series of nasty text messages about you!"

"Huh?" Everyone clustered around to look at the messages on Tommy's cellphone:

'Jess Harris skank Runner!' 'Jess has AIDS!' 'Not Jess Harris, but Jess Herpes!'

"Who is doing this!?" Jess screamed in horror, so loud that she startled several nearby parents who were busy collecting their offspring.

Jess was too frustrated and angry to care who was staring at her. Had this occurred between Monday and yesterday, she'd have been able to purge herself of the bad vibes by running them off, because she'd discovered that while running, she hardly thought of anything else.

But today was Friday—there were no track and field activities for her level, just for the high school kids.

"Someone's real mad at you," the goth boy named Mitch said. "My older sis got bullied like this at her old school. She almost went nuts from it. When she told our parents they thought she was sleeping around. And we never found out who was doing it."

Jess meanwhile had noticed that the phone numbers from which the texts had been sent to Tommy weren't in his contacts list either. She wished she'd not been so fast to delete the messages sent to her last night. Then she could compare the numbers.

"How are they doing this?" she asked her four friends. "How do they get so many cellphone numbers?"

"That's easy," Tommy said. "There's cellphone apps that allow you to create virtual phone numbers that you can text and call from."

"Yeah, that's true," Mitch agreed. "I've got Hushed on my phone, which does that, but I've never used it for anything. I'm saving it for when I wanna prank someone."

Jess was about to ask Mitch to let her see the Hushed app, when she spotted Nicole Harper and her trio of friends emerging from the school building.

Jess pointed them out to the others. "Are *they* the ones doing this or not?" she asked.

Right then, both Tommy's and Mimi's phones beeped.

Tommy studied the screen of his phone and groaned. "More bad messages about Jess," he said.

"Yeah, same here," Mimi seconded.

Everyone turned and stared hard at the quartet of girls who were now looking condescendingly around at everything and everyone at the front of the campus like they owned the school. This was Nicole's usual attitude because her parents were rich.

"I'm sure they're responsible," Mimi whispered as Nicole and company headed towards them. "We just need to prove she is."

The four approaching girls paused when they reached Jess, Mimi, and the others.

"Hi, Jess," Nicole Harper said in a dismissive and insulting highfaluting manner, something else that she had most likely either inherited or copied from her rich parents. "Hope sports practice helps you practice for sextracurricular stuff too!"

"What?" Jess thundered at her. "What are you getting at?"

Nicole laughed. "Oh, I'm sure you know what I mean. We got texts about you too. Saying how *talented* you are in other areas."

Nicole's three companions began laughing uproariously at this, and they all walked away.

"She's clearly responsible and I'm gonna prove it," Mimi said angrily.

Jess felt like her cheeks were burning. She felt exposed to public ridicule.

"I feel like beating Nicole up," she grumbled as she watched Nicole Harper step outside of the campus and climb into her mother's swank car.

And she really did. Jess felt like grabbing hold of Nicole's hair and faceplanting her in one of the stadium's sandpits and then rubbing her face in the sand until she'd completely rubbed that conceited smirk off of Nicole's face. And after just one week of track training, Jess realized that she was probably strong enough already to beat Nicole Harper to a pulp.

"I really, really feel like beating that girl up," Jess repeated.

Except that maybe God won't approve of me doing that.

"Hey, I thought Christianity didn't allow that," Mitch said.

Tommy gave Mitch a dark look. "What are you talking about?"

Mitch shrugged. "You know, dude, alla that stuff 'bout turning the other cheek that they preach in church? Isn't she supposed to follow that?"

"I still feel like beating Nicole up," Jess grumbled. "Even if I get suspended from school for doing so."

"If you beat her up, you'll get thrown off the track team," Tommy pointed out. "You don't want that to happen."

Jess sighed miserably. "You're right. I don't want to be thrown off the track team. That would be a disaster for me."

CHAPTER 55

That Sunday morning, Jess sat in church in a less-than-happy mood.

She'd received one more blast of insulting texts on Friday night, and had once more deleted them after seeing the contents of the first one.

Saturday had been better, she'd gone with her mom to visit her grandparents, who lived in the town of Salem, about a half hours drive from their home in Bridgeport. This meant that she'd missed that afternoon's church Aspire Youth meetup, but Rosemary Hodder had told her not to worry about it.

But Jess had worried about it. One of the reasons why she'd so much wanted to attend yesterday's youth meeting was so she could ask Ms. Hodder questions about bullying.

And now, sitting in church with her parents again, Jess almost felt like God was bullying her, too.

I keep praying to him to 'let this cup pass over me,' as it were, but I'm still on the receiving end of the stick.

Then Jess sighed melodramatically to herself. She'd just remembered that God hadn't 'let the cup pass over' Jesus either: he'd wound up being nailed to the cross despite his clearly stated request to the contrary.

Jess wondered if maybe she should have chosen a different biblical example to illustrate her case when she asked God for help.

Her father and mother sat on her left, singing along with the congregation to the worship team's lead.

Both of her parents clearly liked this church, which she was very pleased about.

The worship team finished their song and Pastor Bryan Howard took over the microphone from the choir leader.

"Let's bow our heads in prayer," he told the congregation.

Jess bowed her head with everyone else, but while Pastor Howard prayed that God would bless everyone within hearing range of his voice, Jess prayed that God would deliver her from bullies, and help her run better.

"Now, brothers and sisters," Pastor Howard began once this time of prayer was over, "today I want to speak about the work of God's Holy Spirit in the life of the born-again believer."

Jess listened.

"Remember what Jesus said in the Gospel of John, Chapter 16 and Verse 7, where he said he would send the comforter to us. And the scripture is clear that by 'comforter,' our Lord meant the Holy Spirit, who later fell on the first believers and the apostles on the blessed day of Pentecost."

Here, Pastor Howard wagged a finger at the congregation.

"Now, my brothers and my sisters," he went on. "We need to ask ourselves: What exactly is the work of the Holy Spirit in our lives? Why did our lord God Almighty consider it essential that we receive the Holy Spirit? Well, first off, let's answer this first question: The Holy Spirit, the Spirit of God as he is also known, is the third person of the Trinity, and an equal member of the Godhead with God the Father and God the Son. Do you remember what our Lord Jesus said? What did our Lord say? Jesus said, 'But ye shall receive *power*, after that the Holy Ghost is come upon you: and ye shall be witnesses unto me both in Jerusalem, and in all Judaea, and in Samaria, and unto the uttermost part of the earth.' "

Here, Pastor Howard stopped speaking for a while to consult his sermon notes and Jess processed what he'd just said:

Power, the pastor said. *Yeah, that's exactly what I need, 'cos most times I feel so powerless, I could puke on myself.*

Pastor Howard resumed speaking: "And so, right there in that verse of scripture, we discover the first, and might I be so bold as to say, to my mind, the *primary* reason why our lord God Almighty, in his boundless wisdom, has blessed us with His Holy Spirit. And what is that reason, folks? It is so that we can *witness* the Gospel to others. Yes, so that we can *witness!* The Holy Spirit in us *empowers* us to tell the world about Jesus. Do you all remember what the apostle Paul said in First Corinthians 2, Verse 5? Where he states that 'your faith should not be based on the wisdom of men, but in the *power* of God?' " Pastor Howard laughed. "But I'm getting way ahead of myself already. "What does the scripture say about our Lord Jesus himself in the Acts of the Apostles? It says, 'How God anointed Jesus of Nazareth with the Holy Spirit and with power, who went about doing good and healing all that were oppressed of the devil; for God was with him.' There it is again, right there, brethren, the Holy Spirit and *power!* Power, Power, *POWER!*"

By this point in the sermon, Jess felt like the pastor was speaking to her personally. She felt like she was the only person in the church, as if the rest of the congregation, her parents included, had faded out of being somewhere beyond the corners of her eyes.

Pastor Howard preached for a good while longer, explaining exactly what the function of the Holy Spirit was in the life of born-again believers, and how one became baptized in the Holy Spirit.

At the conclusion of his sermon, Pastor Howard gave an altar call:

"Okay, now, brothers and sisters, I believe you've all understood the gist of today's message. Now I want any one of you here in the congregation today who hasn't yet been baptized in the Holy Spirit to come forward and receive the baptism of the Holy Spirit now. It doesn't matter whether or not you're baptized in water yet—in the acts of the apostles, the Holy Spirit fell on Cornelius's household before they even knew there was anything called water baptism, so that's not any kind of a prerequisite for receiving the baptism of the Holy Spirit. So, brethren and sistren, come forward if you want to receive the Holy Spirit baptism with the evidence of speaking in tongues."

Jess was aware of her mother's surprise when she got to her feet. But her mother made no attempt to stop her, and Jess wiggled her way past the people seated between herself and the nave of the church, and headed for the front of the church to receive the baptism of the Holy Spirit.

She wasn't alone in going forward. She was one of about fifteen people who gathered there at the altar.

While the worship team sang a gentle worship song to the Lord God Almighty, and the congregation either sang along with them or prayed under their breath, Jess and the other believers with her were led in prayer by Pastor Howard.

Jess could feel the words of the worship song speaking to her spirit as it was performed in the hall, "…I'm gonna sing a victory, I'm gonna sing a victory, for the battle belongs to you Lord…"

The battle belongs to YOU, Lord! Jess thought as though they were delivering a message from God just for her. She did not need to fight this battle alone. God was with her.

And then the Pastor descended from the altar and began laying hands on the heads of each one of them.

Jess already knew that something odd had happened to her while they'd been praying. But she didn't expect that once the pastor laid his hands on her head, she'd fling up both of her hands in the air and begin speaking to God in a weird language she'd never heard before.

She wanted to stop speaking the weird words, but at the same time, she felt deep peace in her heart and a gentle urging to continue speaking out what she suddenly remembered the scriptures described as the 'tongues of angels.'

And the pastor was right; Jess did feel spiritually empowered.

CHAPTER 56

On the way back home from church, Willow Harris felt as if she'd been tripped up by God and next tied up in a confused package by him.

What was that that just happened back at the church?

Her unspoken question of course, referred to her daughter Jess going out to receive the supposed baptism of the Holy Spirit.

Willow had been raised Catholic, and as such, she had the normal Catholic suspicions and prejudices regarding Protestant misinterpretations of the Bible.

But, of course, along the way, she'd come to realize that the Protestants also accused the Catholics of having twisted scripture to suit themselves.

After all, she knew that Martin Luther had led the Reformation on the basis of his belief that God's salvation to mankind was based on faith in Him and not on works done to please Him, which had previously been the Catholic viewpoint on the matter.

And so, Willow had married a Protestant, a Methodist.

Initially, that in itself had been trying enough, as she'd navigated the weird differences between Catholic and Protestant rituals of worship, and had sometimes even comically translated her newly acquired Protestant expectations of worship back home when visiting her parents' Church.

But then David had decided he liked *Pentecostalism.*

Willow viewed Pentecostals as religious extremists. To her mind, the Pentecostals' sole difference from Islamic extremists was their non-violence.

But they amped up just about everything else as far as it could go, until the needle was well up into the absurd.

Willow felt like commenting on today's church service, but her husband David was concentrating on the road ahead, and silently humming a tune to himself.

As someone who focused nervously on the road while driving, Willow was superstitious about interrupting similarly attentive drivers. It was always best to let drivers drive.

So, as the countryside streamed past their car, instead of striking up a conversation with her husband, she turned her attention to the backseat to look at her daughter.

Jess had in the meantime fallen asleep in the backseat. She was lying on her side and looked serene, her face wreathed in a smile as if she was dreaming of angels.

Willow sighed.

Jess looks so peaceful. It's just that I don't understand all of these doctrines. I believe—no, no, I KNOW—that simple Christianity is more than enough for us to live our lives. Why do modern preachers—Pentecostal preachers—have to drape Christianity with frills as if God is simply looking for ways to trip us up.

However, Willow couldn't deny what she'd seen in church.

No, Jess didn't suddenly grow a halo after she'd been prayed for, but the look in her eyes as she made her way along the pew back to our side. She looked glorified, exalted even.

That look had scared Willow, because it meant that she, who liked to keep things properly planned out and well-regulated, no longer knew what to expect from her daughter.

Staring at sleeping Jess, Willow forced a smile.

***

"So, what happens next?" she asked her husband later, after lunch, when Jess had gone upstairs for an afternoon nap.

Willow was displeased by how tired Jess seemed today. That never used to happen in the past. But Willow understood what the problem was. Jess had clearly tired herself out with all of that unnecessary running she'd been doing all week.

"How do you mean—what happens next?" David asked pleasantly. Food in his belly and feeling well-disposed to the world, he'd retired to the living room with a glass of iced tea, and was attempting to tune the TV to a ball game. All he was getting so far, though, was ESPN previews.

"I'm talking about our daughter Jess," Willow told him. She'd followed David into the living room, but she didn't sit on the couch next to him, like she normally did. Instead, she sat in an armchair that almost faced him. "What happens next with *her?*"

"You've lost me," David said.

Willow leaned forward and rested her elbows on her thighs and her chin on her fists. "What happened today worries me," she told him.

"Her receiving the baptism of the Holy Spirit? What's strange about that? She wasn't the only one that Pastor Howard prayed for."

"It felt creepy, like he was telling us that our regular Christianity isn't good enough."

David set down the remote control and frowned at Willow. "You're just putting your usual overthinking spin on things. I don't see that it's a *negative* thing that she's received the baptism of the Holy Spirit."

"David she was speaking in tongues!"

This made David look at her seriously. "She was?"

Willow nodded. "Yes, she was. You didn't hear it 'cos she was seated next to me not next to you. And I clearly heard her speaking some weird stuff that made no sense to me. No sense at all."

David thought on this for a while. "Well, I don't think any harm's done. The Bible clearly says that on the day of Pentecost, the first believers all spoke in new tongues." He grinned at her. "Hey, honey, maybe you and I need to get the baptism of the Holy Spirit also. Maybe then we'll understand what she was saying."

Willow was not in the least bit amused. Her eyes narrowed at her husband. "You're not taking this seriously. You're trivializing the issue."

David moved along the couch until he was seated at its edge, and was closer to Willow. "Well, I don't see what we can do about it, honey. It's not like she's possessed by the devil. What do you suggest that we do? Take Jess back to Pastor Howard and tell him we want to remove the Holy Spirit from her?"

Willow removed her chin from atop her fists, straightened up in her chair and now began banging her fists on the arms of the chair. "This is just so annoying."

"Calm down, honey. You don't wanna annoy God now, by saying something dumb about the Holy Spirit. I think there's no forgiveness for that."

His comment brought Willow sharply back to her senses. Shaking at the thought of how close to uttering blasphemy she'd come, she grudgingly decided that yes, the Holy Spirit could have Jess if he wanted her that badly. No point ruffling the Heavenly Father's feathers over something so trivial, even if it was annoying that it was one's own daughter who might decide tomorrow that she wanted to become the next Mother Theresa instead of a lawyer or a famous scientist or astronaut.

Unable to think of a sensible comeback that wouldn't place David in the right, Willow abruptly changed the topic:

"David, this running of hers has got to stop."

David frowned at her comment and then burst out laughing. "That again? What is it with you and her running?"

Willow rolled her eyes as theatrically as she could manage. "You're asking me that? You saw her conk out in the car, didn't you? And back at home now, it was all she could do to keep her eyes open long enough to eat her lunch."

"Honey, please lower your voice, or you're gonna wake her up."

"Don't tell me to lower my voice," Willow replied. But she did lower her voice to about half of its previous volume. "David, don't tell me you can't see that all this running she's been doing is tiring her out. Where is she going to ever find the time to read, when she spends all of her time running?"

That stated, Willow theatrically flung herself back into the armchair and waited for her husband's response.

"Well, honey," David said slowly, after a few moments reflection, "we need to put things into proper perspective. We need to consider where Jess is coming from. Barely a year ago, she was a depressed suicidal mess, and now—"

"And now, she's running herself into the ground," Willow finished for him. "What's the difference?"

David now got a familiar look on his face that made Willow sigh:

Now, he thinks that I'm arguing just for the sake of arguing, just because I feel like venting on him, and not because I actually want anything to change. But that's untrue! I'm actually very worried here!

"Okay," David said finally. "Let's simply weigh the positives of this situation against the negatives. I'll list the positives as I see them, and you can list the negatives. So, first of all, our previously suicidal daughter is happy again, and—" here David wagged a finger in the air "—and she's not gone goth like her best friend Mimi has—"

"Ugh!" Willow interrupted him. "I don't know what those two see in each other. I swear that kid Mimi is gonna be pregnant by the time she's sixteen. I can practically smell it on her."

"Maybe," David said carefully. "Okay, second . . . Jess is now getting her spiritual relationship with God together, which can only be a good thing, 'cos—"

"Just stop lecturing me already," Willow impatiently cut in on him, raising her voice while doing so, even though she'd intended to keep their conversation at a low volume. "You know what I'm worried about as well as I do. I'm scared that she's simply bounced from one extreme to the other. She used to be moody and depressed, now she's running all over the place like someone's after her, and now the tongues thing . . . David, it's what manic people do—first they're sad as hell and then they're as happy as heaven, maybe literally in this case."

Willow began weeping. "David, don't you get it? I just want our baby girl back the way she was, without all of these excesses."

David walked over to her chair, grabbed her hands and pulled her up to her feet. She went grudgingly, and felt just a little bit better when he wrapped his arms around her.

"I do too, honey," he whispered in her ear, while she wept and trembled against him, both needing him to comfort her and resisting him as well.

"I too want our daughter back just the way she used to be," David said. "But, honey, you and I both know that that ain't ever gonna happen. That old Jess is gone for good now. All that you and I can do is give this new version of our daughter all of the love and support that we can, and hope and pray that with God's help, she grows up into a beautiful person like we want her to."

Willow pulled back from him a little so that she could look up into his eyes. "But, darling, I'm worried," she told him. "Okay, so I agree that I can't argue with her running to God for help, but all of this other running she's doing at school can't be healthy for her. I don't want Jess to wear herself out, that's all. She's already been emotionally exhausted; we don't need her to suffer a physical collapse also."

David nodded solemnly to that. "Let's wait and see," he said. "It's still early days yet. We'll give it a month or so, then we can reevaluate how things stand; check her report card out; see if she's keeping her grades up." He smiled at Willow. "What do you say to that, honey?"

She nodded back at him, glad that he'd validated her concerns. "Okay, I'm willing to do that. Yeah, we'll both watch Jess and see that she doesn't go off the rails."

David laughed. "Well, I won't put it like that, but fair enough."

She walked with him over to the couch and they both sat down, and laughing, now began playing the popular husband-wife contest called 'Own The TV Remote.'

CHAPTER 57

Monday morning, and a fresh storm was brewing over Jess's head.

By now, Jess's euphoria over being baptized in the Holy Spirit was wearing down. Aside from feeling an even greater peace than she had since getting born again, she mostly felt like her regular self again.

This Monday morning began like any other.

But by the middle of the morning, halfway through Mr. Fisher's brain-tasking arithmetic lesson, and with lunchtime looming, Jess suddenly became aware that all wasn't right in her young world.

Mr. Fisher was an old man who sometimes stared vacantly into space as if he could actually see the equations that he taught his students calculating themselves. This absent-minded attribute of his enabled students to send themselves text messages during his math lectures.

The first inkling of trouble that Jess had was when her attempts to unravel the formula Mr. Fisher had instructed them to study were interrupted by suppressed giggling from the seat on her left. She glanced that way, and saw Anna Mendez sneaking peeks at her cellphone and trying hard not to laugh.

Oddly, once Anna noticed Jess looking at her, her giggles increased, then she looked away, returned her attention back to her books. But then she looked at Jess and began giggling again.

Jess was neither friends nor enemies with Anna Mendez. She tried not to think about Anna's strange behavior.

But less than a minute later, while Mr. Fisher solemnly regarded the strange configuration of numbers, lines, and symbols that he next intended to torment his 8th grade captives with, both Terrence Darby and Bobby Larsen, both seated in front of Jess broke into loud giggles also. Then both boys also turned and looked at Jess and giggled even louder.

"What's so funny?" she asked the two boys.

"You don't wanna know," Terrence whispered back at her, and then turned away giggling even louder.

Jess began looking confused. She heard loud alarm bells ring in her mind.

They're texting again. Everyone this time. Oh, God no!

Desperate, she looked over at both Mimi and Tommy. Both of them shrugged back at her. Neither of them seemed to know what was going on.

Five minutes later, almost the entire class was sneaking glances at Jess and giggling like mad. No one, was paying the slightest attention to their arithmetic studies. Fortunately, for them neither did Mr. Fisher seem to be. The mathematics teacher was staring at the whiteboard with his familiar far-off expression on his face, and the boys and girls all knew that until he returned to Ground Control, they could all get away with murder if they wanted.

The thing was, no one in the class would show Jess exactly what they were laughing at on their cellphones.

Tommy Bradley finally convinced the girl next to him to forward whatever it was to his phone. When she did so, Tommy glanced at it, and very theatrically facepalmed himself. Then, shaking his head, he forwarded the unknown source of the class's hilarity to Jess.

And so, Jess finally got to see what had everyone in her class so amused.

Jess wasn't amused at all.

There were two memes, though actually one was a .gif file.

The meme was simple. It showed a baby with Jess's face photoshopped on it and with a feeding bottle between her lips. 'Jess Sucks,' was the caption below the image.

This made no sense to Jess.

The gif file was even more absurd, although more obviously offensive. The gif showed a black-and-white cow, once more with

Jess's head photoshopped in place of its own, dropping a turd on a highway. The gifs animation was such that the cow turned its Jess-face to everyone and grinned broadly and then walked into the middle of the highway to defecate.

'Jess Poops!' was the caption heading the gif file.

Jess felt bewildered. Across the room, Tommy and Mimi were deep in huddled conversation. Both of them looked traumatized.

"What does this mean?" Jess asked aloud. "I didn't poop or suck on anything."

"You don't get it?" whispered Anna Mendez. Anna leaned over and whispered in Jess's ear: "There's a rumor going round school that you had sex with Barry Lindsey and that you liked it so much that you pooped yourself while you two were doing it!"

On hearing this, Jess moaned like she was in physical pain. "OH, GOD. NOT AGAIN!"

Her moan was loud enough to stir Mr. Fisher from those esoteric realms of mathematics that only he had a visa to visit. He turned from staring at the whiteboard and regarded Jess with curiosity.

Of course, with Mr. Fisher on the ball again, everyone in class was back staring at their notebooks like they'd never been doing anything else.

"Are you okay, Jessica?" Mr. Fisher asked in his scratchy old voice.

Jess blinked back tears. "Yes, sir. I just need to go to the bathroom really bad."

"You can go, Jessica," Mr. Fisher told her.

Jess immediately fled the class.

She felt like killing someone to make this torment stop, maybe even herself.

CHAPTER 58

Jess felt empty.

After fleeing the math class, she hid in the girls' toilets and wept until she ran out of tears.

She felt nauseated also, but could only dry-heave.

Then she washed her face and tried to pull herself together. It was around this time that she considered praying to God about her new set of bullying problems.

Seeing as God seemed to be letting her go through this, Jess didn't think God really cared all that much about her at the moment, but she prayed anyway.

After praying, she did feel better, well enough to head to the cafeteria and wait for her friends to show up there.

***

"Yes, it's true," Mimi told Jess during lunch. "Barry *has* been spreading those stories about you pooping yourself during sex with him. It's not just those only. He's saying lots of other horrible things about you, also. I didn't wanna tell you so you didn't get depressed again."

"But why?" Jess asked. "I've never done anything bad to him at all."

"Sour grapes," Mimi said. "I think he wants you back. And since he can't have you back, he's gonna spoil you for anyone else."

"But I don't want anyone else," Jess moaned in a pathetic whisper. "All I want is to be left alone!"

Mimi looked sad, and Jess felt sad. Tommy looked confused.

"What are we gonna do about this?" Tommy asked. "By now just about every kid in school with a cellphone must've seen these horrible memes."

"I feel like I wanna die," Jess told both of them. "If I die this will be over."

She looked around. The memes had clearly spread around. Lots of the kids in the cafeteria were looking her way and giggling, only to look away once she stared directly at them.

Not all of them, though. She suspected that those kids who weren't giggling had no idea who she was: those kids most likely imagined that the gif referred to a girl in the adjacent high school.

Tommy and Mimi were belligerently trying to outstare some of the kids, but two stares against sixty wasn't much of a contest.

Jess caught sight of one girl pointing her out to another one. The girl who'd just learnt her identity began laughing loudly, and Jess felt sick and quickly looked away.

"Let's get out of here," Mimi said on seeing that Jess was about to break into tears again. "I'm not hungry anymore."

Coming from Mimi Richards, this was a sincere, empathetic statement indeed.

***

As they left the cafeteria, they ran into Nicole Harper and her trio of 'goons' as Jess had begun thinking of Rachel, Leah, and Emma.

Nicole laughed on seeing Jess. "Wow, Jessica, you're so *popular*. I wish I had your followers!"

"Hey, leave her alone!" Mimi protested violently.

Nicole looked Mimi up and down like she was poisonous. "We don't *want* to touch her," Nicole said.

"We don't even want to be *near* her," Leah said.

"No, we don't," Nicole agreed. "The internet says Jess is a slut. And my mommy and daddy say that sluts carry lots of nasty diseases that can rot you up inside."

Nicole laughed and nodded to the other three girls with her. "We don't want to catch Jess's nasty diseases, do we, girls?"

The three girls faked exaggerated expressions of horror. "Oh no, we don't!" they laughed.

Jess began crying, she turned and ran off.

Behind her, Nicole Harper and her entourage swept into the school cafeteria like they owned it.

CHAPTER 59

When David Harris picked Jess up after her running practice that evening, he immediately noticed that something was wrong with her.

Jess looked sad and her eyes were red like she'd been crying. This was so far from the young girl he'd come home from church with yesterday that David was alarmed.

"Are you okay, hon?" he asked, though she clearly wasn't okay.

She didn't reply. As they drove home together in silence, David wondered if she was on her period.

But no, she's been crying. When she's near her monthlies she just gets grumpy like her mom does. At the moment, she looks like something's gone wrong at school again. But what? More bullying texts? Could that be the problem again?

When they got home, David instantly led Jess into the living room, sat her down on the couch next to him and took both of her hands in his.

"Okay, sweetie, you know that daddy loves you and cares about you. Now, we don't want what happened to you the other time with you growing almost suicidal to repeat itself, now do we?"

David waited until Jess shook her head, before going on:

"So, honey, you need to tell daddy exactly what's going on with you, okay? That way I'll be able to help you deal with it."

Jess continued looking down, so David placed his fingers beneath her chin and gently tilted her face upward until she was looking directly at him.

"Now, honey, what is going on? Did something go wrong at school today?" A fresh source of her misery now occurred to him. "Or did you get kicked off of the track and field team? That didn't happen, did it? If that's the problem, I'll come talk to Coach Simpson first thing tomorrow."

And then Jess flung herself at him and held him tightly and really began weeping on him.

"I don't know what to do, daddy! That nasty boy Barry just won't leave me alone!"

And then she showed David the nasty memes about her that were now circulating around the school.

CHAPTER 60

"I'm truly sorry about this, Mr. Harris," Thompson Middle School principal Garrison told David the next morning in his office. "But just like before, there's nothing we can do."

David had discussed the matter last night with Willow, and though she'd advised against him doing so, he'd thought he should let the principal know what was happening.

"So, there's really nothing anyone can do about this?" he asked angrily. "My daughter hasn't done anything to deserve being treated like this, and now look what she's going through."

Principal Garrison shook his head. "No, sir, there's nothing we can do. Unless we tell them all to stop using cellphones; which unfortunately is impossible." The principal sighed. "Unfortunately, these kids are still too young to really understand the consequences of their actions. They view bullying as a sport like baseball or football. And it's not just your daughter. I regularly get complaints like this from parents."

"Maybe if you had stricter punishments?"

The principal smiled a sour smile, which suddenly told David that he wasn't really as sympathetic with Jess's predicament as he claimed to be.

"We're regulated by the Harrison County Board of Education, Mr. Harris. They've very strict regulations about what we can and cannot punish students for, and the extent of those punishments."

Principal Garrison smiled for real now. "And so you see, Mr. Harris, in this situation concerning your daughter, my hands are literally tied."

GARY LEE VINCENT

David left the principal's office feeling even more frustrated than when he'd arrived there.

"I told you so," Willow told him that evening, when she got back from work. "That old fool Garrison and his yes-woman veepee Shelly White are more concerned about keeping their jobs than they are about their students' welfare."

CHAPTER 61

It got worse for Jess; a whole lot worse.

By Tuesday morning, the memes and rumors of how much of a slut she was were all around Thompson Middle School and Thompson High School as well.

Jess discovered she was infamous.

Those students who hadn't known who she was yesterday now stared at her in amusement or disdain when she walked past.

"Hey, is it true that you were pregnant?" Anna Mendez whispered to her during the break between first and second period.

"What?" Jess asked in horror. "Pregnant?"

"Keep your voice down," Anna whispered. "You don't want the whole class hearing it. There's a rumor that you got pregnant by one of Barry's friends and that your mom had it aborted. Is that true?"

"That's a lie," Jess said angrily.

But that was merely the tip of the iceberg.

***

When Jess went for running practice that afternoon, one of the other 8th grade girls pulled her aside and told her, "Hey, you shouldn't be running if you're pregnant."

Jess gaped at her. "But I'm not pregnant!" she replied in a whisper.

She'd realized just in time that she needed to keep her voice down.

The girl who'd called her aside gave her a knowing look and said, "Okay, if you say so. But that's not what I heard."

Jess almost broke down crying. She couldn't believe what she was hearing.

And the strange thing was, the meanness was entirely restricted to her peers.

Apparently, Coach Simpson and the other coaches had no idea what was going on. Coach Simpson simply decided Jess was more suited to running the 400 meters than the 100 meters and told her he wanted her to train for relays, too.

Jess discovered that the girls she'd been training with were no longer as welcoming as before. She'd greet some of them, and they'd ignore her or move away as if she were tainted with disease.

Their prejudiced behavior made her feel unclean, like she was nobody, like she was nothing.

Still, she prayed to God to help her, did her warmups, practiced her runs and then went home.

***

Wednesday brought a fresh trial with it.

At lunchtime, a tall and admittedly handsome high school student walked over to her and introduced himself.

"Hi, I'm Jimmy Lee," he told Jess. "I've heard a lot about you. Would you like to hang out sometime?"

Jess stared at him in shock for a few seconds.

"What do you mean?" she asked as horrified realization settled on her.

"No need to be coy," Jimmy Lee told her. "I just wanna be friends with you." How 'bout you and me get together sometime, maybe over at the bleachers? I'll bring us something to drink and we can party a bit."

Jess almost fainted at the request.

"I can't, I've got running practice every day," she gasped at him and then ran off looking for Mimi.

She looked back once. Jimmy Lee was laughing and walking away.

She thought that saga was over, but it wasn't.

***

On Thursday, while Jess was drinking water from a fountain, a tall high school girl named Tina grabbed her by the hair and pulled her back and spun her around.

"Hey, let go of my hair!" Jess howled, aware that even though she wasn't alone there, no one else would come to her rescue.

Tina looked as angry as a she-bear searching for her stolen cubs. She was both taller and more muscular than Jess and Jess really couldn't fight her off.

"Listen, slut," Tina told Jess. "If I see you near my boyfriend Jimmy Lee again, I'll end you!" She tugged painfully on Jess's hair. "I'll end you for good."

She let go of Jess's hair. "Understand?"

Jess nodded. "But I didn't—"

But Tina wagged a hand in her face to silence her and then spat on her. "Dirty skank."

Then Tina walked off to meet up with a group of high school girls who were laughing as they waited for her.

This attack was so unexpected that Jess couldn't even cry.

She'd run out of tears.

She felt like she was living in a war zone, with enemies on all sides.

Oh, my God, why hast thou forsaken me?

The question ran through her head like a poisoned river.

***

"I told you that you're damaged goods," Jeffrey the goth told Jess, when he, she, and Mimi were sitting on the grass of the football field during track practice. "You're like, badly stained, and everyone can sense how dirty you are, and there's no real cure. And so, stained and unclean people are attracted to you. They want to feed on your dirtiness."

"I'm not stained or dirty," Jess angrily retorted. "I'm a child of God. Jesus washed me clean, and God loves me."

But in reality, she felt worse than stained.

Jeffrey Dean had proved to be no good at sprints or longer track and field running, but since he was tall, he'd been steered towards the high jump and long jump instead.

He disliked both sports equally and was currently scheming the safest way to pick up a career-ending injury that would remove him from sporting competition forever.

"I've told you that the only surefire way is to break a bone," Tommy Bradley told Jeffrey when he joined the others. "Preferably an arm or leg bone, so it's got to be put in a splint."

"Dude," Jeffrey groaned back at him, "I've told you that broken bones won't stop my dad from sending me back here once I'm healed up. I wish I could play guitar like you do, then I'd have something to distract dad's attention with."

Listening to them both, Jess wished that her own problems were that simple. She would count it a blessing if she could repair her smeared reputation merely by breaking a leg.

CHAPTER 62

School was becoming hell for Jess again, and worst of all, she couldn't tell her parents about it.

No, it wasn't that she couldn't, but that she chose not to.

She had the suspicion that by this point even her father was tired of the endless series of problems she kept bringing home to him.

Each time she saw him nowadays, he looked ill, as if she was infecting him with her bad luck.

As far as her mother was concerned, Jess understood that the less she said about her troubles, the better; her mom seemed unable to effectively process her daughter's suffering and offer any real comfort.

The only person to whom Jess regularly unburdened herself was Rosemary Hodder, her youth pastor at the Good Faith Assembly church.

There were several other teens in the youth group who were also being bullied, and Rose's number one piece of advice to them all was to 'endure and pray for God's deliverance from that bad situation.'

CHAPTER 63

Rosemary Hodder was also in the habit of reminding her young charges that being a teenager and being in middle or high school were merely transitional stages in life.

"No matter how long it seems at the moment, being your age won't last forever," she reminded them often. "One day, you'll wake up in the morning and 'bang!' you're an adult, with an adult's rights and privileges. So, if you're experiencing hard times now, pray to God for his help in getting through them. And keep in mind that the bullies won't be there forever. What is most important is to not let Satan bully you into becoming like them. Once you start to hit out at others, you're no different from the monster you're fighting against."

It helped Jess a little to remember this. But she was just thirteen years old, and being eighteen, or even sixteen, seemed so far off.

Very far off indeed, when, with a total lack of evidence, you've been confirmed to be the class slut.

After the 'Jess Sucks' and 'Jess Poops' memes had made the rounds of possibly everyone in school except the teachers (and even that wasn't conclusive as Principal Harris had shared the memes with some of them), belief seemed to settle on one and all who'd seen them that Jess was 'guilty until proven innocent.'

And other than Mimi Richards, Tommy Bradley, and Jeffrey and his goths, no one seemed to care that Jess might be innocent. The young populations at the Thompson Middle and High Schools were perfectly content for Jess Harris to be as guilty as sin.

But as with everything else in life, after a while, the nastiness became normal. Most times, Jess was simply shunned. Oftentimes, she was ignored like she wasn't there and had to speak several times to elicit a response from classmates whom she was asking questions.

Soon, Jess, perceiving that she'd become undesirable, stopped bothering to socialize with anyone except those who still accepted her. But those numbers seemed to diminish by the week.

In the cafeteria, it wasn't uncommon for the kids to refuse to let her sit with them at their tables. As one particularly mean young fellow put it: "It's not that we don't like you, Jessica; we just don't want to catch your STDs."

So, if Mimi and Tommy weren't with her in the cafeteria, Jess either sat alone, or if all the tables had unfriendly kids seated at them, she had nowhere to sit at all.

Then she'd stand there in the cafeteria, looking around in a daze and praying to God to help her not lose it and start weeping or screaming in frustration.

Then she'd take her lunch outside to eat.

**

But at least Jess still had her track and field training.

Outside of her involvement in the Good Faith Assembly church's youth group, track and field sports were the one positive thing in Jess's life.

Despite the fact that Susan Martins, for instance, still thought that Jess was pregnant and shouldn't be competing with them, Jess still found enough satisfaction in her running to take her mind off of her other troubles.

Prompted by anonymous text messages, Susan Martins was so convinced of Jess's pregnancy that she went to the extent of mentioning it to Coach Lita Rodriguez. Thankfully, the lady coach had no time for such teenage foolishness and publicly reprimanded Susan, and warned her that next time she spread such rumors about her teammates—any teammate at all—she'd be kicked off of the team for good.

Jess won a reprieve after that. Although Susan's reprimand didn't make the girls like her any better, none of them now dared bitch at her during practices.

As for Jess, she just knuckled down and kept training.

Jeffrey Dean was still doing track and field, and was still trying to get out of it. He'd comically argued to head coach Simpson that he had flat feet and shouldn't be running or jumping at all, but was told by the coach that Usain Bolt also had flat feet.

After such an Olympic-grade defeat, Jeffrey kept on training.

Tommy had left to play in the school band. He'd also decided he preferred playing soccer to running.

Mimi was still there with Jess.

Some days Mimi was serious about training, and other days she wasn't serious about training. She knew the coaches wouldn't kick her off the team anyway; their policy was the more the merrier.

But Mimi clearly would never make even junior varsity. She just did what she was told by the coaches with minimal effort and spent the intervals chatting with the boys and girls, the boys in particular.

"I'm not sure now if I'm here because I want to be out of the house like lots of the other kids here, or if I'm here because my mom wants me out of the house," Mimi complained.

"How pregnant is she now?"

"Very. She seems bigger every morning. She makes me scared to grow up and get married."

Jess nodded. Then she saw her 4 x 400m relay teammates waving and went off to run with them.

One thing was fast becoming clear on the racetrack: Jess might not have been the kids' popular choice to be on the varsity relay teams, but she was all of the coach's first choice and this entirely by merit.

And the girls understood this.

The other girls had quickly realized that they all ran better and with more confidence, and *won* their races, when Jess ran with them and so they wanted her to be on their practice teams, even if, in their teen ignorance, several of them were still scared of catching an STD when she passed the baton to them.

So, to forestall this, someone (actually it was Susan Martin again) suggested to Coach Rodriguez that Jess run their anchor leg, which meant that rather than her passing the baton to one of them, they'd pass it to her (and in this way prevent her passing her infection to them).

Coach Rodriguez didn't know the girls' reasons for making their request, but she agreed, and was pleasantly surprised.

Jess (who also had no idea of why she'd suddenly been promoted to anchor of the 4 x 400m), performed even better now, leading her teams to win by even greater margins.

All of this was, of course, still practice.

But as the days and weeks passed, the middle of March rolled around, and the first track and field meet of the season soon arrived.

CHAPTER 64

Jess's first track meet was against Rose Park Middle School and was held at the Jamieson Stadium near her school.

Jess had rarely felt this excited.

She arrived at the stadium about an hour before the meet.

After her parents had handed her over to the coaches and gone off to find a seat for themselves on the bleachers, Jess joined up with the other kids from her high school.

About a hundred and thirty teenagers would be competing today. The stadium locker rooms would be used by both teams.

A film crew from a local TV station was present to cover the meet, as were both schools' media departments.

It was amusing to see students carrying video cameras and cellphones to film everyone with.

About half of Jess's teammates had begun doing track and field in the 5th and 6th grades and so had experience competing in track meets. These young veterans could be recognized by their more relaxed or (paradoxically, in some cases), their more nervous attitude.

But for most of the athletes, excitement and boundless enthusiasm was the order of the day. It would be hard to prevent a huge group of 10-to-13-year-olds from turning any gathering with their peers into a festive atmosphere.

They were here today to compete and compete they would.

Jess felt like she was looking into a mirror. The kids from the other school were exactly like her own team.

The only difference between us and them is in the team colors that we're each wearing.

Jess saw several girls who were plainly novices like herself, teens full of awe and enthusiasm, but clearly also shy at competing in an unfamiliar environment.

And then, Jess could also make out the more experienced athletes amongst the visitors. Just like those on her own side, these seasoned young veterans seemed almost blasé, while some others mingled about randomly, getting into just about everywhere they could and tripping on the sheer exhilaration of being alive today.

And the team leaders amongst the visitors were taking instructions from their coaches and passing them on down the line.

And the coaches themselves:

"Shot put boys, head over there with Coach Barkley. High jump girls, you're with Coach Farrow; Janie and Shaniqua, make sure you don't stray from her side, this isn't a mixer. 100 and 200-meter sprints, both genders; you wait here with me after the others go off. I got some last-minute instructions for you. Look here, Jimmy, this is my last warning to you. You get in a fistfight again like you did last time, and you're off the team. Got it?"

"Yeah, coach, I got it." Spoken glumly like Jimmy knew he'd be fighting someone or other very shortly and the coach knew it too.

"Good! Now listen up, guys and girls. These Rose Park School kids may have a reputation as being tough nuts to crack, but don't let them faze ya. They're all bark and very little bite. We just need to do what we came here for, and that's to win! You got me?"

"We got you, coach!"

Jess looked around, saw her mom and dad, and waved at them. Her father saw her first, pointed her out to her mother, and then both of them waved back at her.

Jess was delighted that her mom had come today.

The officials, volunteers, and team coaches were having a hell of a time keeping the kids organized and separated from each other. Even before the meet started, and while their parents and siblings were still filling up the bleachers, some kids were already getting into arguments about which of their schools was better.

Jess walked around a bit and found Mimi. Mimi wasn't competing, but she didn't mind being here.

"You know, like I wish our team the best and the opposing team the worst," Mimi said.

"That sounds like something Jeffrey would say," Jess replied. "Hey, where is he anyway?"

Mimi turned and pointed their goth friend out.

Jeffrey was standing with a group of equally tall male and female teens from both schools, each of them studying the set-up high jump equipment like it was the gallows they'd be hung from if they failed to rack up points for their side.

Staring at their combined moody expressions, Jess agreed that this was serious business indeed. Very serious business.

***

Since Jess's arrival, several announcements had been passed over the stadium's PA system, welcoming people to the track meet, passing instructions to the teams about the use of the stadium facilities, and in between doing those, playing music to forestall parental boredom.

But after a while, the music stopped and a man's voice announced:

"First call, 4 by 800 meter relay, varsity girls, to the track please. 4 by 800 meter relay, varsity boys, standby to go on after them."

And just like that, the Thompson Middle School vs Rose Park Middle School track meet had started.

***

The spring evening weather was chilly, but the fire of the young competitors' zeal trivialized this. Kids warmed up before events, got cold again while waiting to be called for their events, and then warmed up again only to once more cool down.

Jess competed in the 400-meter and came in second. In between running the 200-meter and waiting for the 400-meter relay at the end of the meet, she spent the time waiting with Mimi, hurrying over occasionally to speak to her mother and father, and watching Jeffrey compete in the high jump and long jump.

Jeffrey Dean proved to be a better athlete than he thought he was. He placed second in the high jump and fourth in the long jump.

***

The points added up. First, Thompson Middle School was leading, and then Rose Park was leading. They were almost tied, and then Thompson had the lead for about an hour. Then Rose Park won a bunch of races and was leading Thompson Middle again.

Four hours gone and no one willing to concede defeat. The Rose Park middle schoolers meant business.

And then it was time for the final events of the meet: the 4 x 400 meter relays.

"4 by 400 meters relay girls finalists to the starting line please!"

Jess's excitement was now very tempered by worry.

With Thompson and Rose Park practically tied on points, everything had come down to these last two races.

Jess wasn't sure about the math on the boys' side, but for the girls it was simple enough: If Jess's team won the 4 x 400 relay and earned these last five points, Thompson won the girls' half of the meet. If her relay team lost, Thompson lost. It was that simple.

There's no margin for error! Jess thought nervously as she and the other three girls on the Thompson team approached the starting line.

She looked at her teammates. Each girl's face was tense like hers was.

While the officials checked the contestants' names and made sure everything was in order, Coach Lita Rodriguez pulled Jess and her team aside for some last-minute coaching.

"This is no time for worry," the coach told the four of them. "You've all trained very hard, and you're the best that Thompson Middle School has to offer. Remember that: You're the best! The best here at this meet. You're better than those Rose Park kids. Much better than those girls. So, get out there, and just focus on whatever you focus on while running . . . and run. Run like the wind, run for the team, run for Thompson Middle School!"

"Yeah, the best!" Jess and the girls all screamed.

And then, accompanied by the coach, Mindy Lewis, who was running the first lap of the race, went over to the starting line.

Susan Martin, a competition virgin like Jess, was visibly nervous. "Why aren't you worried?" Susan asked Jess. Susan would be running the third leg of the relay and passing the baton to Jess.

The final girl in their relay team was Melanie Owens, a black girl who Jess suspected was even faster than she was.

Melanie had run the anchor leg for the relay team before Jess had been 'promoted' to that crucial position. Coach Rodriguez's idea in having Melanie run the second lap now was so she'd make up any distance that Mindy lost in the first lap and thus ease the pressure on Susan, who, though a good and reliable runner in her own right, was of an extremely nervous disposition, and could mess things up with a bad baton change if under pressure to catch up to the opposing team.

Jess was surprised by Susan's question as to why she didn't seem worried. Jess didn't know that she didn't look worried. She thought about it and realized that though she did feel tense, she wasn't apprehensive about the race's outcome.

"I think God is helping me stay calm," she told Susan. "And besides, we've trained as hard as we can."

Susan shook her head at that and rolled her eyes.

But Melanie laughed and said, "I wish God would help me calm down, too."

Then it was time to run.

***

Mindy took off like a bullet, but the girl from Rose Park Middle School was equally fast. In fact, as the Rose Park girl came around the second turn of the lap, she spurted forward and edged well ahead of Mindy to make her baton change first.

The Rose Park fans in the bleachers began screaming.

And then it was Melanie Owens's turn to play catch-up. But it was here that Lita Rodriguez's genius in putting Melanie on the second lap showed. Melanie Owens ran like she was liquid, and by the time she cut into the inner lane on the backstretch, she'd caught up to the other girl. Coming down the homestretch, she'd passed her by and put a distance of ten meters between them.

Now it was the Thompson parents and students cheering.

Susan took off fast and maintained the lead for a good while. But clearly, the Thompson coach had been just as canny as her counterpart in selecting who ran each leg of this relay. By the time Susan came down the final 100-meter stretch of the relay, the girl from Rose Park had caught up to her, and they were running neck and neck.

Jess waited, poised on the start line with her heart pounding and her left arm outstretched backwards. She could see the exertion on Susan's face as she struggled to keep pace with the other girl.

Jess began praying that Susan wouldn't drop the baton.

Oh, Lord Jesus, anything but that!

Susan didn't drop the baton, but the girl from Rose Park got away first. That didn't bother Jess as much as receiving a smooth baton change from Susan did. Once the metal tube touched her palm, she clasped her fingers tightly around it and hit her personal accelerator pedal.

Jess had no idea if she was faster than the other girl or not, but she knew that the girl in front of her was in for the race of her life.

Jess ran like her back was on fire and the water was at the finish line. On the backstretch, she realized she was catching up to the other girl and ran faster still, pushing herself more than she ever had before during training.

As they came round the second turn into the homestretch, the girl from Rose Park was only about a meter in front of Jess.

By now, everyone in the stadium was up on their feet screaming. The announcer had been calling out a play-by-play account of the race, but now his voice was completely swallowed up in the cheers and jeers.

"Run, Jess, run!"

"Run, Tammi, run!"

Their names blurred into RunJessTammiJessRunTammi JessRunTammiRunJessRunTammi! Until it sounded like the stadium itself was alive and was cheering them both on.

Jess ran. She ran past her parents without seeing them. The spectators faded from view. All that existed now was the strip of red she ran on and the white line at its end.

Fifty meters to go. Now she was neck and neck with her opponent and the noise in the stadium was deafening.

Twenty meters, ten . . . five . . .

Then she crossed the finish line, and there was complete pandemonium in the stadium.

The crowd was screaming her name. "JESS! JESS! JESS!"

Jess ran herself to a standstill, and turned around. She saw that her teammates were all running towards her to hug her.

I won! We won! she thought and began crying as they all surrounded her and lifted her off of her feet.

Looking over at the bleachers, she saw both her father and her mother jumping and yelling along with everyone else and hugging each other.

That made her victory and happiness complete.

***

Thompson Middle School also won the boys' 4 x 400 relay, but not in as dramatic a fashion. The opposing team fumbled their second baton change and lost the race trying to pick it up.

So, all in all, Thompson emerged victorious at the track meet.

And Jess Harris was the undisputed heroine of the day.

CHAPTER 65

By Monday, Jess's performance at the track meet had spread through all the Thompson schools and she sensed a new respect for her, a grudging respect if not admiration.

Those kids who'd watched the race even stopped to congratulate her and chat a little.

"Hahaha, you're famous!" Mimi told her.

So, Jess could breathe easy.

Thank God, she thought, when she noticed that the smirks had reduced a little.

Time passed. The school participated in more track and field meets, several of them against multiple schools, and Jess continued to perform equally well and help her team win.

She was now less of an outcast in the cafeteria too, and more students made an effort to talk to her, although there were still those (mostly friends and associates of rich Nicole Harper) who insisted on giving Jess a hard time.

***

Jess was sitting in the school cafeteria with Mimi one lunchtime when Nicole and her group walked in and demanded that she leave where she was so they could sit down.

"We don't want you infecting us with your diseases," Nicole told her. "As fast as you run, I'm sure your STDs catch on fast, too. And besides, I don't want to spend my lunch time sitting beside a slut who'll make it with just about anyone."

Under other circumstances, Jess might have done as Nicole snottily suggested, but Nicole had been so sure of her intimidating power over her victim, that she'd raised her voice too loud and several students at other tables had heard what she said.

Some of the kids found Nicole's insults funny and others didn't. Some laughed and some didn't.

The kids all watched to see if Jess would leave the table like Nicole was demanding.

"No," Jess said, aware of all of the eyes on her. She felt that if she backed off now from Nicole, all of the gains in status that she'd salvaged through her running would be lost.

"What did you say?" Nicole asked, her voice incredulous that her victim dared refuse her order.

"I said, no!" Jess told her firmly. "There's lots of other places here in the cafeteria. Go sit somewhere else."

Nicole looked furious.

"Hey, let's move," Mimi told Jess, while tugging on her arm. "There's space over by the window where Erica is."

But Jess shook her head. "No, let Nicole go and sit over there if she wants to. I'm tired of her trying to boss me around. First, she wanted Barry Lindsey and now that she knows I'm not with Barry, she wants something else." She got up from her chair and leaned over towards Nicole and whispered in Nicole's ear so that she alone heard what she said: "I think you're jealous of me, 'cos I'm athletic and you're not."

"What?" Nicole jerked back from Jess, her lips trembling furiously. "I'll get you for this!" she said.

"What did she just say to you?" Leah asked Nicole.

"Don't worry about it," Nicole spat back at her. She turned her regal gaze around the cafeteria, ignoring the 'peasants' who had watched her exchange with Jess.

"Let's sit over there!" she finally told her entourage. "I'm sure she's dirtied this table just by sitting on it. We don't want to catch Jess's icky social diseases, do we, girls?"

"Hell no, we don't!" her friends loyally responded with a chorus of contrived giggles.

The kids seated closest to Jess's table seemed to think they were supposed to support Nicole's mockery and some of them laughed, albeit a little uneasily.

Satisfied for the moment, Nicole Harper turned back and smiled wickedly at Jess. "I'll deal with you later, bitch!"

"Ooh, you shouldn't have done that," Mimi said in a worried voice, as she and Jess watched Nicole sit down at a table across the room. "She's gonna put you on her poop list for sure."

Jess laughed. "Everyone in school is already on Nicole's poop list."

Mimi nodded. "True. But what do we do if she does some more memes about you?"

Jess's face paled now. "Do you think she would? Oh, my God. I wasn't thinking about that."

Worried thoughts filled Jess's mind. There had been no more obscene texts sent to her or nasty memes about her for ages. Since she'd become a sort of pariah, the sender of the nasty texts must've concluded that their work was done. And since Jess had achieved minor celebrity status on the school track and field team, the bullying had died down.

Or maybe the bully-wolves had just decided that she'd served her term as their tasty rabbit and shifted their undesired attentions elsewhere.

But now, I seem to have accidentally started it up again, all by myself. Oh, God, why didn't I listen to you and simply turn the other cheek just now?

"Don't worry about it," Mimi said. "I don't think she'll try anything yet. People saw what just happened and heard her say that she'll get even with you. So, if new memes about you come out right now, they'll know she's responsible, and some kids might report her. She's not anyone's friend."

"I hope so," Jess said. But she was unable to shake the feeling of apprehension that now settled over her.

CHAPTER 66

After classes ended two days later, Jess and Mimi were on their way over to the stadium when Mimi suddenly pulled up to a halt.

"Oh shoot!" Mimi said.

"What's the matter?" Jess asked.

"I forgot that hairpin I borrowed from you in the class."

"Oops," Jess said. The hairpin belonged to her mother. It was handcrafted and uniquely designed, and very expensive, and her mother loved it. Her mother had loaned her the hairpin today because Jess had broken all of her own.

"We'd better hurry back before someone finds it and keeps it," Mimi told her.

"If that happens, I'd better not go home anymore," Jess said. Then she groaned and gestured at Mimi's hair. "How could you forget it? You were using it to hold your hair down."

"I took it off to hand it back to you, and then I forgot. Listen, let's just hurry back before it gets stolen."

The two girls hurried back through the school entrance.

The school corridors were deserted now as just about everyone who didn't have some after-class activity had gone home.

After dashing past their Math teacher Mr. Fisher, who stared after them like he was wondering where they were in such a hurry to get to, they arrived at the hallway leading to their class.

"Ouch," Mimi grunted all of a sudden and stopped running.

Jess halted too. She watched Mimi grab her belly like it hurt and walked back to her.

"What's the matter?" Jess asked.

"I need to use the toilet. It's been bugging me for a while . . . but now I gotta go."

Jess looked around. They were close to the restrooms.

"Okay," she told Mimi. "You go in there and I'll pick up the hairpin."

"Okay, it must've fallen beneath the desk," Mimi said and then hurried off into the toilet.

Jess smirked at the pained expression on her face and walked over to the classroom.

"Lord, please, let that expensive hairpin not be missing," Jess prayed. *" 'Cos, Lord, if it is, mom is gonna make bacon out of me."*

She ducked into the empty classroom and looked over beside Mimi's desk. Her mother's hairpin lay wedged between a leg of the desk and the hallway wall.

Oh, thank you, Jesus! Jess thought in relief and hurried over to pick the hairpin up.

After picking up the pin, she straightened up again and found Nicole Harper smiling at her from the classroom door.

"Hi slut!" Nicole greeted her brightly, now walking inside the class and letting Jess see that she wasn't alone, she'd brought her regular entourage of Rachel, Leah and Emma along with her.

Once all four girls were in the classroom, Nicole shut the classroom door behind them.

Oh, God, no! Jess thought. She realized that with the four girls blocking the door, she was trapped inside here, with no way out. She glanced over at the windows. No way out there either.

"Ha ha, you're alone now," Nicole said while dropping her schoolbag on one of the front desks. "We were just leaving for home when we saw you and that brat Mimi head back in, so we decided to follow you."

"And we saw Mimi go into the restrooms," Rachel said. "Whatever the matter with her was, it was quite serious."

"Which means you're all alone in here," Leah said. Leah Randall was a plump girl who looked more masculine than lots of the boys in school.

"She's trying to decide if she's got gender dysphoria or not," was Mimi's verdict about Leah.

With a mean smile on her face, Nicole began clapping her hands like she was a movie villainess.

"Git her, gurls," she ordered.

The other three girls swarmed over Jess.

Jess tried ducking away from their hands, but there was really nowhere for her to run to. After two successful evasions, she was grabbed by Emma and Leah and further restrained by Rachel, who now had a firm grasp on her hair.

"Ouch!" Jess groaned as the three girls shoved her forward to Nicole.

"Now, we've got you," Nicole said gloatingly. She wore a multicolored scarf draped around her neck, and now began fiddling with the ends of it, pulling it first left and then right across the back of her neck.

"Let go of me!" Jess grunted and tried to get away from the three girls holding onto her. But Rachel's grip on her hair was really painful and had the effect of keeping her firmly in place.

"Help!" Jess began protesting, but she'd left her cry for help too late.

Before Jess could get the word out, Nicole slipped her scarf around Jess's mouth and gagged her with it by knotting it behind her head.

Rachel looked out of the windows. "We'd better hurry up. Someone might come."

Nicole shook her head. "No one is coming. Everyone's going home now." Then she grinned down at Jess. "I hate you," she told Jess. "You're dumb and poor and stupid and you think you're someone special."

Jess was still processing this, when Nicole slapped her hard. The slap snapped Jess's head to the left and dazed her. Nicole slapped her again.

Jess began wondering how long it would take Mimi to finish in the bathroom. Surely, Nicole and her friends wouldn't continue beating her in front of witnesses.

Nicole seemed to consider hitting Jess again and then decided against it. Instead, she walked back and forth in front of her angrily.

"Listen, slut, if you dare go near Barry again, I'll pluck your eyes out!"

Jess of course, couldn't reply. But she could scream silently when Leah handed Nicole a large pair of scissors from her bag.

"I'll blind you with these," Nicole threatened. "Do you get that?"

Nicole was holding the scissors in a stabbing grip and now looked sufficiently angry to give Jess a demonstration of the blinding process, and so Jess hurriedly nodded her head to let her understand that she would never, ever go near Barry Lindsey again.

But I haven't gone near him since that one time last year! she thought in fright. *Nicole is crazy! Or if she isn't, who keeps telling her these lies about me?*

Nicole lowered the scissors. "And next time I tell you give up your place in the cafeteria to me and my friends, you do it. Understand?"

Jess nodded that she understood. Rachel's grip on her hair was so tight that it felt like she was tugging her hair out by the roots.

Nicole nodded. "The slut understands her place now. Let her go."

Jess sighed in relief as the gag was removed from her mouth. Then she caught the wink that Nicole gave Leah, but it was already too late for her to prevent what came next.

Next thing Jess knew, Leah was pulling her back by her hair, dragging her haphazardly across the classroom until she slammed Jess against the hallway wall.

Half-stunned by the impact, Jess watched for a long five seconds while Nicole and her friends left the classroom.

It was quite a while after Nicole had sauntered off before Mimi ran into the classroom. Mimi saw Jess leaning against the wall and hurried over to her side.

"Hey, are you okay?" Mimi asked. "I'm sorry I'm just getting here."

"What kept you?"

"Nicole and her goons stopped me inside the bathroom—I finished pooping and they were waiting for me in there—and they warned me to warn you not to mess with them."

"It's okay," Jess said, her mouth bitter. "You were right. I won't *ever* mess with Miss Fancy-Pants again."

"Did they hurt you?" Mimi asked in a worried voice. "If they did, we can go report to Mr. Fisher or another teacher."

"Forget it," Jess said, although her head hurt from where Leah had slammed her against the wall and she felt like screaming her frustration at the entire world.

"You're sure you're fine?" Mimi asked.

"Let's just go for track practice," she told Mimi. "Coach Rodriguez will be wondering where we are." She wagged the expensive hairpin at Mimi and managed a smile. "I'm glad they didn't notice this and break it. I'd rather put up with Nicole's harassment again than face my mom if I broke this."

CHAPTER 67

David Harris had been feeling overly tired for a while now. He knew what the problem was:

Getting this new consulting business set up requires me overworking myself. And that ain't a good thing when you're getting on in years like I am.

He'd just arrived home from fetching Jess from her track training. He was sitting at the dining table, sipping water.

Jess was upstairs now, probably having a shower. She seemed to prefer to come home all sweaty and clean herself up here. Though the stadium, of course, had showers in the locker rooms, there were apparently too many kids to use them.

David frowned.

I can sense that something's wrong with Jess again. I got the feeling once she got into the car with me. She's got that same kind of nervous tension about her that she had when those obscene memes were circulating.

"Ouch!"

David winced at an indefinable discomfort, the kind that seemed to come from everywhere at once, but which couldn't be pinned down to any source in particular, so that afterwards it always felt to him like his whole body was complaining about how he was living his life.

The problem was that of late, he'd been having these sorts of feelings more and more regularly.

I'm overdue for a visit to the doctor. But if I go to see the docs, their prescription for me will surely involve slowing down and altering my current lifestyle by reducing stressors. He frowned. *And until I get the business up and running, I can't afford to slow down.*

He laughed at the Catch-22-like situation and made a mental note that once he'd gotten the consulting business up and running, a visit to the doctor would be his number one priority.

But then his smile soured again.

But what's up with Jess? Her state of mind is more of a priority than the state of my body. Hey, it had better not be that kid Barry messing with her again!

Then David both looked and felt confused.

But I honestly don't get it. How in the hell can one young punk cause an innocent young girl so much trouble and absolutely nothing be done about it? What the hell is our school system coming to if the principal won't punish a rapist?

David slipped into an aggrieved reverie about how he wished Barry Lindsey was about two years older, so he could beat the living crap out of him and not be accused of abusing a minor.

"Dad, can I talk to you about something?"

David snapped out of his reverie.

Jess was standing there with a bothered look on her face. David's heart immediately went out to her, and he gestured to the nearest chair at the dining table.

"Sure thing, honey. Have a seat."

She sat down and he looked her over. He wasn't really a great judge of things like this, but to his eyes, she looked fitter than she'd been before.

She's taller anyway. Not by much, but she's growing up on me before my very eyes.

"So, what's the matter, hon? What'cha wanna talk to daddy about?"

Suddenly, her eyes seemed hurt and unsure, and his heart went out to her again. "C'mon, Jess, don't be shy and don't be afraid. You know your father loves you. If I can do what you want, I promise that I'll do it for ya."

She nodded and said: "Daddy, in three months I'll be finished with middle school. Can I go to high school somewhere else that isn't Thompson High School?"

David sucked in a deep breath. "Hmm, now I wasn't expecting this." His eyes narrowed and he tapped his fingers on the side of his water glass. "Is that punk Barry bothering you again?"

She shook her head and seemed to force a smile. "Not really. I mean, I haven't seen him in months. But, daddy, I don't wanna go to the same high school that Barry Lindsey does. If I attend Thompson High, I'm gonna be seeing Barry and his friends every day."

Jess looked like she was going to cry while making her point, and David instinctively reached over his hand to cover hers on the table. Then he smiled as reassuringly as he could.

"Don't worry about it, hon," he told her. "I'll have a talk with your mom about it tonight, and we'll see what we can do about that."

"For real, dad?"

David nodded. "Yep, for real, hon."

Smiling, Jess left her chair and crossed over to his and hugged him. "Thanks, daddy."

That hug made David Harris feel like he'd just won the 'Father of the Year' award.

***

After Jess had gone to bed, David put the matter of changing her school to Willow.

As David had expected, Willow had her reservations about changing Jess's school.

"If I'm right, Thompson's the *best* of the three high schools in this county," Willow pointed out. "Where else can we put her?"

"I'll ask around," David told Willow. "There has to be another high school in driving distance that she can attend. And it isn't like she wants to change immediately, meaning we've got a few months to look into it."

Willow sighed and shook her head. "It's not that I'm unsympathetic, it's just . . ." She shook her head. "Yes, you're right, do some research and let's see where else she can go. Hopefully, it'll be close by."

The next day during the morning school run, David told Jess that her mother had agreed that they needed to find her a different high school.

He was delighted by the smile on her face, and the spring in her step as she walked off into the school campus.

CHAPTER 68

The next track meet was a quadruple meet against three other schools, and it was being held at one of the other schools' sports stadiums. It even included running clubs, which included 6th graders who showed promise and could run with a given the middle school team if sponsored.

That Saturday morning, Jess woke up feeling an uncharacteristic nervousness.

She knelt down by her bed and prayed to God to see her through the day. But even after praying, her nervousness continued.

"Are you alright, dear?" her mother asked her at breakfast. "You look a little upset."

Jess looked over at her father, who nodded back at her. "Your mother's right, hon. You do look stressed."

Her mother, who was sitting beside her on her left, reached out a hand and felt her neck and then her brow. "Well, you don't appear to be running a temperature."

"I'm fine," Jess assured them. "I'm just a little bit anxious about today's meet. We're competing against Wheeling Central and they're the state champions."

Her mother responded with a knowing smile, and said: "Well, that's great, dear. Competition is good for one; it toughens you up. Competition is how small businesses become big ones." Willow Harris glanced at her husband before going on: "You start off as no one, and then by progressive stages, you take on and conquer the competition and take over their spots."

"Dog eat dog and cats also," Jess's father said.

"Exactly," Willow agreed.

Jess nodded that she got the point. "Thanks, mom."

But later that day, riding to school in her father's car, Jess was still worried.

The problem was that, during that week's track practices, while urging her charges to give their best at today's meet, girls coach Lita Rodriguez had done too good of a job of emphasizing to her girls how tough their opponents from Wheeling Central Middle School were, with the result that in addition to inspiring the teens to train harder, she'd also unconsciously instilled a fear of the other team in them.

Jess wasn't the only girl on the team who was more than a little worried about today's contest.

"We're gonna get slaughtered," Mimi told her once both girls had met up at the stadium. "These kids are gonna squash us like bugs."

Mimi too, would be competing today. Somehow, simply because, like it or not, she'd been practicing with the others, Mimi had improved as a runner despite herself and had somehow found herself on junior varsity. And since today's meet would have a lot of kids competing, Mimi had found herself selected to both run the 200-meter and compete in the long jump.

Mimi wasn't thrilled by the prospect of her debut for the school, not after the coach had told her how tough Wheeling Central Middle School was.

"Don't look at their faces," Jess told her. "Remember what Coach Simpson told us. It's just posing."

Mimi looked around at the other boys and girls at the meet; particularly at the girls. "But, Jess, they all look so tough; like they're gonna eat us for lunch."

"They don't look tough. They're just trying to intimidate us. They're as worried about us as we are about them."

Jess understood what Mimi didn't: that the other kids here at the meet were being competitive and putting on their best game face to frighten their rivals.

However, even though she got Mimi to relax a little, Jess was unable to quiet her own misgivings about today's events.

Coach Rodriguez had spent quite a bit of time explaining how Jenny Martinez, Wheeling Central's star in the 400-meter, had a deceptively 'slow' gait while running that might lull the competition into thinking she was on her last legs, when in fact the girl was ready to burst into full flight on the homestretch.

Jess knew she couldn't compete feeling like she was.

I really need God's help now.

And then, like God's answer to her unspoken prayer, an idea came into her mind. After waving to her father who was seated over in the stands, Jess walked over to Head Coach Simpson, whom she'd earlier noted was holding a red Sharpie, along with his regular pens.

Coach Simpson was discussing something with the male shot putters, but paused when he noticed Jess by his arm.

"Hey, kid, what can I do for you?" the coach asked her fondly.

Jess gestured at the pen in his pocket. "Coach, can I borrow your red Sharpie for a few seconds?"

"Why sure!" Coach Simpson said and handed over the pen.

Jess hurried away to a spot near the bleachers where the kids were fewer in number, knelt down on the grass, and in block capitals wrote, 'I CAN DO ALL THINGS THROUGH CHRIST WHO STRENGTHENS ME! PHIL 4:13 on her left forearm.' After doing this, she studied the two lines of large red text for a few seconds, and touched up a few letters that didn't scream at her loudly enough.

"There, I can't forget that God's helping me now!" she told herself and went to return Coach Simpson's marker to him.

The head coach was finished with the shot putters now, and was busy examining something on his clipboard. Then he nodded to himself and after gesturing at Assistant Coach Helen Smith to come over, he began looking around for someone or something amidst the general turmoil of arriving athletes, parents, spectators, and the officials in the sports field.

Jess tapped on his arm to get his attention and returned the Sharpie to him.

"Thanks, coach!" she chirped brightly.

As she turned around to leave, Coach Simpson stopped her with a firm hand on her shoulder.

"Hey, wait up, kid."

Jess turned around to face him again. "Yes, coach?"

Coach Simpson nodded at her left arm. "Jess, what's that you've gone and written on yourself?"

She raised her arm and showed it to him.

"I can do all things through Christ who strengthens me," Coach Simpson read off.

"It's from the Bible, coach," Jess said brightly.

"I can see that, girl," Coach Simpson told her. "You even went so far as to write out exactly *where* in the Bible it's written." Then he laughed. "Well, I hope that Jesus really does strengthen you today, kid. With the number of schools competing today, we could use some divine assistance." Then he looked over Jess's head, out across the field. "O.K., run along now. Coach Rodriguez is waving at me like mad, and I believe it's you she actually wants."

Jess turned and ran over to where Coach Rodriguez was huddled with the other sprinters.

CHAPTER 69

The meet began.

Once the contests started, Jess's nervousness reduced. The excitement of being there with everyone else was infectious—very hard to ignore.

And in addition to that infectious vibe in the air, there was also the fact that Jess quickly found herself involved in all sorts of things.

For one thing, Coach Rodriguez kept sending her off to take messages to the other coaches, if she couldn't get them on their phone. And then, when Jess wasn't doing this, she found herself with the responsibility of calming the nerves of the lower-grade girls who would be competing today.

"Listen, guys, this isn't Little Red Riding Hood versus the Big Bad Wolf," she told some 6th graders before the 200-meter dash preliminaries began. "We're just as rough and tough as they are. You just gotta get out on the track and give it your all. Stop thinking of it as if you need to win the race. Think of it like you need to work and gain points for the team."

She could tell that the 6th graders were confused. Not by the advice that she'd given them, but by herself.

And she understood their confusion. These young girls would have seen the memes and have heard the rumors about her, and because they'd had no personal interaction with her, would likely have concluded that she was a really nasty, trashy person.

And now they meet me in person and find that I'm not like that at all.

One girl in particular, Charlotte, kept staring at the Bible verse written on Jess's forearm.

The girls went off and gave quite a good account of themselves in the heat, with two of the three qualifying for the next round.

"Maybe you should stop running and take up coaching," Mimi joked afterward. Mimi had been disqualified from the 200m heats for jumping the gun.

"I'm relieved," she told Jess afterwards. "It wasn't like I was going to win anyway. Now I only have the long jump to worry about."

"You could at least have made an effort."

Mimi laughed. "That was the problem: I made too much of an effort and got disqualified."

"2nd call, 400-meter preliminaries, girls."

"Okay, that's me," Jess told Mimi. "See you after the race." She glanced at the Bible verse on her arm. "God, help me. I mean it, seriously."

With Mimi laughing at her for saying that, Jess headed over to the track and began warming up.

The race went better than she'd expected. Keeping in mind to pace herself in this race so she didn't wear herself out before the competition got tougher, she qualified for the final by finishing in second place.

"Very good, Jess," Coach Lita Rodriguez told her afterwards. "I don't want Wheeling Central to have any idea of how fast you really are."

Now that she'd qualified for the final of the 400 meters, Jess would have relaxed, but she was immediately commandeered again by Coach Rodriguez, who wanted her help in keeping an eye on the Brown twins, hot-tempered if talented jumpers from the 6th grade, to ensure they didn't get into arguments with any girls from the opposing teams.

Jess kept watch on the Browns and prevented one fight from occurring.

Then, thinking the twins would be unlikely to cause any further trouble soon, she took a quick break from watching them and ran over to hug her father.

"You did great, kiddo," her dad told her happily. "But why weren't you running as fast as you could?"

"Coach told me not to let on to the girls from Wheeling Central how fast I am before we reach the final."

Her father nodded and then looked over at where Coach Rodriguez was organizing a group of girls.

"Smart woman; good tactic," he said approvingly."

Then he noticed the Bible verse written on Jess arm. He read it and laughed. "Yeah, I think the Lord means business with you, girl," he said.

"What do you mean, daddy?"

Her father smiled. "It don't matter, honey. Just go back over there and give all those other girls hell."

"But I'm a Christian, dad. Shouldn't that be 'give them heaven?' "

"Girl, they can go to heaven tomorrow. Give 'em hell today!"

Jess laughed and ran back to join her teammates.

After discovering that in her short absence the Brown twins had gotten into another loud argument anyway, Jess went off with Mimi to watch the high jumpers.

Jeffrey Dean was still in the running, and the bar seemed dizzyingly high already.

"He's got real talent," she told Mimi admiringly as Jeffrey cleared yet another increment in the bar's height.

"He don't wanna do it tho'," Mimi said. "I agree with him. Goths shouldn't be athletes. It makes us happier than we wanna be."

Jess gave Mimi a knowing look. "Meaning yourself?"

Mimi nodded. "But, whatever, right? Parents ruin our teenage lives."

They stood there for a while, watching the high jumpers and listening to the announcements coming over the venue's PA system.

Two of the girls from Wheeling Central were walking past them when they apparently recognized Jess.

They stopped and smirked at her.

"We've heard about you," one of them said.

"Yeah, that you like boys a lot and that you can run very fast after them," the second girl added.

Jess gaped at them, struck speechless by the 'like boys a lot' comment.

"Hey, leave us alone," Mimi said.

The girl who'd spoken first, stepped up close to Jess. "Listen, man-eater, it doesn't matter how fast you run, you're simply not fast enough to beat Jenny Martinez."

"Or any of the rest of us," the other girl added. "Chew on that."

The two girls haughtily walked off.

Jess stared at Mimi. "Did you hear what they just said?"

Mimi burst out laughing.

"What is so funny about me being called a man-eater?" Jess asked angrily. "That's like another word for slut."

Mimi shook her head, but still couldn't stop laughing. "No, it's not that. I'm just understanding what you meant by them trying to intimidate us. Those two were trying so hard to look tough, they both looked like Cruella DeVille."

Jess still wasn't amused.

She stared down at the Bible verse on her arm. "Oh, yes, Lord. I can do all things with your help, and that includes not lose my temper."

***

Jeffrey came in third in the high jump.

Right after Jess and Mimi had gotten through congratulating him, the PA system announced the girls' long jump was about to start. Then the announcer told everyone about low-priced pizzas at one of the concession stands.

"See you guys later," Mimi said and headed for the long jump sandpit.

"I'd better be going too," Jess told Jeffrey. "I can see coach looking around for me."

"See ya later," Jeffrey said and Jess hurried off back to the coach's side.

"Where were you?" Coach Rodriguez asked her. 'Start warming up, it's almost time for the girls' 400-meter dash finals." She placed both hands on Jess's shoulders. "Remember, you don't hold back this time. Give 'em hell!"

Jess almost remarked to the coach that her father had recently told her exactly the same thing.

***

The girls' 400-meter final consisted of Jess and Melanie Owens from Thompson, Jenny Martinez and the two girls who accosted her and Mimi from Wheeling Central, and three girls from the other two schools.

Jess was in the fifth lane, sandwiched between the girls who had earlier had words for her. Staring back and forth along that staggered row of runners, Jess felt a return of the butterflies to her belly.

Oh, no! I'm not getting scared now!

As the officials checked their stopwatches, Jess looked at the scripture on her arm.

Heavenly Father, I'm counting on you now. Please, Jesus, don't let me make a fool of myself.

"On your marks, get set . . ."

The starter pistol barked like a dog and Jess was off running.

Once more, as it always did, her mind quickly shut off everything external to the track. She became aware of just the red strip that she ran on.

Even the noise faded to just the sound of running feet; hers and her opponents' feet.

Soon she was on the backstretch, and then coming around the second turn into the homestretch.

And it was now, with the stadium almost deafening with the noise of the spectators, that Jess became aware that the only runner she could see was sprinting superstar Jenny Martinez from Wheeling Central.

Jenny seemed to be slightly ahead of her, but not by much.

Help me, Jesus! Jess howled inside of herself and pushed herself harder than she'd yet done.

And then she and Jenny Martinez crossed the finish line, and there was literally no end to the noise in the stadium.

It took a while for Jess to understand why:

It was a photo finish. She and Jenny had both crossed the finish line at the same time. Nobody in the stadium, neither the crowd, nor the officials was certain which of them had won.

Thank you, Lord Jesus for not letting me down!

She and Jenny both stared at each other in confusion. Jenny Martinez, who'd apparently written Jess off after watching her run the preliminaries and the semi-final, looked shocked to discover that Jess was so fast on her feet.

The other two girls from Wheeling Central looked equally shell-shocked.

Then, teammates surrounded each of them and added an additional layer of excitement and confusion to the mix.

Jess grinned, while the officials and judges tried to sort out which of them had won the race.

The order in which everyone else had crossed the finish line was obvious: first, one of the other two girls from Wheeling Central, then Melanie Owens, then the third girl from Wheeling Central. And then the three other runners.

It took about two minutes of consultation and examining and reexamining video footage before the judges reached their decision.

Jess Harris and Jenny Martinez had clearly crossed the finish line at exactly the same time. And so, both girls would share the points for first place, and each of the other runners would be promoted up a position.

"Ha ha ha!" Melanie Owens told Jess as they walked over to the stands to greet their parents. "They think lightning just struck 'em."

"They aren't happy," Jess told Melanie afterwards, while they walked back to Coach Rodriguez. "They're gonna really bring it during the 4 by 4 relay."

"Let 'em bring it," the black girl replied. "We'll bring it too."

Jess figured that was the right attitude to take.

Jess and Melanie arrived back at Head Coach Simpson's and Assistant Coach Rodriguez's sides to hear the most shocking news of the meet:

Mimi Richards had won the varsity girls' long jump.

"How?" was Jess's question, which was echoed by Melanie.

Even Coach Helen Smith, who'd trained Mimi in her long jumping, was astounded.

But win, Mimi had.

"Everyone else just jumped badly today," Mimi said deprecatingly. "I wasn't expecting to win anything, but the star girl from Oakland Middle School kept making bad jumps and I got so annoyed watching people screw up, so I decided I'd show her how it was done. So, I just like, ran hard and put my heart into it and . . . Ha ha ha! I got the best distance."

All the coaches and team were delighted with Mimi, as it meant the team's points tally was rising.

The Thompson boys were doing well too, giving a very good account of themselves against the other schools. But no single middle school had really done anything definitive to take a clear lead over the other schools.

Thompson had done excellently in the sprints, but were mediocre at best in the middle and long distances, and there the other schools made their gains.

But the events continued, and finally, as the meet drew to a close, it was time once again for the 4 x 400 meter relays.

By this time everyone in the stadium, athletes and spectators alike were pumped up for this race. Even the officials had an air of expectancy.

But Jess suddenly discovered that Thompson had a problem.

"I'm too nervous," Susan Martins told her three teammates as they walked towards the starting line. "I wanna run with you girls, but I'm frightened that I'm gonna drop the baton when I try to pass it to Jess."

This was like hearing one's death bell toll. Jess knew that without Susan running on their team, Thompson stood no chance whatsoever of winning the relay race. Maybe they could beat the other two teams with a last-minute replacement, but definitely not the girls from Wheeling Central, who were spoiling for revenge, and who had three of the girls from the 400-meter final in their team.

And yet, what Susan Martins was saying was true. Even on a good day, Jess was always scared that Susan, who ran the penultimate leg, would drop the baton while passing it to her.

"What are we gonna do?" Mindy Lewis asked.

"This is real bad," Melanie Owens said. "Tanya can replace her, but she's nowhere as fast as Susan is."

"I've got an idea," Jess told the others, and explained what it was. The problem was they had no time to discuss it with the coach first.

And so, when it was time for the first lap runner to head over to the staggered startup line, Susan went instead of Mindy.

(How that played out was, Coach Rodriguez actually sent Mindy off, but then Melanie distracted her with a complaint about her bib, and by the time Lita Rodriguez got through with Melanie and looked back at the starting lineup, she discovered that Susan was over at the starting blocks in Lane 4 instead of Mindy.)

This change of arrangement created a problem not just for Coach Rodriguez, who had no idea what her girls were doing, but also for the opposing teams, who had all clearly watched previous relays run by Thompson and had arranged themselves accordingly.

But Susan was already in position, well up ahead in Lane 4 and there was no calling her back and switching her without it looking really weird.

Coach Rodriguez looked over at Jess and mouthed a "What the hell are you girls doing?" at her.

Jess, who had no explanation, simply grinned back at her.

***

"On your marks . . . Get set . . ."

Bang!

No false starts here. The four girls running the first leg took off, and the cheering started.

Susan ran like the wind, and Mindy walked onto the track and got ready to receive the baton from her.

Jess's idea had been simple: since Susan's problem was her fear of dropping the baton at the most crucial stage of the race, the other girls should let her start instead. Then she'd be under much less pressure, seeing as all she had to do was hand the baton to Mindy. Mindy could then feed Melanie the baton, and Melanie could pass it to Jess.

By the time the four teenage runners came down the homestretch, there was little separation between them; all four of them were still as staggered in their lanes as at the starting line.

Susan might have slowed down a little while making the baton change, but it otherwise went smoothly enough. And then Mindy was off running, too, chasing down the one girl from Wheeling Central who hadn't been in the girls' 400-meter final.

Mindy cut across to the innermost track at the beginning of the back straight and turned on the speed.

"Let's do this," Melanie Owens said, walking onto the track.

By the time Mindy passed the baton to Melanie, there was once more little difference between the sides.

The race for first place was now clearly only between Thompson and Wheeling Central schools. The two other relay teams were playing catch-up, fighting for third place.

And now was where Jess's switch in the deployment of Thompson's runners made its first crucial impact. Carrie-Ann Windom, the girl that Melanie Owens was running against, was the same girl she'd beaten into fourth place in the 400-meter finals. Aware of this, Melanie figured she could beat her again.

By now, the crowd was yelling like crazy. Yes, Carrie-Ann Windom was fast and at first pulled ahead, but by the time she and Melanie were on the backstretch of the track, Melanie had caught up to her and was going neck and neck with her.

And the two of them ran like that, neck and neck, around the second turn and all the way down the homestretch to where Jess and Jenny Martinez both impatiently awaited their turn in the race.

The crowd was screaming like mad now, with fan noise indistinguishable from foe jeers for both sides.

Once Melanie slipped the baton into Jess's palm, Jess grasped it firmly and then took off at full speed. She'd run maybe ten meters or so when she heard the crowd's screaming hit a weird, subdued note for a second. Still running, she chanced a glance back.

She was shocked. Somehow or other, Carrie-Anne had dropped the baton and Jenny Martinez was scrambling about to pick it up.

Jess turned her gaze back to the track and ran. She forgot everything else in the world and hit her personal gas pedal.

She could hear loud cheering as Jenny Martinez fought to catch up to her, but it was to no avail, and Jess knew it. She'd gotten too good of a head start for Jenny to reach her, except if the other girl suddenly sprouted angel wings and took to the air.

She crossed the finish line five meters ahead of Jenny Martinez and the race was decided.

And after all the celebrations and the victory lap, it was time for Jess and her team to explain to the coaches why they'd switched the orders of the runners.

And from then on, that became the new order for their relays.

The Thompson boys' relay team came in third, with the winners in that one being the Wheeling Central boys and East Fairmont Middle School placing second..

Wheeling Central were the overall girls winners of that day's track and field meet, with Thompson coming in second place.

But despite that, Jess was once again something of a school heroine.

CHAPTER 70

It was after school on the Monday after the quadruple school track meet and Jess was on her way to the sports field.

Uncharacteristically that day, Mimi (who most students viewed as Jess's 'shadow' because they were together so much) wasn't with her. Mimi had vanished off somewhere after class and Jess had no idea where she'd gone off to. Jess had both phoned and texted her, but Mimi wasn't responding.

Mimi did that sometimes nowadays. Vanished like a bird in a magic trick.

Jess figured that Mimi would enlighten her about where she'd gone once they met up later. She'd begun wondering if maybe Mimi now had a boyfriend that she was still too shy to talk to her about.

Jess was wondering how she and Mimi would continue their friendship once her parents changed her school for her high school years.

It won't change much, since we live closer to each other now.

Despite Mimi being her bestie, Jess had not yet told her about the planned switch—she didn't want Mimi getting all excited and broadcasting it to everyone before it happened.

Jess was walking past the high school now, and as she stared at it, a feeling of intense dread threatened her when she thought she might have to continue her education there come fall.

Because what happens if Dad and Mom can't get me a good high school for some reason, and I have to keep attending Thompson here, and Mimi has already told everyone I'm leaving?

"Hey, Jess!"

Jess turned to see who'd called her.

214

Two younger girls were hurrying after her. She immediately recognized them as two of the girls whom she'd advised before their races. One was named Charlotte, the other Johanna.

"Hello," she told them.

"Hello," they replied shyly. "Can we walk with you?"

"Sure," Jess nodded.

Together they set off for the sports field.

"Actually, I've something I want to ask you," Charlotte said before they'd gone very far.

"What's that?" Jess asked her.

"That Bible verse you wrote on your arm during Saturday's meet, what was that for?"

Jess smiled. "It was to help me remember that Jesus is my strength. I was worried about the other teams being better than us, so I needed that reminder."

"Wow!" Johanna said. "That's cool."

"I dunno," Charlotte said sadly. "I used to go to church too. I enjoyed church, but then my parents got divorced and I live with my dad now and he doesn't let me go to church anymore even though there's one just a few blocks from our house."

Johanna laughed. "My dad and mom never go to church, except for weddings and funerals. Us kids want to go sometimes, but they never wake up on time on Sundays, so I watch televangelists instead."

"I don't understand, Jess," Charlotte said. "If you're such a nice person, why do you get bullied so much?"

Jess shook her head and fingered the cross around her neck.

"Only God knows," she told the girls. "But you know what? I'm glad Jesus helps me overcome all of that stuff now. 'Cos I felt like killing myself when he didn't."

The three girls all laughed and walked on to their practice. Jess's two new friends asked her questions about her life and about Jesus, and she shared good answers with them.

CHAPTER 71

Jess had realized that running had become real therapy for her, a way to purge herself from negative emotions. When she ran, she felt free, like she'd literally left her problems behind her. But it was more than that now. It wasn't just therapy—it was communion.

Each stride became a prayer. Each breath, an offering. As the wind rushed past her cheeks and her shoes thudded rhythmically against the track, Jess felt herself moving not just across a field, but through healing. With each lap, it was as if God whispered into her soul, *"You are not what happened to you—you are who I say you are."*

Sometimes, she would start a run in tears—tears from a harsh word at school, a memory she couldn't shake, or the weight of worry that maybe she just wasn't good enough—that the stigma the mean kids labeled her with was somehow true. But by the time she rounded that final curve, those tears would dry. Peace would settle in. Her legs, burning and tired, felt redeemed by purpose. She wasn't just running for herself anymore—she was running for every other kid like her, broken and bruised, who needed to know that God could turn pain into perseverance.

She often wrote scripture on her arms with a black marker before each practice. Philippians 4:13 had become her favorite: *"I can do all things through Christ who strengthens me."* The words were sometimes smeared with sweat, but they stayed etched in her spirit. Even Coach Simpson, who wasn't particularly religious, had begun noticing her pre-race rituals. "Whatever works, Jess," he'd said once. But she knew it wasn't *whatever*. It was *Who*.

Running was her battlefield and her sanctuary. Her race wasn't just against time—it was against despair. And every time she crossed a finish line, Jess imagined heaven cheering. Because with each step forward, she was declaring to the world—and to herself—that healing was real, and that through Christ, she was not just surviving, but overcoming.

CHAPTER 72

And so, the spring progressed. A familiar pattern had now been established in Jess's life and was adhered to.

She had classes. She studied and tried to live up to her mother's academic expectations for her.

She and her parents continued attending the Good Faith Assembly church. Jess became one of the most vibrant members of the church's youth group.

She trained hard to run faster. She participated in track meets. She inspired her teammates to win. She became increasingly popular with her coaches.

Largely due to Jess's inspiring contributions, Thompson Middle School became a force to be reckoned with in West Virginia middle school sports circles. They didn't win all the time, but Jess's never-say-die attitude soon infected the entire team.

Mimi, for instance, never repeated her brilliant long jump win, but she did put in more effort afterwards and helped the team win points.

Jess became the heroine the kids hated to love.

The occasional text bullying spree still happened. Usually, this occurred when the 8th-grade humorists ran out of topics to laugh about and remembered her.

The year's most classic meme was called 'Jess's Training Regime' and depicted Jess as running at full speed along a racetrack while being chased by a squad of angry girlfriends of boys she'd seduced.

Even Jess had to laugh at that one.

Every now and then, Jess heard stories of Barry mouthing off about her to his friends. Several high school boys asked her if the rumors about her sexual talents were true and then asked her for dates.

After turning the boys down, Jess would feel like killing Barry. But now that she was born again, she knew this wasn't God's way, and so she would pray for him instead.

And God helped her. After a while, she discovered that she no longer hated Barry Lindsey anymore. She disliked him for being such a jerk; but most of all, she pitied him.

She could see how shallow Barry was, how empty he had to be to keep reminding himself of how he'd raped her as if it was some kind of crowning achievement in his life.

CHAPTER 73

And so, Jess's life rolled on.

And then came another landmark day in her life.

This was a Saturday in May, after the track and field meets for the season had been concluded, and the 8th graders were all looking forward to attending high school next academic session.

Jess was at Saturday's Aspire Youth group meeting at the Good Faith Assembly church.

During the meeting, Jess remembered Mimi and smiled.

Mimi has no idea what she's missing by not coming here with me.

But Mimi had said she wouldn't be available at all today, because first, she had to go shopping with her mom, and then after that, they were driving across town to visit her grandparents.

Jess smiled as she remembered her own grandparents. Her father's parents lived out-of-state in London, Kentucky. But her mom's parents lived in nearby Salem.

"Now remember, kids, that in John 16:24, Jesus said, 'ask and ye shall receive, that your joy may be full,' " youth pastor Rosemary Hodder preached to her congregation of 13-to-15-year-olds, the youths once again being split up into three groups which were seated at different parts of the main auditorium. "This means that our Lord God wants you to be happy and that he knows that there are things that make us happy. For instance, considering the fact that all of you teens are in school, you'd want God's help in your studies, right?"

After the class nodded, she added: "So that's something to pray about—that our Lord and Savior should give you the sort of wisdom he gave Daniel and Shadrach, Meshach, and Abednego. Now that's one clear instance of how you can all request from God for something that'll give you joy. Other things are . . ."

Jess listened with all seriousness, like she always did. Some kids at the youth Bible study didn't take notes, but Jess made sure to do so. Afterward, when she got home, she made certain to read through her notes and compare what her Bible teachers said with what the Bible itself said, just like she'd heard that the Berean Christians did in the book of Acts of the Apostles.

"And so, my message to us all today—myself inclusive—is that we not be afraid to ask God for what we need him to do for us. Our lord God is a loving father, and he wants us to be happy. Just remember to ask in faith, for without faith it is impossible to please God."

That was the end of the sermon.

Rosemary shut her Bible and placed it back down on the pew beside her.

"What we are going to do now," she told everyone, "is pray to God in faith from our hearts and ask him for those things that we desire him to do for us. I'm talking here about things that have bothered us for ages. Remember, kids, that nothing, absolutely nothing, is impossible for God. Every impossibility that we consider is entirely in our human sense of limitation. Okay, everyone, let us pray now. You can get on your feet if you want to, or you can remain sitting down if you want to, or you can even kneel down, but make sure that you commune with God in your heart, in faith and in all sincerity, because the word of God says that the true worshipers of God shall worship him in spirit and in truth."

Jess got to her feet and prayed with the others. She had one particular issue bothering her heart.

So far, her parents hadn't yet gotten back to her concerning their progress in switching her school.

"Oh, Lord Jesus, please, please, please, help me get out of Thompson. I don't want to be anywhere near Barry Lindsey when we resume school after the summer break."

After praying thus, Jess felt a sense of peace.

Surely God has answered me now. I believe he has.

***

Afterwards, Pastor Hodder held short counseling sessions with some of the kids.

"So, how are things at school now?" she asked Jess when it was her turn. "I mean with regards to your bullying problems."

"Much better," Jess replied with a grin. "People mostly leave me alone now. I still don't know why they even believed all of those lies about me in the first place."

Rosemary Hodder shook her head sadly. "The devil is everywhere, Jess. You see it in the news every day. Satan stalks people like a roaring lion, seeking whom to devour. And *he* turned those kids against you, seeking to devour you, but God has not allowed it. Yes, Jess. Thanks be to God who endlessly gives us the victory in Christ Jesus."

"Yes, God has really, really helped me," Jess agreed. "I'm like, popularly unpopular now." Then she frowned. "I've told my parents I don't want to attend senior high school there."

"That isn't a bad idea at all," Rose agreed. "And what do your parents think about it?"

"They're going to try to change me to another school in the summer, but I don't know which one yet."

The youth pastor nodded. "Let's pray about this now, and trust God to bring it to pass in your life."

And so, she and Jess prayed concerning the matter.

After they had finished praying, Rosemary Hodder was silent for a few seconds. At first she looked troubled, and then suddenly she smiled.

"Listen, Jess," she said. "The Lord just revealed to me that you'll discover something quite surprising very shortly. It will be something very upsetting to you. But God doesn't want you to worry about it at all. He is revealing this to you just so that you will know that he's with you at all times, and that he's constantly protecting you."

Jess couldn't help but look worried. "Oh no, they aren't going to start bullying me again, are they?"

"Don't look so worried, girl," Rosemary Hodder replied. "No, I don't think that's it at all. Yes, it is related in some way, but not like that." She smiled reassuringly at her young companion. "Our glorious Lord has won a great victory for you, and you'll soon find out what it is."

And so, Jess went home smiling but quietly confused. She couldn't stop wondering exactly what she would soon find out.

Nothing else happened that day, and she almost forgot Rosemary Hodder's words.

But the next night, back in her room after dinner, she got a video call from Tommy Bradley.

This was in itself a surprise, as Tommy hardly ever called her.

"Surprise, surprise," she laughed after picking up. "So, you finally got round to calling me? You know today isn't my birthday, right?"

"Listen, Jess," Tommy went on as if she hadn't spoken at all. "You are not going to believe what I just saw."

"What?" Jess now remembered Ms. Hodder's word of wisdom for her. And Tommy looked very serious; like the world was ending around him and he'd rather be on another planet right now.

"You won't believe it if I tell you," Tommy said, "so I'll just forward the video I watched to you and you can watch it for yourself."

"Okay, send it over," Jess agreed.

Tommy hung up and then Jess waited impatiently for the video he'd mentioned.

Despite Rosemary Hodder's assurance that this discovery (whatever it was) was for her good, she could not help feeling nervous.

The WhatsApp beep came in and Jess immediately clicked on the video link.

CHAPTER 74

The video showed the interior of a large house. From the furniture on display, the owners of the house were *very* wealthy.

This was confirmed a few seconds later when the video panned to show Nicole Harper.

Oh, so this is Nicole's house? Jess thought.

Nicole was wearing a pink bikini and had a towel wrapped around her waist.

The camera followed Nicole outside and down several steps to a pink marquee set up in the rear garden. As both Nicole and the camera moved, Jess saw a few teenagers, both male and female, seated beneath the huge tent, which was erected a few yards from a huge swimming pool in which even more kids were swimming.

The swimming pool had to be heated, because this week hadn't been particularly warm.

Some of the seated kids wore swimwear themselves, and others were dressed in regular clothes. The seated kids were helping themselves from a lavish buffet table.

The camera panned slowly across the swimming pool to show a group of women seated around tables, talking and drinking on the opposite side.

Jess suddenly realized what she was looking at.

Oh yeah, yesterday was Nicole's birthday!

After the last incident in the classroom, both Jess and Nicole had kept their distance from each other.

Jess's reason for avoiding Nicole was simple enough to understand: she had no desire to get rough-handled again.

Nicole's own motivation, however, seemed more difficult to comprehend. Mimi had recently suggested that Nicole's sudden aversion to Jess, other than to occasionally smirk at her from a distance, was because she was scared that she might have gone too far last time.

"Maybe the security cam in the classroom caught her and the others beating you up, and she got warned to leave you alone or else she'd be kicked out of school?"

Jess still didn't know, still didn't care, and still wasn't interested in finding out. She was relieved enough that Nicole had stopped making a nuisance of herself in her personal space.

And I thank Jesus for that, she thought.

The kids at the party were having a lot of fun, so much fun that Jess almost wished that she and Nicole were good friends and that she'd been invited to her birthday bash too.

She recognized several of the 8th graders and some kids from the lower grades also, including some girls from the track and field team.

And then, while the camera panned back across the swimming pool, Jess recognized one of the teenage swimmers in particular.

Hey, that's Mimi! she thought in shock, with the blood simultaneously draining from her face. *But what is she doing here? I thought she was going to visit her grandparents yesterday! That's the reason she gave me for not attending the church youth group with me!*

Down in the swimming pool, Mimi was having lots of fun. While the video camera remained focused on the kids, she stopped swimming and lounged in the shallows of the pool, laughing boisterously as something that boyish Leah, of all people, was saying.

Seeing how chummy the pair of them were, Jess felt immensely betrayed. She remembered Leah dragging her across the classroom by her hair and slamming her against the wall.

Okay, I can't understand Mimi going to Nicole's birthday party because their moms are friends and because Nicole's mother invited Mrs. Richards, but Mimi's being this friendly with Leah doesn't make any sense. And Mimi not telling me that she was going to Nicole's house makes even less sense.

Or . . . Jess tried to give her best friend the benefit of the doubt. *Or, was Mimi scared of my reaction if she told me?*

Jess glanced at the progress indicator for video playback, and saw that there was still more than two-thirds of the video left to play. Dread filled her mind as she wondered what else she was going to discover.

***

There was quite a lot more to see and it got increasingly worse.

After a glitch in the video that clearly indicated where it had been spliced together, the visual shifted inside the house.

Outside, it seemed to be drizzling (yes, it had drizzled yesterday afternoon) and everyone seemed to be inside the house now and were dressed in their regular clothes again.

With less focus on showing who was in attendance now, the camera moved across what appeared to be Nicole Harper's parents' living room, where most of the teenagers and parents were involved either in playing board games or watching a movie on the giant TV wall, and paused near a small group of teenagers.

The recording was also more jerky now, as if this cameraman or camerawoman wasn't the same one who had filmed the outside scenes.

Now, the camera concentrated on recording this particular group of teenagers.

Jess, who by now had begun to suspect where all of this was heading to, wasn't really surprised to see that the group consisted of Nicole, two members of her goon squad Rachel and Emma, and Mimi. She was very surprised, however, to see that also included in their group was Barry Lindsey and two of his friends, both of them boys who had asked her about her reputed sexual ravenousness and afterwards asked her out on dates.

Nicole was pressed tightly against Barry, who had an arm draped over her shoulders as if the two of them were now an item.

Similarly, one of the other boys had his arm draped over Mimi's shoulder and was whispering something in her ear while Mimi giggled like mad.

From the familiarity evident between the two young couples, it was obvious to Jess that these were two long-standing relationships.

Neither of the two girlfriends, for instance, showed the slightest concern that their mothers were present at the party, meaning that their parents both knew and approved of the young men they were dating.

Jess was of course stunned by this additional revelation.

"Hey, happy birthday!" the person filming them said, her comments now causing everyone to turn towards her. "So, for your fans and for the record. How do you feel today? How does it feel to turn fourteen?"

Jess easily identified the speaker/recorder as Leah.

Nicole turned from nuzzling against Barry and grinned broadly at the camera and waved at it.

"I feel really great!" Nicole replied. "Guys, as you can see, we're having a great party here, a really great party!" Then Nicole frowned and looked mock-serious. "Downer. We're having to watch some crappy action movie, however, instead of a nice rom-com like I wanted."

"That's just girls for you," Barry said then, leaning into the camera in front of Nicole. "We're watching 'Expendables 3' and it's great!"

Everyone in the group laughed at that.

Nicole now made a grand show of pushing Barry out of the way and hogging the camera to herself.

"Hey, stop filming *him*. Film *me* instead. It's *my* birthday, not his. Hey, you know what's best of all, everyone?" Nicole now grinned broadly, showing all of her perfect teeth. "I'll tell you what's most perfect in my life now." Now she leaned over and pulled Barry into view beside her. "It's that I'm finally with the love of my life, Barry!"

She turned his face properly towards her and kissed him on the nose. Then she pushed him away again. "And do you know who I have to thank for this most of all?" Nicole asked.

Mimi now pushed her way into the shot. "She has to thank me, guys, for getting that nasty dirty slut Jess Harris out of her life!"

"Hey, lower your voices over there; we're trying to watch the movie!" a woman yelled at them.

Nicole now pouted in the direction of the voice. "Mom, we're recording."

"Go record in your dad's study then," the adult voice insisted. "And shut the door behind you."

Nicole shrugged at the camera. "You heard that, everyone. I'm fourteen now, but some things never change."

"Guys, let's go," Barry said.

There was a period of transition while everyone got their feet and crossed the living room. This crossing took longer than it might have because Nicole kept stopping to hug her friends and explain to them that she'd soon be back outside, and that once the movie ended, the DJ would start the party music.

And then Nicole and her inner circle were inside her father's office, filming again while surrounded by bookcases.

"Okay, Leah, let's go," Nicole told their camera girl. "Yeah, now where was I?" Then she smiled. "Oh yes, my new BFF Mimi Richards was just telling you all how much she's responsible for my current happiness. Mimi used to be best friends with Jess Harris instead, but I helped her see the error of her ways, by telling her that since her mother and my mother are such good friends, we should be good friends too."

"Hey, can I talk now or do you intend to hog all of the limelight?" Mimi asked.

"Be my guest," Nicole said theatrically and stepped back, telling Rachel and Emma and the boys, "I'm thirsty. Come on, let's raid the kitchen for food and drink."

"What Nicole says is true," Mimi told the camera, when it was focused solely on her. "I used to be besties with Jessica Harris, but now we're not. Though she looks so sweet, and now even says she's a born-again Christian, Jess Harris is just a hypocrite. Jess has spent the last year trying to ruin Barry's reputation by accusing him of horrible and nasty things. One of the reasons why she now pretends to be a Christian is so that we will all believe her when she lies about Barry because Christians are known to tell the truth."

"You mean, all Christians tell the truth *except* Jessica Harris," Leah said from behind the camera.

Nicole, soft drink in one hand and potato chips in the other, leaned back into the picture now. "Guys, Mimi is the one who designed all of those memes you love so much!" She nudged Mimi with her elbow. "Hey, bestie, tell everyone about that!"

Mimi shrugged and for the first time seemed a little unsure. "Maybe that's not a good idea? What if someone else watches this?"

"No one else is going to see it," Barry called out, then added to Nicole. "Babe, can we get some booze?"

"Forget it," was Nicole's reply to him. "Duh. You know we can't drink alcohol with all of the kids here and my parents in the house too. Hey, Mimi, stop being such a scaredy cat. Tell everyone about the damn memes."

By now, Jess was totally confused. The revelations kept piling on themselves.

'I don't believe what I'm watching and seeing,' she texted Tommy. 'How did you get a hold of this?'

But for the moment Tommy didn't reply, and Jess was left to try to make sense of what she was watching on her own.

So, Mimi was responsible for those memes that had caused her so much heartache and agony? It seemed impossible to believe and so Jess listened attentively to confirm to herself that it was not true.

"Yeah, that's true," Mimi said. "I got into hating Jess so much by then that I had to do something. I just had to do something to get back at her. Like I told you already, Jess seems nice on the surface with her fake competitive attitude, but down inside, really inside she's just rotten, a totally nasty person. And that is why I made the memes to show everyone what she's really like. And that is what I honestly feel about Jess."

Mimi now leaned in towards the camera so that her face was huge in the video recording and when she spoke again, she spoke slowly, clearly pronouncing each word so that no one could possibly miss or misunderstand what she meant.

"Jess Harris sucks. Jess Harris is total poop. And Jess Harris steals other girls' boyfriends and afterwards lies about it. I hate her, and all of you should too."

Her eyes bugging out in shock, Jess thought that she'd heard it all now. But she was again proved wrong.

"And something that you don't know, Jess," Mimi said. "Remember the day in the classroom? I set that up: I intentionally left your mom's hairpin in class, so we'd need to go back and get it. And my belly was fine that day; I didn't need to use the bathroom at all. I just wanted you to be alone when Nicole was laying down the law for you."

After making this additional confession, Mimi looked as if she'd exhausted herself. She turned away from the camera and asked someone: "Hey, guys, pass me a Coke or something."

Her place in the video was now taken up by Nicole again.

"Okay, everyone," Nicole told the camera. "You've heard now the truth about Jess Harris." Then, Nicole laughed almost maniacally. "Who the hell cares about Jess Harris anyway? "Today is *my* birthday, not hers. That's right, *my* birthday! I'm fourteen, fourteen, *fourteen*! Yay!"

Barry leaned back into view also. "Yes, peeps, everything that Mimi said about Jess Harris is true. She's a slut and she was all over me like white on—"

"Hey, stop talking about *her*," Nicole interrupted him in mock anger. "You're all *mine* now and she can't ever have you back." Nicole gestured like an empress around her father's study. "Hey, everyone, let's go rejoin the party, before my mom thinks we're all making out in here!"

Then, Nicole Harper leaned in towards the camera one final time and said, "And that, guys, is the reason why I feel so wonderful today."

***

After watching and listening to this, Jess felt shell-shocked.

For minutes, she literally had no words whatsoever. Her mind felt like a complete blank.

Slowly, comprehension of what she had just watched came to her.

She wanted to weep, she wanted to rage, she wanted to scream at the top of her lungs until she was taken away in a straitjacket like had happened to Mr. Riley, who lived down the street early last year after he lost his job.

What Jess finally did, however, was to get down on her knees beside her bed and pray to God.

"Dear, God, thank you so much for revealing this to me," she prayed. After some thought, she added: "please forgive Mimi for doing this to me. Please forgive her, Lord. She doesn't know what she's doing."

(Actually, Jess partly blamed herself for what had happened because, fearing that Mimi wouldn't be able to keep the matter secret, she had never told Mimi the truth about what had transpired between herself and Barry.)

After praying like that, Jess forwarded a copy of the video over to Mimi with the caption: "Why, why, why, Mimi?"

It took a few minutes before she got a reply to her message.

The reply from Mimi was simple: 'GO TO HELL, SLUT.' followed by a cascade of rolling-on-the-floor-laughing smileys.

CHAPTER 75

At school the next day, Mimi completely ignored Jess.

It was almost as if Jess had ceased to exist for her.

Jess shrugged and concentrated on the day's studies.

At lunchtime, Tommy Bradley explained how he'd gotten hold of the film.

He and Jess sat together near a cafeteria window and talked. Mimi and her new friends were seated at the opposite side of the dining hall from them. It looked as if both parties were doing their best to be as distant from one another as they could manage.

"What happened," Tommy said, "was that Barry's friend James took the vids home to splice them together."

Jess was ignoring her food. "The same James who asked me out, who was at the party?"

Tommy nodded. "Yep, James is a tekkie. James took the films home to edit them together. While doing so, he sent a copy over to Barry as an example of what they'd look like afterwards. Or, maybe he did it as a joke. But James didn't have Nicole's phone number and wanted Barry to forward the vid to Nicole. But by that time, Barry was drunk, apparently on a bottle of brandy that Nicole had stolen from her dad for him." Tommy laughed. "So, what happened was, that Barry accidentally forwarded the video to his sister Mary instead. Either he did that directly, or he sent it to both of them, but Mary's was accidental."

"And Mary forwarded it to you," Jess finished for him.

Tommy nodded. "She said she doesn't have your phone number anymore."

"But why did she out Barry like that?"

"Mary told me that she hates how Barry's been spreading fake rumors about you. She said that at first she believed what he said about you, but not anymore." Tommy frowned. "I think he treats her badly, too. Mary complained that Barry was turning into a copy of their dad."

"Wow," said Jess, who was still trying to process the info. "I still can't believe that Mimi did all of that to me." Then she frowned at Tommy. "But what are *we* gonna do with the video now? Share it with everyone?"

He shook his head. "No point doing that. The only thing new in it is that Mimi was the one who set you up for them."

Jess laughed now. "Yeah, and if we publicize her meme-making skills, other bullies might want her to make some for them too."

So, Jess and Tommy didn't share the revealing video with anyone. But someone (maybe Mary Lindsey again) clearly did, because Jeffrey and the goth kids somehow got a hold of it too.

Jeffrey Dean was mad at Mimi's betrayal of Jess.

The goth kids summarily kicked Mimi out of their company.

Mimi told them they could all go to hell and ditched her gloomy face paint. She'd already begun toning down her gothic makeup anyway, because Nicole thought it made her look both cheap and creepy.

Thereafter, Nicole and Mimi were always seen together on campus. Everyone accepted that she'd now become Nicole's shadow instead of Jess's.

The other thing Mimi did, which Jess counted as a blessing, was drop off the school's track and field team. Jess never found out if this was because Mimi was worried about their teammates' reaction if they, too, discovered that she was responsible for the bullying memes or if Nicole simply didn't want any jockettes in her social circle.

Jess figured it had to be the latter. And besides, if Nicole expected Mimi to hang out with her all the time, where would she ever find the time for sports?

Whatever the reason for her ex-bestie's departure, though, Jess was intensely relieved that Mimi would no longer be attending practices.

It meant there wouldn't be any nasty scenes on the sports field that might negatively impact her concentration.

Jess's attitude was: *New friends, new life, new running team.*

But it's the same God for me! Thank you so much, Jesus, for revealing who my real friends are!

Then she'd sighed and fought down the worry that rose up inside of her.

And hopefully a new high school for me too. 'Cos now that Mimi is on Barry's side, high school will surely be hell otherwise.

CHAPTER 76

It took an entire week for Jess to make up her mind to share the video from Nicole's birthday with her parents.

Her hesitation was because she feared her father's reaction to watching the video. She knew he would explode like a bomb and it would take all of her mother's calming him down to prevent him doing something drastic.

But finally, she made up her mind to show her mother and father the video, for the simple reason that it would add fire to the gasoline of her desire to change schools.

She decided to show her dad the video after church on Sunday. After lunch to be exact.

He's usually in a great mood then, and shouldn't lose it too badly.

So, after church on Sunday, which Jess enjoyed immensely, she had lunch with her parents and afterwards, when they were both sitting on the living room couch, began to tell them about Mimi's betrayal.

"Dad, mom, there's something I want to show you."

"Oh, what is it, hon?" her father asked, being in the expected well-fed and pleasant state of mind that Jess had counted on. At the moment, David Harris looked so calm and serene and at peace with the world, that Jess doubted even an earthquake could change his mood.

Her mother, however, had a stormy look about her face that Jess disliked. It seemed that she'd mistaken which parent to be worried about.

"Okay. I found out something that you've got to see!" she told them both.

But then she discovered that she'd left her cellphone upstairs in her bedroom. "Hold on, please," she told them. "I'll go get it."

Jess hurried upstairs and found the cellphone, picked it up, and hurried back downstairs, only to find her parents, whom she'd left in a calm and peaceful state, having an argument.

The quarrel grew louder as she descended the stairs.

What happened?

"What I'm saying, David," her mother was thundering, "is that you're being too soft with our daughter. Yes, I love her as much as you do, but—" Willow was up off the couch now and was standing facing David with her feet firmly planted and her hands on her hips, "—if she rides out the bullying it will toughen her up. That's what I think!"

"Ride out the bullying?" David asked in dismay. "Honey, this is our daughter we're talking about here, not some child statistics on TV."

"You don't have to remind me that she's my daughter. I'm talking like this because she's our daughter and I want nothing but the best for her."

Jess sat on the bottom step of the stairway, unnoticed, and listened. She was still surprised that they'd gotten into this argument before she'd even played her video for them.

"And do you honestly think that leaving Jess at Thompson for her high school years is the best thing for her?"

"I do. I do."

"You seem to have forgotten what happened last year."

"No, I've not forgotten about that." Willow glared over the top of her husband's head, either saw Jess and didn't care or didn't notice her at all, and returned her attention and her anger back to David. "This request of hers to get out of the Thompson Schools is simply another weird step up from the endless running that she does and that Pentecostal baptism nonsense."

David looked worried when she said this. "Hey, watch what you say!"

But Willow breathed in and out furiously and thundered instead: "Why should I keep checking my speech because you Protestants hate hearing the truth!? Dammit, I should have listened to my late dad and married a Catholic instead!"

Now it was Jess's father's turn to raise his voice: "So why didn't you then? Huh?"

David Harris got to his feet too now, and he was much taller than Willow, so that seeing him angry like that had the automatic effect of making her shrink back from him, even though Jess had never seen her father hit her mother.

"I don't care what you think!" her father told her mother. "I'm totally tired of hearing you bitch about everything where Jess is concerned. And now I don't care—I don't give a damn if you leave me or not over this—but our daughter is changing schools this summer and that is that!"

"But . . . but . . .!" Willow rallied nervously but angrily. "But . . .!"

"But nothing!" David roared back at her. "I'm the one who mostly drives her to school and back and so I don't see what concern of yours it is if her new school is at the other end of the damn state!" His voice lowered somewhat but he was still clearly angry. "You seem to be forgetting that these Thompson schools that you're so insistent on our daughter continuing to attend are the same ones who did nothing to help when she was raped! All that those fools did was shovel the evidence under the carpet! So, what happens if someone else tries to hurt Jess? What then?"

"Surely, you don't think . . .?" To Jess, her mother seemed to be under immense emotional pressure.

"Willow, it doesn't matter what I think," David Harris told his wife firmly, but not as angrily now. "What is important is that Jess not have to spend her high school years in such a toxic environment, with the same kid who hurt her so badly. And I intend to ensure that she doesn't."

"You can't decide that alone!" Willow shouted at him. "I'm her mother."

"So, act like her mother then. Act like you care about more than how good her grades are each term. All you do is complain about how she should run less and study more, without taking into account the fact that running makes her happy."

"That's unfair to me," Willow Harris said. "I just want Jess to do her best for herself; to become the best she can be. I want her to have more of a future than being a baby-making machine. I don't see how running can possibly help her achieve any lasting success in life." Now that her husband sounded less angry, she looked furious again. "And . . . and, David, you sound like you don't think I'm necessary to this family."

"No. You are understanding me wrong," her husband replied in a tired voice. "But if you're tired of being married to a Protestant, then leave. But, honey, please, when you leave, leave my daughter behind, so she doesn't turn out as lopsided in her beliefs as you."

On hearing her father say that, Jess turned and fled up the stairs.

***

Jess sat in her room totally confused; confused because she didn't know if it was God or the devil at work now.

The muffled noise of further angry words being exchanged downstairs seeped through her bedroom door.

Jess sat in bed with her hands clenched into fists by her sides and tried to fight off the stress that she felt invading her.

Sure, her parents had had fights before, and a few loud ones at that, but today's fight had an added edge to it.

And the intensity of her parents' current argument wasn't an isolated incident either. From what she'd heard, she thought they must have been fighting about her when she wasn't around to hear it.

The prospect of her mother leaving them was a scary one. Jess loved her mother, even if she was overly strict sometimes. She didn't know what she'd do if her mother took up her father's dare and left them both.

Lord Jesus, please don't let that happen to me!

Then, feeling slightly better after praying this way, she remembered the video she'd been about to play for her parents.

Oh, what do I do now? If mom and dad are already fighting about the school before I show them what we found out, what are they going to do when they see the video? Because I never mentioned to them that Nicole and the others beat me up in class.

Jess decided there and then that she wasn't about to breathe a word about what had happened to either of her parents.

No, I'm not telling them a single thing about any of it!

She still felt stressed out, and prayed to God to help her cope with the stress.

And, Lord Jesus, she added silently in her heart, *No matter what happens to me, I'm going to keep myself focused on doing what you want me to.* She grinned. *And I'm also going to keep on running!*

PART THREE:
TRIALS AND TRIUMPHS

CHAPTER 77

And so that year's West Virginian student track and field season ended.

Those athletes who didn't play other sports now waited for the cross-country season, which began in the summer and extended through the fall.

Jess was one of those waiting for the cross-country season to start.

Since the track and field season had concluded, with Thompson Middle School doing very well, Jess had felt a kind of emptiness inside of herself. Its cause was obvious; for the time being, she had nothing to strive for.

Jess still had church, however, and she participated enthusiastically in the Good Faith church's youth fellowship.

She still went to the stadium and trained several days a week, but now with the cross-country season in mind. She tried out her legs at longer distances and worked to strengthen herself and build up her endurance for the 5K, or 3.1-mile, exertion that she next intended to participate in.

Her 8th-grade year soon ended.

Jess was almost beside herself with joy when her father told her he'd arranged for her to transfer to College High School over in Morgantown.

Morgantown was 35 miles away from Bridgeport and three counties distant but Jess did not mind in the least. She was simply relieved at being given the opportunity to make a fresh start somewhere where the past didn't lurk around every corner to haunt and stalk her.

Summer arrived, and Jess went off to College High summer camp.

At the end of July, the College High cross-country tryouts were held, and Jess participated.

She wasn't exactly a rookie here. The other boys and girls at the summer camp and the cross-country coaches already knew about her from her middle school running performances.

Once she showed that she had the stamina to run longer distances, too, she was happily welcomed to the team and quickly made varsity.

Jess couldn't have been happier. She really felt that now she was on top of the world.

CHAPTER 78

It was now, now that she'd begun running cross-country, that Jess really discovered how freeing running could be. Unlike when she'd competed in the man-made atmosphere of a stadium, the natural ambience of the countryside she ran through while training with her teammates never failed to thrill her.

And somehow, maybe because Jess herself felt different on each day, each practice session felt similarly different to her, even when she was running along a familiar trail.

Uphill, downhill, level ground, around a lake, through a tunnel of tree leaves created because the trees grew so thick on either side of the trail that their branches overlapped.

The switching locations never really mattered. What did matter was the thrill of physical exertion and the knowledge of the waiting destination.

Jess would relax, permit herself to flow in tune with nature, and run. She *ran*.

Startling rodents and birds with the measured but fast patter of her feet on the grass trail.

After a while on those runs, her mind seemed to detach itself from her body, as if watching over her body from a height like an angel might do, or how Jess believed God Almighty watched her.

Her mind became as clear as the pure streams that she and her teammates ran past. And her soul seemed as free as the birds that circled overhead in the clear blue sky.

It was meditation. While she ran, she felt herself communing with God, her mind bubbling over with verses of scripture, with extracts from sermons she had heard and Christian books she had read, and with her own personal reflections on the goodness and greatness of God.

She utterly loved how easy it was for her to focus on God when surrounded by the things he had made.

Out here, with the clear evidence of God's glory all around her, it was easy to become lost in the beauty of it all.

After these training runs, Jess felt completely rejuvenated. It didn't matter what she was dealing with in her personal life at that moment; cross-country running felt like she was taking a bath in God's divine glory.

***

Once again, days became weeks and weeks combined into months.

Sooner than Jess had expected, summer vacation was over, and she was resuming her freshman year at College High School.

CHAPTER 79

"Bye, honey, have a good day in school."

"Bye, dad, see you later!"

Jess waited for a few moments to watch her father drive off. And then she headed into the College High School campus.

Jess felt happy now. Coming here each morning held the same pleasant anticipation and excitement as arriving at Thompson Middle School used to hold for her before her fall from grace.

Here at College High, Jess knew she was the same as every other student. There was no stigma attached to her. Here, no one considered her an outcast, no one viewed her as too insignificant to talk to.

Almost as proof of this fact, another 14-year-old female freshman fell into step beside Jess almost immediately she was on the high school campus.

"Hey, Jess, how was your weekend?"

Ashley Roach, the speaker, was also a member of the high school cross-country team. She and Jess had met at summer camp. The girls had quickly discovered that they had a commitment to Jesus Christ in common, though Ashley attended a different church from Jess.

"Hi, Ashley, the weekend was great," Jess told her friend. "Our youth group went out on evangelism in Stonewood."

"Yeah? How did that go?"

Jess shrugged as they stepped into the school's front building. "We didn't get the kind of response we were hoping for, but we'll be going back again this weekend."

Ashley sighed. "I wish you didn't live so far away from here. Then we could hang out together and attend church together."

Jess sighed also. "It's crazy that my dad has to drive such a long distance to get me here every morning and pick me up after practice every evening."

"Maybe you guys will move closer before you finish high school?"

Jess laughed. "I doubt it. My mom still isn't the greatest fan of me attending here, but my father insisted."

As they turned into the hallway that led to their classroom, another girl joined them.

"So, guys, how was your weekend?" Sandra Parker asked. Sandra wasn't an athlete, but she had become firm friends with both Jess and Ashley and also lamented the fact that Jess lived in Bridgeport, three counties away, and so they couldn't get together and hang out or have sleepovers at each other's houses.

The trio arrived in class and greeted the other boys and girls.

Then the days' education began.

The different teachers arrived and departed like an assembly line was processing them: Mr. Holmes for Math, Miss Jenkins for Biology, Mrs. Thompson for American Literature; the list went on and on. Information flowed from the teachers' minds and lips into the ears and dreams of their students, hopefully not down the mental drain afterwards.

Jess absorbed it all. She couldn't get over how relieved and refreshed she felt being here at College High.

Thank you, Jesus. Thank you for answering my prayers, Lord Jesus. I am so grateful to you for doing this for me. I feel like you've rescued me from hell on earth!

Sometimes, on reviewing how far she'd come over the past two years, Jess felt like she was dreaming. She felt like a captive who'd been set free. She now realized that she hadn't understood how restricted she'd been at her previous school.

Wow! I can't believe how much pressure and stress I was under back at Thompson Middle School. Only God helped me survive that toxic environment with Nicole and Mimi and all of that gossip and slander and bullying. Thank you, Jesus, for plucking me out of that horrible situation.

Then she would sigh, and her good mood would dull a little.

I just wish that mom would be more understanding about why I have to do this, why I have to make this move here. It's almost as if she prefers me being at Thompson, simply because it's a more convenient distance.

But her mother's feelings on the matter were really just a minor issue.

What really matters is that I am finally here, here where I can be myself!

CHAPTER 80

After classes ended that afternoon, Jess, Ashley, and another high school freshman named Tiffany Welsh piled into Toby Green's Toyota.

Toby was in 12th grade and was on the boys' cross-country team.

The cross-country team had this arrangement where the older students who had cars helped to ferry those students who didn't have cars over to where each day's cross-country training practice would be held.

"So, girls, how's your day been?" Toby asked. "Did Mr. Holmes sufficiently terrorize you with algebra and coefficient binomials?" That said, he laughed loudly.

"Oh, dude, they're not that hard," Jess replied, while the other girls giggled.

Toby shook his head. "Maybe not for you, li'l sister. But I'm no good at math. Never have been, never will be."

"What do you want to study in college, Toby?" Tiffany asked as Toby started the car and reversed out of the school parking lot.

"Hey wait!" Jess said as Toby began driving off. "We've forgotten Josh."

"No, we haven't," Toby replied. "Josh didn't come to school today."

"Do you know why?" Ashley asked. Like Toby, Josh Bellamy was a senior, too, and it was obvious to everyone that Ashley really liked him in a girlfriend sort of way.

"Dunno. Not really sure. Tho' I suspect maybe it's a problem with his mom's car again."

Toby Green drove them over to Van Voorhis Trailhead, where they held their Monday cross-country training.

Toby kept on joking as he drove, and Jess relaxed.

This is something else I've discovered since arriving at College High, she told herself as they rolled through the town. *Here, I'm completely accepted by my teammates; no doubt about it. Thanks for that too, Lord Jesus.*

Indeed, the difference was like chalk and cheese. Where formerly, Jess had had to fight through deep prejudice for every shred of self-respect that she could salvage for herself, as a member of her current school's sports team she was respected not just for her sporting accomplishments (since she'd competed against several of her current teammates at the middle school meets earlier that year) but simply because she was a good human being.

That means the world to me, more than anyone can imagine. Over at Thompson, it was clear that lots of the girls distrusted me. They only tolerated my presence on the team because they knew I'd help them win races and gain points for our school. Those girls and boys knew me personally, and yet they still believed and acted like I was as bad as I'd been painted.

Here, however, even the girls and boys who've heard the rumors don't accept them at face value; they're waiting for me to either act that way or not.

And, best of all, I'm not anywhere near Barry Lindsey anymore! Thank you, Jesus!

Finally, Toby drove his car into the Van Voorhis Trailhead parking lot. He parked, switched the engine off and then turned to grin at his three passengers.

"Well, here we are, ladies," he said. "Let's go do some running!"

Then they all got out of the car and stood waiting for the rest of the cross-country team to arrive.

They had a big interschool cross-country meet this Saturday, and everyone wanted to be ready for it.

CHAPTER 81

Saturday came, and it was time for the big cross-country meet.

Seeing as today's sports meet was being held in Clarksburg which was closer to Bridgeport than to Jess's school, David Harris was heading there directly.

(This was a case in reverse. Oftentimes, since Morgantown was right at the northeastern part of the state, and Bridgeport further south, the school sports bus actually ran past Jess's home on their way to their cross-country meets.)

David glanced away from the highway ahead and smiled at Jess. "You're really enjoying yourself at the new school, aren't you?" he asked.

Her replying smile told him everything he needed to know and filled his heart with delight. *The long drives to and fro every day of the week are worth it just to see her smile like this each day. Sure, yeah, her mother still thinks it's folly, her attending school so far away, but she's agreed to go along with it as long as I'm the one doing all the driving.*

David smiled to himself. *And I clearly don't mind at all. So long as it is for Jess's good, I'm willing to make the sacrifice.*

David glanced over at Jess again, saw that she was reviewing a Bible study plan, and didn't bother her with any more comments.

She had told him that whenever she got nervous before a sports meet she liked to read her Bible as it helped her to calm down.

Suddenly, as David drove them towards Liberty High School in Clarksburg's west end of town, he felt tired and frowned to himself.

I just hope that I don't break down from all of this overwork I've been doing. 'Cos I'm the most aware of anyone that I need a rest and real soon at that.

David was particularly concerned about the shortness of breath which he now kept experiencing after exerting himself. And also, about the occasional pains he had recently been begun getting in his chest and arms.

He looked over at his daughter again.

Yeah, I really need to see that doctor and fast! 'Cos if I break down now, Willow is gonna raise holy hell about taking Jess to school and bringing her back home again. And that's not even talking 'bout Jess's running practices and meets. Yeah, I need to take better care of my health, just because of her.

After a while longer driving, David drove into the parking lot at Liberty.

"All right, kiddo," he told Jess. "Here we are. Do your best!"

Then they both got out and walked over to where the team tents were set up.

CHAPTER 82

Jess and David had arrived at Liberty High School two hours before the cross-country meet was supposed to begin.

Once her father had driven off back home (intending to return when the races started), Jess got down to the serious business of preparation.

In reality, this wasn't much different from when she'd been participating in track and field. Jess had discovered that the critical element here, aside from doing one's warm-up exercises and stretches, was to avoid being intimidated by their opponents.

This last was hard to do because every girl competing today looked fitter than the next.

But thankfully, Jess had come prepared with her secret weapon.

Sitting in the tent, she began getting ready.

"I can't get over how you always do this," Ashley said as she watched Jess pull off her tracksuit to reveal both her running clothes and the Bible verses that she had written on her arms and legs at home.

Jess laughed. "At first, I was really self-conscious about writing so much God-stuff on myself. But now I don't mind. As well as helping me, it honors God too, so I like it."

Team captain Cassie Henderson crossed the tent to stare at Jess's unusual body art.

The verses were written in different colors of Sharpie and all in block capitals, along with where exactly they could be found in the Bible.

Most prominent of all was Philippians 4:13, which Jess always wrote on her left forearm: 'I CAN DO ALL THINGS THROUGH CHRIST WHO STRENGTHENS ME.'

Jess's dad often joked about that verse, saying that maybe she should get it permanently tattooed in place.

"I thought all Jesus people sucked until I met you," Cassie told Jess. "Yes, it's true," she insisted, seeing the slightly taken aback look on Jess's face. " 'Cos as far as I can see, attending church takes all of the fun out of life. And what is being alive for, if not to have fun and enjoy oneself?"

"God doesn't disapprove of people having fun," Jess replied. "It's just that God's idea of fun and our idea of fun is different."

"Don't even think of going there," Cassie told her sharply. "I'm not about giving up alcohol and boys and sex before marriage. After marriage, sure, but not before."

Ashley laughed at that. Cassie seemed not to notice however; her concentration was focused on the verse that Jess had written on her left thigh.

"What does that one say?" she asked, before walking around behind Jess so she could read it, because Jess had written the Bible verse upside-down so that she could read it too. "They that wait upon the Lord shall renew their strength?"

". . . They shall mount up with wings like eagles; they shall run and not grow weary," her younger companions finished up for her.

"Is that from the Bible too?" Cassie asked.

Jess nodded. "Yep. Isaiah 40 verse 31."

"Mounting up like eagles is kinda cool, since our team is named the Hawks," Cassie said. "You know, I like that sort of stuff in the Bible. It's the hands-off-boys policy I can't get with."

"I know what you mean," Jess agreed. "But you can't have one without the other. It's like an exchange: you do what God wants and then he does what you want. You are never really going to get God's benefits without following God's rules."

Coach Jane Bixby leaned under the tent awning then and waved the girls over.

"Come on out, all of you, time to take a look at the course."

Outside, Jess stood with the six other girls on her team and took in the surroundings.

She could not remember how many teams were actually participating in today's meet, whether five or six.

The tents for the participating cross-country teams, along with the row of chemical toilets—or 'Porta-Johns' as they were often called—were set up in an enclosure that was both bounded by the running course and was about fifty yards from the starting line.

Additional tents for the officials, timing crews, and medical support/paramedics were set up across the head of the trail.

Then there were lots of concession stands.

After waiting for the College High boys' cross-country team to join them, Jess and the rest of her teammates followed the coaches over to the start of the course over which they would be running.

The girls walked in front and the boys behind, with each senior coach lecturing their team as they moved on.

"Alright, ladies, now listen up," Coach Bixby said as they walked a gentle decline in the countryside, "yeah, we can all see that the trail initially goes downhill here. But remember what I told you earlier, you've got to pace yourselves. Don't think that because the trail goes down at first, you can speed up. You have to pace yourselves. Remember, there will be surprises ahead. Or else you'll wear yourselves out and have nothing left later when you need to make that push to the finish."

The College High girls' cross-country team wasn't the only one walking the course.

Jess could see at least three other teams of girls and boys, two ahead and one behind (and all wearing numbered running bibs), doing the same thing that she and her team were doing, trying to get a feel for the terrain, a fast-food familiarity as it were, for the countryside that they would shortly be charging through.

"See what I mean?" Coach Bixby pointed out once the ground leveled out. "The hill terrain starts right over there." She called a halt for a moment and gestured back at the start line, maybe 300 yards away. "So, if you go too fast coming down the slope, it'll prove at best irritating when you need to run up the hill."

Jess soaked all of this in. She had, of course, heard it before, but it never hurt to hear it again.

After walking the course, the team checked in with the officials again, and then they returned to their tents and worked their minds into a proper competitive attitude.

Then it was time for final warm-ups and switching their regular sneakers to running spikes, and using the restroom or drinking water.

And then the man with the big bullhorn loudly announced that it was time to run.

CHAPTER 83

Jess had run in two cross-country meets so far.

On neither occasion had she cracked the top ten runners, but she'd positioned well both times, once finishing in 13th place and the second time in 15th position.

She attributed her so-so performances to her inexperience in cross-country running and the fact that the older girls were bigger and stronger than she was.

"Yes, your age *is* a factor in how you perform, but it's not a huge factor," Coach Bixby had told the freshman runners during a team pep talk. "Because you need to consider height-to-weight ratios as well. Because you're not as tall as the older girls, that means you also weigh less than Cassie or Flora, for instance. And that means that when you check your height-to-weight ratio compared to theirs, you'll come out about even."

"Or let's view it another way," the coach had added after a moment's thought. "You've all seen the marathon runners on TV, haven't you? How do those women look?"

"They're all skin and bones," Ashley Roach replied. "Particularly the Kenyan ones."

"That's not all," Coach Bixby told her. "They all tend to be very small also. They're never as big as their American or European counterparts, and yet they run just as well. In most cases, better even." She'd frowned at everyone. "So, you younger runners, you need to have a completely positive mindset about what you can achieve now. Don't postdate yourselves and imagine that you'll only be able to place in the top three positions when you're in your senior year."

"I can do all things through Christ who strengthens me," Jess had mumbled gently to herself that day.

But the coach's exhortation had made perfect sense to her also, it had filled her with the conviction that she too could be among the top-placed finishers.

It had affected the way she ran from then on.

CHAPTER 84

Soon, everyone was at the starting line.

Jess had a quick look. Thirty-three young-adult females ranging in age from fourteen to eighteen, spread along a wide line, numbered bibs implanted with digital tracking chips on their fronts and backs, hair uniformly pulled back into aerodynamic buns and ponytails, all bunched in starting boxes according to their schools.

Then the starter pistol went off, and it was every young woman for herself—and for the team, of course.

At first, Jess kept pace with the other girls from College High, but after receiving a nod from team leader Cassie, she and Ashley began pressing forward through the throng, jostling for positions at the front of the press, but not too far ahead.

One didn't win a 5-kilometer race by running it like it was the 100-meter dash.

***

Like Coach Bixby had pointed out, that first descent was easy going. Too-easy going, even, and Jess had to remind herself not to speed up, even though she saw some girls passing her by because the downslope made for easier running.

But then the ground evened out again, and soon they were rising up through the hills. Those girls who'd run the initial stretch too hard now realized their mistake, and the more experienced runners amongst them now slowed themselves down and paced themselves better.

The end result was that, except for two girls who kept on going ahead, those early sprinters were soon back in the main mass of runners again.

It was hard to explain 'just running,' except to say that you 'just ran.'

At first, Jess found the going easy, almost like she was doing a sightseeing jog with a group of friends. Though running fast, she could still appreciate the pleasant terrain, and the pockets of spectators that lined the running course, along with the occasional vehicle that rumbled past on the highway that ran parallel to the course for a short distance.

But as the second kilometer transitioned into the third, the lactic acid began really building up in her muscles, and the pain began setting in.

Now she'd reached the point where that initial leisure feeling gave way to a feeling of exertion.

"It's like what one would experience if you turned your hobby into your day job," Head running coach Tom Forrest had once explained to everyone. "If you did that, you'd still have all of the same tasks to complete, only now the delight at doing them would take a backseat to the pressure of deadlines and the necessity to make that previous pleasant pursuit now pay cash dividends."

Jess agreed it was like that.

And that was all there was to it now, pushing the body where it really didn't desire to go, making it do more than it wanted to.

This was mind-over-matter, the mentality that being tired was okay, but one must get to the end of the race regardless of how one felt.

The runners were further spread out now, but she was still near the front of them, with Cassie Henderson up ahead on her right and another senior, Brooke Lawson, over on Cassie's right. As if Jess were a grandmother clock and Ashley was its pendulum, Ashley Roach was occasionally ahead of Jess and occasionally behind her.

Meanwhile, Cassie was monitoring their mile splits on her wristwatch.

By this point in the race, Jess could practically run on autopilot. Little conscious thought was required; all she had to do was keep pace with everyone, make the turns as indicated by the signs or officials along the course, and zone into her private, peaceful space.

What she always tried to do now was meditate on scripture. Jess didn't meditate just on those Bible verses that she'd written on herself, although those were always at the center of her mind. All she had to do to remind herself that she could 'do all things with Christ's help' was raise her left hand up a little.

While her feet trod the grass and she ran steadily towards her destination, Jess also reflected deeply on how far God had helped her come over the past two years, how he'd purged the emotional agony that she'd been through from her heart and really made her into a new person.

And then she rejoiced in the knowledge that God and Jesus both loved her.

In this meditative state of mind, Jess ran past the 5K split, and Cassie looked back and gave Jess and Ashley a look that reminded them it was almost time to start contesting for their final positions.

***

The race had begun long ago, but suddenly it felt as if the race had just begun.

One kilometer left. Just over half a mile to beat this.

Yes, suddenly, the remaining distance was equivalent to an 800-meter race, and it was time to draw on one's reserves of energy and hope you had enough left in the tank to put the competition behind you.

"Time to start overtaking," Jess gasped at Ashley.

"I'm right behind you," Ashley gasped back.

Jess looked behind her. The runners were now spread out over quite a distance. She counted about fifteen girls ahead of her, which meant there were a similar number behind her.

The first indicator that the course was drawing to a close was the increasing number of spectators lining the side barricades. She heard someone call her name, and it was one of the coaches urging her on. Then she heard some members of the boys' team doing the same.

Their cheering was an injection of adrenaline that made Jess even more determined to do her best.

She noted that most of the girls ahead of her seemed to be seniors. They were all taller than she was and more muscular, too. Then she put that daunting fact out of her mind and began really running.

Now, she wasn't running like she was running cross-country, but as if she was running in a 400-meter relay.

That had just occurred to her; that the distance remaining was approximately the same, and, except for the exertion that she'd previously made, the conditions could be identical, mainly because for this homestretch, they were running over a flat grassy plain.

The real question now is how much gas do I have left in my tank? Well, there's only one way that I'll find out. Help me now, Lord Jesus.

Jess began pushing forward.

Ironically, or amusingly, the first person she passed was her own team captain, Cassie Henderson.

Cassie gave her a surprised look, and increased speed herself, but Jess was running her own private race now and soon left Cassie behind.

300 meters. Now, Jess really exerted herself.

She caught up to the next girl and swiftly left her behind, then passed a group of three girls who were running neck and neck.

Then she passed another girl.

By now, the crowd had noticed her and begun cheering her on. Jess passed two more girls. The finish line was fifty meters ahead and there were four girls ahead of her.

For a moment, Jess wondered if she'd be able to catch those four girls in time, and if she even had the energy reserves to do it.

But then . . .

"Go go go!" she heard Cassie gasp behind her. And then Cassie was beside her and was running past her. And Jess, not wanting to be beaten by Cassie even though she was the team captain, ran after Cassie like mad, while the crowd kept howling like crazy.

They'd left their break too late to catch the first girl (who, surprisingly, had been one of the two fast-starters who'd not fallen back into the multitude after the initial run downhill), but Cassie finished in second place and Jess in third place. Brooke Lawson crossed the finish line in sixth place, while Ashley Roach finished seventh. Grace Tolbert, the fifth girl from College High to cross the finish line, placed eleventh.

After both young women had gotten over the obligatory state of total exhaustion and (in Cassie's case) sensation of nausea that followed their high-demand physical exertion, Cassie grabbed Jess and hugged her tight. Then their other teammates crowded round and they all shared a group hug.

"I'm sure we did great today!" Cassie said.

After all the celebrating with her teammates and coaches, Jess located her father cheering for her in the crowd and ran over to celebrate with him too.

She really wished her mother was here also, to share her joy.

***

Long story short, Cassie Henderson was right, her team had done great: College High School's girls had the lowest total from five runners and won that day's cross-country meet.

Which was something they'd not done for a while.

CHAPTER 85

After this victory, from being in the competitive doldrums for a while, College High School really started picking up some cross-country wins.

Jess was clearly critical to this. Before her arrival at College High, Cassie Henderson had been the only cross-country runner who'd consistently placed in the top five finishers at meets.

But now that had changed.

Though neither of them ever finished in first place, either Jess or Cassie would place second or third each time and the other would be right behind her.

The same went for Brooke and Ashley: as if in competition with the two frontrunners on their team, they too kept switching around positions. And they were never far behind the front two either, which made it difficult for the other teams to get high points against them. Even their not-so-fast teammates rarely placed outside of the top twenty finishers, with at least one of them generally being inside of the top fifteen.

Things were really on the up and up.

The girls developed a habit of winning cross-country meets.

The victories piled up.

Soon Jess and her team were getting to be the favorites to win the West Virginian high school cross-country championships, and after that maybe even the national cross-country title.

CHAPTER 86

One Saturday afternoon, while out evangelizing with the Good Faith church's Aspire Youth group, Jess saw Barry Lindsey again.

Since her arrival at College High, Barry Lindsey had existed for her as a shadow, a mirage, just something that she might have imagined. He was no longer real.

But then she saw him that Saturday, and the old, evil dread threatened to return and overwhelm her again. For a few seconds, she felt like she'd faint, but then she rallied.

I'm a new creature in Christ, she told herself. *Old things have passed away, all things are made new.*

To her surprise, it worked.

Barry saw her too and smirked at her, but she seemed to see through him, like he was transparent.

She caught the look on his face when he saw that she wasn't bothered by him. And they were in a public place where he wouldn't dare bother her either.

She watched his facial expression turn troubled, then angry, and finally, she watched him turn away from her while angrily slapping his fist against his thigh.

He looked completely defeated.

Oh, yes, I'm free of him for good now. Thank you, Jesus, for the victory in your name, Jess thought, smiling, as she walked away from him also and rejoined the teens from her church.

CHAPTER 87

Jess was still friends with several kids from Thompson High, in particular Tommy Bradley, Jeffrey and the goth kids, and surprisingly Mary Lindsey.

They all texted and occasionally phoned each other, but Jess hadn't seen any of them since leaving the school.

According to Tommy, he had a rather weird problem now. Spurred on by Mimi's spurious tales about his sexuality, Leah, who was herself unsure if she was a boy or a girl, was now blackmailing Tommy into dating her, insisting that if he didn't go out with her, she'd have Mimi 'meme' him up claiming he was in the closet.

Unfortunately, Tommy couldn't stand Leah. She was too pushy.

On hearing this, Jess felt relieved that she'd escaped from that toxic setting and those nasty teenagers.

"Just be careful with them," she warned Tommy. "You know how mean and nasty they are."

CHAPTER 88

Occasionally, Thompson High and College High participated in the same cross-country meets, and on those occasions, Jess ran into some of her old middle school teammates who were now high-schoolers like herself, and their team coaches.

The latter were always delighted to see her, the former not so overjoyed. The Thompson High girls believed that Jess had deserted them.

Jess understood how they felt. Since College High School generally trumped the competition at those meets, she couldn't exactly expect them to be pleased.

But, girls, that's largely your fault for not standing up for me when I needed you to, she thought. *So, I've simply moved on to where I'm wanted and appreciated.*

CHAPTER 89

David was delighted with Jess's success in her cross-country endeavors. Each time he remembered how good she was at running, he felt a warm feeling in his heart and a smile on his lips.

"I still think she spends too much time training and running," Willow told him one Monday night. "But it's not affecting her studies, so I can't complain too much about it."

That night David and Willow were seated at the dining table after dinner. Jess had gone off to her room, and Willow was sorting out work documents on the table.

"I wish you'd make the time to attend some of her competitions," David said. "I'm certain it would mean a great deal to Jess to have you there cheering her on."

Willow paused from straightening out a handful of glossy real estate brochures and laughed.

"Oh no, buster, I see what you're trying to do," she replied to him.

David didn't understand what she meant by that.

"Simple," she explained once he'd communicated this to her. "First of all, you'll start off by having me attend Jess's track meets, and then you'll ask me to start driving her to them when you don't feel up to it. And then, finally, you'll arrive at what you really have in mind, which is having me drive Jess to school and back each day like you do." She wagged a finger at him. "Oh no, sweetheart, you signed up for this; I didn't."

"Don't be so unsympathetic; she's your daughter, too."

Willow nodded. "Yes, she is. But unlike you, who works mostly from home, I gotta get out and about. You know that most days my schedule didn't even allow me to take her to school in the mornings when she attended here in Bridgeport, and now you're thinking of Morgantown."

"Let's not fight about it." Then David smiled. "Hey, I've an idea! Next Saturday is Knight Night."

Willow looked up again from her stacks of papers. "What is Knight Night?"

"Knight Night is a nighttime cross-country meet that's held at Preston High School in Kingwood," he explained. "Jess and the Hawks will be competing there, and I'm thinking that it'll be great if we both attend it to support her." He wagged a finger at Willow before she could protest. "Honey, it holds at night, and you don't work nights."

"Alright, I'll think about it," she grudgingly agreed.

David gave her a serious look. "Promise?"

Willow nodded. "I promise, darling. Now, darling, please let me finish up with all of this sorting before bedtime."

Satisfied now that Jess would have Willow cheering for her at least next Saturday night, David got to his feet with a smile and walked into the living room to watch Monday Night Football.

He was halfway to the living room couch when he began feeling uneasy.

All of a sudden David felt this sharp pain right in the middle of his chest. The pain felt like he was being stabbed with a huge knife.

As he groaned in pain, he also discovered that he was gasping for breath.

The pain and difficulty in breathing intensified, and soon his eyesight began to blur.

His sole intention now became to reach the couch, which was just two steps away from him. But taking those two steps seemed impossible, and instead of moving forward, he staggered both sideways and backward, as if the pain had taken over control of his limbs from him.

His unintentional retreat across the living room stopped when the backs of his knees hit the coffee table, and even then, he was now so unstable on his feet that it was a miracle that he didn't fall backwards over the coffee table.

David realized he was having a heart attack.

"Dear, God, help me!" he gasped in horror while the agony increased, his breathing seemed to almost shut off completely, and his eyesight faded in and out of focus.

He looked across the living room, back out into the dining room. Willow was still busy sorting out glossy papers. She had no idea of his crisis.

"Baby, call an ambulance!" he howled at her.

His voice didn't sound particularly loud to himself. But in reality, it must have been so, because he saw Willow jerk upright and spin around and look at him. At first, she had a look of irritation on her face because she'd been interrupted, but that swiftly turned to shock and fright.

David saw her scrambling for her cellphone, and then he collapsed forward and hit the floor.

And after that he remembered nothing.

CHAPTER 90

"So, my dad is in the hospital now and my mom is over there with him," Jess told Ashley on the phone the next afternoon.

"Oh, my God! I'm so sorry to hear that!" Ashley replied. Jess had waited till school had ended before calling Ashley, and now she could hear that Ashley was outside in the parking lot, most likely waiting for Toby Green to drive her and the other girls to cross-country practice.

***

Jess had, of course, missed school that day.

She was confused and more than a little bit scared. The craziness of last night hadn't yet left her: hearing her mother screaming . . . running downstairs to find her father outstretched and face down on the living room floor . . . the blaring siren that announced the arrival of the paramedics . . . four men rolling a gurney into the house, collapsing it and rolling her father on top of it . . . Outside, watching her father being loaded up into the ambulance with the flashing red and blue lights . . . Her mother dashing past her and getting into the ambulance also . . .

Afterwards, Jess had felt shell-shocked. Hardly noticing the neighbors who'd emerged from their houses to investigate her mom's screaming, she'd tramped back inside the house without bothering to shut the door after her and wound up sitting at the foot of the stairs and staring at nothing.

Jess had burst out crying. She'd thought her father was already dead, or was going to die.

"Oh, God, please save my daddy!" she'd wept loudly. "Don't let him die, Lord. In the name of Jesus!"

She prayed this over and over again until she felt an overwhelming peace that convinced her that either it was too late to do anything for her father and thus too late to worry about it, or that God had heard and answered her prayer.

Then she'd gotten up from her seat at the foot of the stairs, shut and locked the front door, and then gone upstairs to get her phone so that she could call her mother.

***

"How is he now?" Ashley asked.

Jess heaved a deep sigh of relief. "Thank God that he's fine. Well, not fine like that. He's in the ICU, but he's not dead."

"Oh, praise God," Ashley replied and then added: "I'll tell my parents and we'll pray for your dad too."

"Thanks," Jess said. "I need to call my youth pastor, so she can get the kids to pray for Dad, too."

"Okay, I'll hang up now," Ashley said. "I'll tell Coach Bixby why you can't make it to practice today."

***

"Oh my God, oh my God no," was Rosemary Hodder's response when Jess got her on the phone. "Well, thank God that he didn't die. I trust God that he'll make a good recovery, in the mighty name of Jesus. Okay, Jess, I gotta hang up now 'cos I'm at work, but I'll get in contact with Pastor Howard and we'll get the whole church praying for your father."

***

A short while later, Jess heard a car pull into the driveway. She peered out through a living room window and saw her mother get out of a car, most likely an Uber, since both of her parents' cars were parked outside the house.

Jess ran to the front door and let her mother in.

The two of them stared at each other in silence for a long moment. Jess was surprised at how haggard her mother looked, like she'd not slept all night long. Her eyes were sunken and reddened like she'd also spent most of the night crying.

And then Willow grabbed hold of Jess and hugged her hard.

"Oh, honey!" Willow wept. "Your father really needs our prayers!"

"Oh, God, please help daddy!" Jess wept.

"I was so scared, so scared that he was gonna die!" Willow wept. "He was just lying there on the floor like that, not moving at all, and I thought he was gonna die!"

"I thought he was dead, too, Mom!"

After they'd both calmed down a little, Jess and her mother went to sit in the living room.

"So, how is Daddy now?" Jess asked Willow.

Jess had hoped that her mother would have a reassuring smile and some good news, but that wasn't the case. Her mother both looked and spoke miserably.

"The doctors aren't sure if he'll make it or not." Tears filled Willow's eyes again. "Oh, Jess, you can't even start to imagine how happy I was when your father opened his eyes and recognized me and called my name. But the doctors say that his heart attack was very severe and he's still in serious danger. They say that your daddy had overworked himself almost to the point of no return."

Jess felt devastated by the news. "He's gonna die?" she asked in disbelief.

Willow looked at Jess with hollow eyes, and held her tightly. "I really hope not, darling. I pray David doesn't leave us like this!"

Jess began crying again, too. "Oh, God, no!" she wept. "Don't let daddy die!"

"When can I see him?" Jess asked after once more calming down. "I wanna see him."

But her mother, completely exhausted from being on her feet and being put through an emotional wrench for the past 18 hours, had fallen asleep on the couch.

***

The cross-country team video-called Jess once the day's training practice was over.

Once Jess accepted the video call, Coach Jane Bixby's face appeared on the screen.

"Hi, Jess," the coach said in a sober and sympathetic voice. "Everyone is really sad to hear what happened to your dad. Hope he recovers soon. My thoughts and prayers are with him."

"Thanks, coach," Jess miserably replied. "Thanks for your prayers. We really need all the prayers we can get. The doctors aren't sure if he'll survive or not."

Coach Bixby shook her head sadly. "I hope your dad does pull through this, Jess. I really do. And, I really wish I had as much faith in God as you do." Then she gestured aside. "Jess, the girls and boys want to reach out to you too."

The coach's face disappeared from the phone screen to be replaced by Cassie, Ashley, and Toby's faces, each of them wearing equally melancholy expressions. Jess knew they were all imagining what it would be like if one of their own parents had been the one who'd suffered a heart attack.

"Hello, Jess," Ashley said softly. "We're all praying for your dad too."

"Yes, we are," Cassie agreed.

Toby seemed to be the one holding onto the phone, and he now tilted it selfie-like, with his arm extended, so that Jess could see that the entire girls' and boys' teams, along with the rest of the female and male coaches, were standing there with them.

Everyone looked equally sober and upset by the news. They waved desolately and mumbled a chorus of consolation: "Sorry to hear what happened," "Hope your dad feels better soon," "Hang in there, Jess," "Hope your father pulls through!" and other similar expressions of sympathy and hope.

Jess began weeping. "Thanks, guys," she said through her tears. "You honestly don't know how much your support means to me!"

Toby shifted the camera focus back to himself, Cassie, and Ashley. Behind their framed trio, the rest of the runners now began to disperse, their subdued body language clearly showing that the news about Jess's father had been a total downer to them all.

Jess watched them all walk away with the dissatisfied feeling that she really should have been there with them.

I really should have been. But daddy's health and wellbeing are far more important.

"So, how are you doing?" Cassie asked. "How are you holding up?"

"I'm fine for now," Jess replied. "God is helping me to be strong. I'll be going to the hospital to visit my dad in the ICU once my mom wakes up. She didn't get any sleep at all last night."

"Give him our greetings when you see him," Toby said.

"Guys," Jess said, one problem temporarily overshadowed by another, "what are we gonna do about next Saturday? According to my mom, the doctors say my dad's gonna be in the hospital for a while at least, so how am I gonna attend training with you?" Jess facepalmed herself. "We need to win that Knight Night."

Cassie facepalmed herself too, and then she nodded and looked very serious. "I dunno what we're gonna do."

"Maybe Donna can sub for you?" Ashley suggested. "Are you sure you wanna be running at a time like this?"

Jess shrugged. "If I don't run, I'll go crazy from worry. You should've seen my mom when she came in—like she'd lost half of her mind since last night."

Cassie sighed. "I sort of agree with you both," she said. "Ashley is right that maybe you shouldn't be competing in your current frame of mind, and you're right too. You've told me more than once that running is like therapy for you; that it helps you cope with pressure and difficulties in your life."

"Even though I'm not on your team, I don't think Donna is a good replacement for Jess," Toby said. "She's not varsity level yet. I've watched her run, and she's way too impulsive to take Jess's place in a race as important as Knight Night."

"Donna is fast, but lacks staying power," Jess agreed. "She keeps running the course like she's running the 100-meter dash, and then she blows herself out before it's time to make that final charge for the finish line." Jess began shaking her fist at the screen in frustration. "We need to win the Knight Night meet. We gotta!"

"We need to discuss this with the coach," Cassie told Jess. "Don't trouble yourself about it, or you'll wind up stressing yourself out even more than you already are. Coach Bixby will figure something out."

Ashley nodded. "Just look after your dad and we'll let you know how it goes."

CHAPTER 91

Jess arrived at the hospital with her mother to find her father awake.

Though tethered to more machines than Jess had ever imagined outside a movie, her father looked up at her and offered the slightest smile. Fragile and flickering, it still pierced through her dread like sunlight through storm clouds. In that moment, Jess felt hope rise—however much the doctors doubted his chances, she believed he was coming back to her, that the worst of it was behind him now.

"Hi, hon. Did you miss me?" David Harris gasped and softly wagged a hand connected to an intravenous line at them. His voice sounded like hissing gas, like it wasn't coming from his lungs at all but was being powered directly by the oxygen that twin transparent tubes fed into his nostrils.

"Oh, daddy!" Jess wanted to run over to his bedside and hug him tightly, but she restrained herself because of the nurse who was in the room with them.

Willow sat on the chair beside the bed, and Jess stood beside her, her lips trembling and her heart beating nervously.

"The doctor says you can speak to him for five minutes," the nurse, a large black woman," told the saddened mother and daughter.

"So, how do you feel now?" Willow asked David.

"I feel like I dodged a missile, but then it got stuck in my back," he replied in that same hoarse vocal hiss. "I never knew a heart attack would feel like that. It felt like I was being murdered. In this case, by overwork."

Willow smiled at him. "Well, I intend to see that from now on, you get all of the rest that you deserve."

"I can't wait for you to get well and come home again," Jess said.

Willow frowned. "You're just scared of being alone in the house with me all of the time, 'cos I'm not soft like your father."

David hissed out a laugh. "Okay, maybe some of that, too."

Jess felt embarrassed that the nurse was looking at her.

"What are we gonna do about her school now?" David asked. "I know your work schedule is nowhere near as flexible as mine."

Willow blinked back tears. "Don't worry about it, sweetheart. We'll work it out somehow."

"Okay," David agreed. "See that she gets to run too."

"Rosemary at the church said she'll be praying for you," Jess told her father.

"That's great," David said.

And then suddenly, he looked even weaker than he had when they walked in. The change in him was so abrupt and so drastic that Jess thought he was dying right there and then.

Oh, God, no! Daddy, don't you dare die!

"Pastor Howard also sends his prayers," Willow added. "He's not in town at the moment, but he says he'll be over to see you once he's back from Tampa."

Willow, too, now noticed how tired David looked, and she stared worriedly at the nurse.

"Oh, you've tired him out," the nurse said after examining David. "I'm afraid you'll have to leave now, Mrs. Harris. You can visit him again tomorrow."

Jess was relieved to hear her father wasn't dying, but one look at him made that hard to believe. He lay motionless, each breath dragged in by machines, his body too still, too quiet. It was hard to imagine there was any thought behind those half-closed eyes, let alone words waiting to be spoken.

"But he seemed better when we arrived here," Willow told the nurse in a worried voice. "Better than yesterday."

"Oh yes, but he's not as strong as he looks," the nurse replied while preparing a sedative. "Even the slightest exertion, like having a conversation, can wear him out. As you've just noticed."

Before leaving the hospital, Jess and Willow met with Dr. Smith, the white-haired old specialist who was in charge of David's treatment.

"Oh, I'm sorry, Mrs. Harris," the doctor said, "but last night's prognosis still holds. Your husband's case isn't looking good at all, I'm afraid. We've done all we can, and yet he isn't responding to treatment in the way we expect him to. And we can't give him any more medication because that would endanger him too."

The doctor sighed tiredly. "I wouldn't normally say this to the family of my patients, Mrs. Harris, but your daughter is wearing a cross, so I believe you're both people of faith." He gave Willow a searching look. "Am I correct in my assumption that you both believe in the supernatural and divine intervention in human affairs?"

Willow nodded.

"Alright, Mrs. Harris," Doctor Smith went on after her assenting nod, "the way I view this is that, at the moment, your husband David is more in God's hands than he is in ours."

In spite of how upset she was, Jess actually felt pleased to hear that.

Dad is in God's hands? Well, that's cool, 'cos God has the safest hands of anyone I know.

Jess and her mother left the hospital.

Jess's mood was bittersweet, like she'd gotten her father back, and yet hadn't exactly gotten him back.

CHAPTER 92

With David in the hospital and no discharge date in sight, Willow coped as best she could. In a way, this was easy for her to do, considering that she was a person who planned everything out. Just like with everything else in her life, in this crisis situation also, Willow Harris simply needed to work out what needed to be done and then do it. Once Willow formed a plan of action, she had no trouble sticking to that plan.

It was hard work though.

By the next morning, driving Jess across those three counties to Morgantown, Willow was almost cursing her sick husband for insisting that they moved Jess to a different school.

The trip was smooth and pleasant, but it was so loooong!

David had that kind of free time to spare, but I don't have the luxury of driving thirty-five miles either way, twice a day.

But that didn't matter. She knew she'd have to do it, at least until she could make alternate transport arrangements for Jess.

'Cos I can't pull Jess out of school, this far into the school session, and start looking for another high school for her that's closer to home.

Willow dropped Jess off at the school entrance, watched her walk in with some other teenagers, and then headed off for work.

In her mind, she went over how she intended to handle this:

Dropping Jess off at school and picking her up afterwards is all I can manage. In a way, her daily running practices actually work out for the good here, as it means I don't have to leave work halfway and then hurry back to it again.

Then she frowned.

But all of those cross-country meets are out. I need my rest on weekends. I can't work all week and then spend Saturday watching a group of young adults play silly and unproductive games.

So, no more meets. She does have a commitment to one next week. What was it again? The one I promised David I'd think about attending with him?

Remembering David felt like someone was pouring salt on Willow's wounded emotions. Suddenly, she felt like crying and she did.

She was driving along a long stretch of uninhabited highway and when that depressed feeling came over her, she drove until she reached the next shoulder and pulled over. Then she laid her head on the steering wheel and wept her heart out.

Oh, David!

Of course, she hadn't been to the hospital to see him today, but she intended to drop in on him between house showings.

Each time Willow thought of her husband in his current critical condition, she was flooded with the fear that she'd soon be a widow.

Dear God, please help me! I don't want to lose the man I love!

She wasn't thinking or praying frivolously here. She clearly remembered Dr. Smith telling her that David was 'in God's hands now."

Now that she reconsidered the doctor's words, they had a chilling ring to them; the admission by a medical professional that science was helpless to save her husband; that the intervention of a higher power was required to set him right again.

Oh, Lord, why does this have to happen to me? To us?

Willow recalled making a similar inquiry of God when Jess had been hurt too.

I don't recall God replying to me. No, I didn't get an answer from God then, but I want one now! Lord God, why does my family have to keep hurting like this? We're good people who love you!

Willow snapped out of her blues when a police cruiser stopped to see if she was in trouble.

After assuring the officers that she was fine, but just a little tired, Willow started up her car again and drove back to Bridgeport.

She spent the day showing three houses to potential buyers. The houses were situated in different parts of Harrison County, and none of them were even close to I-79, which would naturally assist her in scheduling her journey back to Morgantown.

In fact, the last house that Willow was scheduled to show that day was down in Lost Creek at the southern border of the county, totally opposite the direction in which she needed to be headed after that meeting.

All the house-viewing appointments had been scheduled before David's heart attack. Willow couldn't bring herself to cancel them— not because she didn't want to, but because she couldn't justify putting her needs above her clients'. Still, each showing felt like a betrayal, a quiet decision to keep pretending everything was normal while her world was falling apart.

But she knew that all future house-viewing appointments would need to be scheduled with whichever building nearest to I-79 last in line, so she could hit the road for Morgantown afterwards.

***

Anyway, Willow made it through that first day's showings, although she mistimed her plan to visit David in the hospital and decided to reschedule the visit to after she'd picked up Jess.

Once she was done with the day's work, she drove over to Morgantown as planned and picked up Jess from her cross-country training.

David had already told her that the College High School cross-country teams practiced at a different racing trail each day, and when Willow had checked the four different locations on Google maps, she'd discovered that they were spread out over a distance with the school in the middle.

At first, she'd been upset by this, but then she'd realized that driving to different pickup locations each day wasn't anywhere near as stressful as driving to Morgantown for the pickup in the first place.

"How's dad doing now?" Jess asked her nervously as they rolled homeward.

"We're going to see him now, darling," she replied with her eyes glued to the road like they usually were when she drove. "I haven't had the time today." Then she glanced hurriedly over at her daughter. "However, the hospital hasn't called me with any bad news, so I'm thinking your father is still okay."

"All of my friends are praying for dad to get better quickly."

"That's great. Pastor Howard called to let me know that he's organized a prayer chain for David."

"A prayer chain? Wow, that's great! Dad is gonna improve for sure now."

With tears threatening to spill from her eyes again, Willow wished that she shared her daughter's depth of faith and trust in God.

***

This time at the hospital, David was asleep when they arrived, and although they were allowed to peek in at him, they weren't allowed to stay longer than a minute.

During their allotted minute, the machines David was connected to chirped, beeped, thrummed, and hummed with such serene efficiency that Willow was momentarily puzzled as to why these miracles of modern science, with their dazzling metal-and-plastic splendor, impressive dials, and flickering lights, couldn't heal her darling husband.

They aren't God, that's why not!

The words rang in her mind. Willow was unsure who'd spoken to her: Jess, God, or herself?

"Did you say something?" she asked her daughter, who'd looked really upset on seeing her father today.

But Jess shook her head.

If God just spoke to me, that is scary, Willow thought. *And if I just spoke to myself, that is just creepy.*

She quickly ushered Jess out of the door and down the gray hospital corridors to the front parking lot.

***

When Willow and Jess got home that evening, they prepared dinner together, and then Willow did her best to act like things were still normal.

She told herself that she was doing this for Jess's benefit, that the girl had already endured one cycle of intense emotional turmoil and didn't need to find herself embroiled in another.

So, for her sake, I need to act like everything will be fine.

"Okay, mom, I've loaded up the dishwasher, do you need me for anything else?"

Willow shook her head, but then asked, "Are you going up to your room?"

Jess nodded back. "School stuff. I've a paper that I need to finish before Monday."

Willow waved her away. But then, she almost called her back and asked her to bring her schoolbooks and laptop downstairs and work on her school paper on the dining table.

But she didn't do it, and after Jess's footsteps stopped sounding on the stairs, Willow regretted not having detained her to keep her company, even for five or ten minutes longer.

Willow felt so alone now. She wasn't used to feeling this way.

Of course, the neighbors had come over to enquire after David's health and offer their help if she needed it.

Her closest friends had also phoned to comfort her over David's heart attack. And her three brothers and their families had too. Her brothers all lived outside of West Virginia and next weekend would be the earliest that any of them could possibly make a trip to visit David in hospital.

David's older sister Rita, who lived in the not-so-distant town of Madison, WV, had planned to drive over yesterday, but then yesterday morning, Rita had fallen sick with a terrible cold and felt it best not to come by for fear of anyone getting ill because of her.

Both families had agreed to keep the grandparents out of the know. It was enough having to deal with David's coronary. No one wished to have either set of their own parents giving up the ghost from shock or apprehension on hearing about their son or son-in-law's critical medical condition.

Inside, Willow Harris was almost cracking up herself. She'd lived with and loved David Harris for so long in continuity that the idea that he might not be with her tomorrow or in the near future held almost indescribable terror for her.

To steady her nerves, she poured herself a glass of wine, sat down opposite the television, and tried to watch something calming, maybe a comedy or a documentary about cute animals.

But her thoughts were too uneasy to remain on anything for more than a few seconds.

And then, it suddenly occurred to Willow that since her husband had suffered his near-fatal heart attack, she had done just about everything else except pray for him, as in a 'get down on her knees and seriously ask God to help him recover' sort of prayer.

She realized that she had gotten so caught up in the whole business of ensuring that David was being properly cared for at the hospital, that she had overlooked the basic necessity of spending a few moments of that time in prayer to her heavenly father.

And that's just so crazy. Jess's friends and teammates are praying for David. The youth group at church is praying for David. In fact, at this very moment, our church has a prayer chain going for David. And yet I, the closest person to David in the whole world, isn't praying for him. So far, all that I've been doing is moaning and grumbling at God. How is God going to take everyone else's prayers seriously when I, his wife, isn't praying about his condition as much as those other people?

Feeling alarmed at how unwise she'd been acting in this regard, Willow now turned off the television and picked up her cellphone instead. On her phone she opened up one of several Bible apps, and spent some time reading passages about God's promises of divine healing.

Then, she got down on her knees and began praying quietly to God.

"Oh, lord God," she prayed, "please forgive me for my unbelief and help me to believe in you and trust you at this important time in our lives. Heavenly Father, please heal my husband, David, who is lying critically in the hospital at the moment. In the name of Jesus, amen."

After a while of praying in this vein, it occurred to Willow to involve Jess in this prayer session also.

So, she went upstairs to call her.

And then mother and daughter both prayed long and hard together for David's speedy recovery.

CHAPTER 93

The new week began like the old one had ended, with Willow Harris feeling like the world was collapsing around her.

She'd not attended church yesterday; instead, she and Jess had both spent the day at the hospital with David.

David was still in critical condition, lying there in bed and smiling at them with all sorts of tubes plugged into him.

"Don't speak and tire yourself," Willow had told him. "Don't speak unless you really need to."

"Yes, daddy," Jess had added with teary eyes. "We just want to be with you."

Later in the day, Pastor Howard, his wife, and several of the Good Faith church's deacons had stopped by the hospital to pray for David's recovery.

"We'll keep praying with you for your husband's recovery," the pastor told Willow afterward. "You just keep believing in God's word on divine healing."

***

That was yesterday, and today, Willow was back with her nose to the grindstone.

Once she'd delivered Jess to school, she drove off to begin Monday's round of house showings.

While commuting between showings, Willow thought of an additional challenge: money.

The money isn't an immediate concern; our health insurance plan covers David's hospital bills for a while yet, and we've got some money saved up along with David's retirement benefits, but with just me earning money now, that money in the bank will soon start dwindling.

Her next prospective clients—a lesbian couple—soon made Willow forget her financial worries when they got into a heated argument over the house that she was showing them.

One lady liked it and the other lady didn't. Willow spent most of the showing preventing their relationship from disintegrating.

Much later in the day, mentally exhausted, she drove back to her office. She didn't relish the thought of driving all the way over to Morgantown to pick up her daughter.

A short while after Willow had left the office to do just that, her phone rang. She glanced at it in its holder on the dashboard, saw that it was Jess calling, and accepted the call.

"Hello, darling," she said in a tired voice. "Are you okay? I'm just on my way over to pick you up."

"Mom, that's what I'm calling about," Jess told her. "You don't *need* to come to the school today. I'm back home already with Coach Bixby and Coach Jameson."

"Really?" Willow was surprised.

"Yes, mom, just come straight home now. The coaches are waiting for you here."

"O.K., I'm on my way home."

Then, feeling very relieved that she didn't have to drive 35 miles feeling the way she did, Willow hung up and turned her car homeward instead.

CHAPTER 94

"Mrs. Harris, on behalf of our entire cross-country team, please let me express our sympathy over your husband's current condition," Coach Jameson told Willow, once everyone was seated in her living room. "We were really saddened to hear what happened."

"How is he doing now?" Jane Bixby asked. "Is he improving?"

Willow sighed at the other woman. "David's exactly the same. He just lies there in bed. He can talk, but the doctors say he shouldn't, that it tires him out too much. So, when Jess and I visit him, we mostly just sit and smile at him until it's time to leave."

"I'm truly sorry to hear this," Coach Jameson said. "Jess has told us so much about how wonderful a father he is to her. I really hope he gets better quickly."

"We're all praying for his speedy recovery," Coach Bixby added.

Willow nodded. "Thanks so much, both of you. You can't imagine how much your support—and that of your cross-country team means to us right now."

She sighed and decided this was a good time to broach the subject of Jess's reduced participation in the cross-country team's activities.

"But, David's illness creates a logistics problem for me," she told the coaches. "I'm so occupied with other things right now, that I've no time to drive Jess to your track meets too. You both know that David was the one who handled that." She shook her head sadly at Coaches Jameson and Bixby. "I really regret having to do this, but Jess will have to stop competing with you for the time being, at least until things settle down around here. I hope you'll both understand and respect my decision."

To her surprise, Jess didn't seem worried at all on hearing that she was going to quit running with the team.

Willow soon discovered why that was.

Jane Bixby laughed. "Oh, there'll be no need for that, Mrs. Harris," she said. "That's part of the reason why Coach Jameson and I are here now. We want to discuss Jess's running future with you."

Willow nodded and listened.

"Well, it's simple enough, ma'am," Coach Jameson said with expansive and demonstrative gestures of his muscular arms. "As you know, your daughter Jess is an important and integral part of our running teams' success, and since hearing about your husband's heart attack, myself and the other coaches have been doing some thinking." This said, he nodded to his female companion to take over speaking.

"That's right," Jane Bixby said. "What we concluded is that, to help you out, we'll take on the task of bringing Jess back home each day after her cross-country training. So that means, all you have to do is get her to school each morning."

Willow hadn't expected anything like this. This sounded like a godsend.

"Really?" she asked. "Are you serious about this?"

Coach Jameson laughed and nodded. "Yes, we're very serious. "You just bring your daughter to school each morning and we'll see that she gets home safely each day. That also includes on Thursdays when we don't have cross-country training."

"Oh, that's just wonderful!" Willow said with sincerity. "That'll take so much of the pressure off of me!"

She looked over at Jess and saw that Jess was grinning broadly, which she interpreted to mean that the coaches had already explained everything to her on the drive over to the house.

The head coach wagged a finger in the air. "Also, Mrs. Harris, we— I mean the cross-country team—will be responsible for picking Jess up for our meets and returning her home afterwards."

"So, you'll have nothing to worry about there," Coach Bixby added. "You know she's perfectly safe with us."

"Thank you, thank you both so much," Willow said, and tried not to cry.

Willow felt so grateful to God for taking this huge burden off of her heart, because prior to this moment, one of her biggest worries had been what David's reaction would be on hearing that Jess had had to quit her beloved running because of his heart attack.

Willow had worried that David's disappointment on hearing this would be enough to finish him off and send him to his early grave.

But now, thank you, God, that won't be happening.

CHAPTER 95

Saturday came along with the big Knight Night meet.

Full of excitement, Jess rode to the meet in her mother's car.

"You should have let the coaches pick me up," Jess told her mother as their car rolled along the twilit highway toward Kingwood, where the nighttime cross-country meet was being held. "You seem out on your feet."

Her mother shook her head and kept her eyes on the road. "I'm fulfilling the promise I made to your father. I told him that I'd decide on whether or not to attend this meet with you." She removed her eyes from the road for a moment, and looked sideway at Jess. The small smile on her face made Jess feel good. But then the smile faded. "I don't think it's fair that I'm going to this cross-country meet and your father can't be there. He wanted us all to be there together."

Jess laid a hand on her mother's arm. "It's okay, mom. I'm sure dad will improve soon."

Soon enough, they arrived at Preston High School, with all of its big tents and bright night lights.

***

When Jess removed her tracksuit, her teammates were surprised by the number of Bible verses she'd painted on her body. Big and small, the Bible verses were painted in marker in a multitude of colors, so that they commanded attention.

Everyone gathered around Jess and had a look at her.

"You look like a Jesus billboard," Coach Bixby told Jess. "How'd you do the ones on the back of your legs?"

"My mom did those," Jess admitted. "I couldn't get those right even using a mirror."

"At least you left your face free," team captain Cassie Henderson told her. "Remember what we've got planned to freak out the other teams here!"

Jess and the other girls laughed at the thought of that. "They won't know what hit them!" Ashley said.

"Okay, everyone, now calm down and let's go walk the course," Coach Bixby said.

So, the girls and boys left their tents and walked the course.

As they tramped along the running trail, which was a little bit wet due to a drizzle earlier that day, Jess agreed that yes, holding a competition at nighttime had a strange beauty and serenity to it. It wasn't just the hanging lights or the tiki torches that were placed along the trail; there was something about the silence, not just 'people silence,' but ambient silence, that made her feel calm.

Coach Bixby said: "You newbie girls, this is the biggest cross-country meet you've been in so far, so I'd better give you a few tips. There's so many girls running tonight that you'll need to be extra-careful to know where your teammates are."

Their group stopped beside a lit-up sign indicating that the trail went left here, and the coach waved a cautionary finger at them. "Hey, hey, don't let too many opposing runners get too far ahead of you, but don't overrun yourselves either. Don't expend too much energy trying to catch up with girls from the opposing teams. Run your own race. And always remember, this is a team play, not an individual one. Our aim here is to get the best five positions we can across the finish line. *Any five* of you, so, everyone, do your best. Today—I mean tonight—may be your own time to shine!"

After they'd warmed up with a short jog down the rest of the course and everyone had either returned to the tents or headed off to mingle with the other contestants before the races began, Coach Bixby called Jess aside.

"Jess, you heard what I said about everyone running for the team, didn't you?"

Jess felt upset and slighted. "C'mon, coach, you know I always run for the team."

"I don't mean it as a criticism," Coach Bixby replied with a smile on her face. "You're one of the best team players I've got. But from now on, I need you to upgrade that a little."

Jess gave her the appropriately confused look to indicate that she had no idea what Coach Bixby meant by what she'd just said.

Coach Bixby laughed. "Young lady, I just want you to realize that now, you're running for your father as well."

"Huh?"

"Jess, your dad really supported your running. And now that he's ill, it's your time to support him by winning. Each time you win—each time you contribute to our team carrying the day—your dad's gonna feel great when he hears about it or watches or reads about it online. Do you understand me?"

Jess nodded. "Yeah, my dad really loves it when I win."

"So, think of him while you're running, to inspire yourself," the coach said, "and hopefully, your performances will inspire him too and help his journey to recovery."

Jess grinned. "That makes sense. Thanks, coach."

"Don't mention it, girl. Remember, I'm always here for you if you need to talk about stuff."

Jess nodded. Coach Bixby walked off to deal with an issue concerning young Grace Tolbert's running shoes.

Jess really liked the coach's idea. She found it very inspiring.

Yes, she decided that she'd start dedicating her races and her wins to her father. If she got interviewed with the team, she'd make sure to mention him, which she knew would make him feel a lot better.

Dad's willing me to win and I'm willing him to win too.

***

Jess stepped outside the team tent to look around and was almost immediately met by a tall boy from another school who said hello.

"Hey, what's all of this you've got painted on you?" he asked next.

She laughed. "They're verses from the Bible to inspire me to run."

"That's really weird," he said. "Do you need that sort of inspiration?"

Jess shrugged. "You know what they say about fire extinguishers, right?"

"That you'd rather have one and not need it, instead of need one and not have it?" He nodded. "Yeah, I'm familiar with that."

"It's the same with me. When I feel my energy flagging, I look at this one—" she tapped her right thigh to indicate the giant 3-D-like ISAIAH 40:31 painted there, "—and I remember that God's gonna renew my strength and it bucks me up."

He looked amused. "You're serious? You really do that?"

"I guess you gotta have faith for it to work?" she replied. "What do you do when you're feeling the pain after the second mile of running?"

He shrugged. "I look inside myself and try to dredge up whatever's left inside the tank."

"It's the same principle, then. Just that you look *inside* yourself, and I look *outside* of myself." Jess raised her eyes heavenward. "One thing I know is, God's always got spare fuel for me."

"Oh, come on, now," a girl's voice said behind Jess. "Do you honestly think that God cares about what we're doing here tonight?"

Jess was about turning to see who'd spoken, but the girl was already stepping in front of her. She was a tall black girl from Ravenswood High School, whom Jess had raced against before."

"Do you think Jesus gives a damn what we're doing, running?" the girl asked. "Do you think that he's gonna help you beat the competition?"

"Yep, 'cos if he did, that'd be a lot like using paranormal performance-enhancing drugs," another boy who'd just joined them said.

Jess laughed. "Well, I don't know about Jesus helping beat others, but I do know that he's promised to help me do my very best in whatever *I* do." She tapped the dayglo words of Philippians 4:13 on her left forearm. "Yes, I really do believe that *I can* do all things through Christ who strengthens me. Okay, I know how silly that may sound, but it works." She grinned at the black girl. "Well, it works for me anyway. You gotta have faith, I think."

"I guess you're right," the black girl replied and went off to answer a team summons.

"I'd really like to believe in God like you do," another boy told Jess, "but everything I see keeps convincing me otherwise."

"Yeah," the first boy that Jess had met agreed. "You got all of these wars and starvation on the news and then there's all of the serial killers and pedophiles and . . ." He ran out of words and stared helplessly at her. "If God loves the world like Christians say he does, why is this place so messed up?"

"Well, everyone seems not to take Satan into consideration," Jess replied. "Every time something bad happens, God gets all of the blame. And yet, most of those bad things are the devil's fault. Take pedophiles, for instance. Nowhere in the Bible does it say that old people should abuse kids. That's all Satan's doing and—"

"Hold on a minute," the first boy said. "But the Bible says that God *made* the devil. So, isn't saying that God isn't responsible for the state of the world like saying the President of the United States isn't responsible for sending our troops to fight wars overseas?"

"Okay, but remember that Satan rebelled against God and—"

And so, the debate continued with other teenagers, male and female, freshmen, juniors and seniors, stopping to stare at Jess's scripture body-art, and occasionally joining in the discussion, while the clock ticked down to the start of the meet.

The impromptu discussion swung both ways, with some runners supporting Jess and others disagreeing about the roles of God and Jesus and the Holy Spirit in human affairs.

The discussion came to an end when College High team captain Cassie Henderson came to fetch Jess away from the others so that they could 'get ready,' as she told her with a conspiratorial wink.

***

"All female teams to the starting line!"

Once all of the girls' teams were assembled along the starting line in their starting boxes, the race official did a last-minute check.

They discovered that one team was missing. One starting box was empty.

Where was College High School's female cross-country team? Everyone acknowledged that they'd been present just a short while ago. Where had they suddenly vanished to?

Had they been abducted? Even the College High School coaches seemed puzzled and worried by their disappearance.

The officials all began worriedly looking at each other.

But then the air was rent by a piercing scream.

Everyone, officials, athletes and spectators, turned towards the noise.

The noise, which someone quickly likened to the cry of a hawk or other hunting bird, came again, and then it ceased.

And then, seemingly from out of nowhere, the College High female team burst onto the track yelling loudly.

They'd emerged from the midst of the spectators, about a hundred yards down the running course, and now they charged crazily at the other teams. One girl was holding up a College High School flag with a rampant hawk emblazoned on it.

Everyone watched the strange spectacle in varying degrees of confusion, shock and fright.

As the girls drew closer, it became easier to pick individuals out of the yelling throng.

Most prominent of all were Cassie and Jess, both running in front of the others, and both with their faces completely painted a glow-in-the-dark neon green, vividly set off against their yellow and red running clothes.

Then, like they were a machine regulated by clockwork, all of the girls stopped running at once.

While stomping their feet on the grass, first left and then right, and with the girl with the flag waving it wildly, they began chanting. They chanted gently at first, but the sound of their voices slowly grew louder.

After a while, the listeners made sense of what they were hearing: "WE ARE GOING TO WIN! WE WILL DEFEAT YOU ALL! WE ARE GOING TO WIN! WE WILL DEFEAT YOU ALL!! WE ARE GOING TO WIN! WE WILL DEFEAT YOU ALL!!! WE ARE GOING TO WIN! WE WILL DEFEAT YOU ALL!!!!!"

The girls' voices rose in volume until the noise seemed to spiral up out of hearing range and hit the clouds above, and then fall again on the listeners.

And then they stopped chanting and made that harrowing bird sound again, which was almost as agonizing to hear as nails on chalkboard, and then they ran forward at the other girls again.

Once more, they stopped and began stomping and flag-waving and yelling that tribal chant:
"WE ARE GOING TO WIN! WE WILL DEFEAT YOU ALL! WE ARE GOING TO WIN! WE WILL DEFEAT YOU ALL!! WE ARE GOING TO WIN! WE WILL DEFEAT YOU ALL!!! WE ARE GOING TO WIN! WE WILL DEFEAT YOU ALL!!!!!"

The officials made no attempt to interfere, they were as amused and bemused as everyone else there.

"Make them stop! They're frightening the other girls," one of the coaches from the opposing teams insisted to the officials.

But a female official laughed and shook her head. "There's no point doing that. They're headed for the starting line anyway."

Since the College High athletes were clearly headed for the starting line, the race officials let them take their time with it. It added to the spectacle of the event, and lots of people had their phones out and were recording them. A lot of the camera attention was focused on

Jess and Cassie, who both stood out starkly in that glowing green face paint.

Their opponents however, weren't amused at all. The strange tribal spectacle they were witnessing affected most of them somewhere deep inside, down in their subconscious minds where such instinctive uneasiness was impossible to either root up or logically reason away.

Most of these girls who were watching the College High girls were tough competitors, young women full of grit, and they pushed resolutely against the jitters that watching Jess and her teammates started in them; but each and every one of them was negatively affected in some way, their confidence shaken by what they were witnessing.

And then, just before hitting the starting line, the College High runners all stopped and yelled in unison:

"THIS IS OUR YARD NOW!

YES, IT'S OUR YARD NOW!

WE'RE GONNA WIN!

YOU'RE ALL GONNA LOSE!

LOSE LOSE LOSE LOSE LOSE!"

And then it was over. While the spectators had a good laugh and the other coaches tried to calm their runners' completely frazzled nerves at this critical last minute, Jess and her teammates calmly joined the starting line.

***

After that spectacle, the race finally happened.

The other competing teams put up a good fight, but their best efforts weren't good enough.

In the end, College High School completely devastated the competition.

That Knight Night, Cassie finished in first position, Jess came in fourth, and Brooke came in sixth. Ashley and Grace came in ninth and eleventh, respectively.

Their team tally of 31 points was the lowest by a long shot. The school that placed second to them had 42 points.

The College High School boys team also won, but not by such a devastating margin.

And then it was celebration time before the trophy was presented. And Jess, her face still painted that weird glow-in-the-dark green, went looking for her mother to share her delight.

CHAPTER 96

It was the Sunday evening after the Knight Night track meet, and Jess and Willow were sitting in David's hospital room.

Even though David was still incredibly weak, the doctors had finally taken him off their danger list.

To David's relief, he'd now been moved out of the ICU, into a private room with fewer machines. He also no longer needed the oxygen tank to breathe.

He could also talk for longer without feeling like passing out.

David was as delighted to see his wife and daughter as they were to see the improvement in his condition.

"Mr. Harris would love to get his feet under him again, but the doctors aren't taking any chances on letting him walk around yet," the attending nurse told them all. Then she smiled at David. "I'll leave you to relax with your family now, sir. Please, use the call button if you need me for anything."

"Thanks," David said, and the nurse left them to have their private conversations.

David listened with keen interest while Willow and Jess filled him in on the details about last night's cross-country meet.

"When Jess and those other teen girls ran out yelling and screeching like that, I almost had a heart attack of my own," Willow said.

David smiled weakly and then managed a full laugh. "I should've been there and seen that," he told his wife and daughter.

"Here I filmed some of it," Willow told him and then held her phone over in front of him to view. Jess hurried over to the bed to watch too.

"Hey, dad, I told everyone I was dedicating yesterday's race to you!" Jess told him.

"Thanks, honey," David told her.

David stared at the video of Jess and her teammates shrieking like madwomen and laughed aloud. "That's just crazy."

"Cassie is supposed to be Mama Hawk and I'm Baby Hawk," Jess explained. "I'm not sure if we won the meet because we were better than everyone else or if we won because we scared them half to death."

"It doesn't matter, dear," Willow said. "What matters is that your team won."

"But, mom," Jess went on, "is what we did even right? Does God approve of us scaring people like that?"

David saw that Willow was giving him a confused look and intervened in the discussion.

"Well, honey," he said, "what I can tell you is that at least we know God doesn't *disapprove* of you scaring your opponents."

He saw Jess was giving him a dubious look. "Yeah? Why?"

David laughed. "Well, remember when the Israelites were besieging the city of Jericho? God instructed Joshua and the Israelites to go round the city seven times on the seventh day and then to shout loudly. I'm sure that that shout would have totally rattled the citizens of Jericho. Scared some of them clean out of their skins."

"And then the walls fell down flat," Willow added. "So, you see, dear, you guys did the right thing to get your win that way."

"Yeah, I guess," Jess agreed.

"Don't count on it working again next year, tho' " David said. "Everyone will be wise to you girls by then and be expecting you to pull a similar stunt."

"How do you feel now?" Willow asked after they'd finished watching the race.

David thought about the question for a while.

"I feel like death warmed over," he replied to her. "The doctors say I'm much better than before, and I can see that, but I don't feel any better." Then he grinned at Jess and patted her hand. "But I'm

out of the ICU now, so something's definitely improved about me."
He grumbled. "I wish they'd at least let me use the bathroom on my
own, but no, I still gotta let the nurses handle all of that. It's frustrating
as hell. If I can get up and walk around, then I'd know for sure that
I'm improving, and I'd make a proper effort to get better. It really
hurts a guy's pride to have women looking after him like this."

David honestly hadn't expected the worried look that immediately
came over his wife's and daughter's faces.

"Oh no, buster, no you don't!" Willow said quickly. " 'Making a
proper effort' is what got you in here in the first place."

David conceded that she was right. "Oh, okay. I'll try to take it easy
then."

"When will you be coming home, daddy?" Jess asked.

David shook his head at her. "Not for a while yet, from what the
doctors say. They say that though I'm improved, they want to keep on
monitoring me, until they're certain that I'm completely out of
danger."

"I agree with them," Willow said, but Jess frowned.

"Why are you looking grumpy all of a sudden?" he asked Jess while
stroking her hair.

She sighed. "Dad, maybe we'll win the state cross-country title and
even qualify for the national championships too," she replied. "If we
do, it'll be great if you can be there to watch us win."

David shook his head sadly. "I'd love to be there to cheer you on,
honey, but that doesn't look like it'll happen this season. Maybe next
year, huh?"

Jess nodded.

David said. "You just keep on winning, kiddo. You guys keep on
giving your opponents hell."

Jess made a face at him. "Dad, we're *Christians*. Shouldn't that be
'give your opponents heaven?' "

David remembered their long-time-ago conversation at the
Thompson race track and laughed. "Just like I told you last time,
honey, give 'em hell that day, and heaven the next one."

Jess burst out laughing.

Then David and Jess had to explain the joke to Willow so she could enjoy it too.

CHAPTER 97

Time passed. Life went on, sometimes it moved as sluggishly as a snail, and sometimes it flew like a bird. Fall became winter, and the year flipped over.

***

Jess immersed herself fully in the Good Faith Assembly's Aspire Youth group and began pestering her parents to let her travel south to Tampa, Florida, for the church's upcoming youth retreat in the summer.

David said, 'Sure,' but Willow said, 'Maybe.'

Jess decided to let God work it out for her.

In the meantime, her pseudo-evangelism at interschool meets continued. Of course, she'd not set out to actually preach to anyone. But even though she'd begun writing the verses on herself to encourage herself in the Lord, the more she kept on doing so, the more attention her unusual body art drew to her.

So, at just about every track meet now, young Jess Harris would find herself the subject of curious scrutiny by male and female teens who wanted to know why in the world she had John 3:16, Phil 4:13, Isaiah 40:31, and other such scriptures brightly drawn on her arms and legs.

Jess did her best to give everyone a sensible answer.

***

Jess and the College High School girls' cross-country team continued to dominate the other high schools in West Virginia. Plus, with College High's close proximity to the Pennsylvania state line, they also had plenty of meets with other out-of-state school districts in PA and Ohio.

Just like Jess had told David that they might do, their school's male and female teams swept the state cross-country championships, and then everyone set their focus on attaining national dominion as well.

The national cross-country championships would shortly be held, and everyone on the teams was training like mad.

By now, even though Jess was still a freshman, she'd become a highly influential and respected member of the team. Just like had happened before while she was at Thompson Middle School, everybody had quickly realized that they ran better when she was on the team. The other female first-year students looked up to her as their leader, and once she'd realized this, she did her best to fulfil that role.

So, Jess excelled on the cross-country trail.

***

Taking her mother's feelings into consideration, Jess did her best in class also.

It was debatable whether she might have gotten better grades had she not been running after school, as she maintained a 4.0 GPA throughout her freshman year. She had even taken two Advanced Placement classes, which were typically reserved for one's sophomore and later years if a student proved they were smart enough to handle the curriculum.

Her father said no, and her mother said yes.

When asked, Jess said she didn't know and pointed to her teammates, who were an eclectic mix of near-genius to near-dyslexic.

"Nothing works for everyone," Coach Bixby told her once.

As it stood presently, her straight A's were good enough for all concerned.

CHAPTER 98

And finally, the national cross company championships arrived.

This year the nationals were being held in the West Virginian capital of Charleston.

The atmosphere on the school bus during the ride over to Charleston was chaotic. Everyone, including the coaches, was super-excited. This was the chance to win the big one.

On arriving in the city of Charleston, Jess felt overwhelmed by anticipation.

Driving through Charleston to the venue, being greeted and processed through by the officials, checking into their hotel accommodation. Everything passed in a blur of teenage excitement and emotions. There was so much to do and so much to see and the fun of it all.

After checking in, they rode out to the cross-country course they would be competing on. The starting point for the race was a beehive of activity, with workmen still erecting tents and concessions, trucks bringing in loads of foldaway chairs and tables and other furniture, volunteers taking all kinds of measurements and putting up signs everywhere, and officials making last-minute tweaks to their logistics calculations.

The College High students jogged around the cross-country course twice to get in that day's practice without taxing themselves.

Several teams from the other states were there doing the same thing.

Afterwards they drove back to their hotel and had dinner with those contestants from the other teams who were rooming in the same hotel.

And then night fell and passed in sweet dreams of glory.

And just about everyone woke up feeling tense the next morning.

CHAPTER 99

After having her bath the next morning, Jess got Ashley Roach to help her with painting her scripture verses on her body. She hadn't done it yesterday because of her fears that the colors would smear once hit with sufficient soap and water.

"I like how you don't joke with this stuff," Ashley told her. "I wish I was as bold as you are. You're a real track evangelist. I love how everyone asks you about the scriptures and you turn them into a witness for Jesus."

Jess laughed and convinced Ashley to at least paint a John 3:16 on her own left thigh.

And then the two girls prayed together for God's help and strength that day.

***

Arriving at the cross-country course again that noon, the atmosphere felt very different.

All of those pleasant emotions that Jess had felt during yesterday's visit here seemed very far away now, like they too were components of last night's dream.

Despite her best efforts to calm herself as she and her team walked towards the officials, Jess felt extremely tense.

Indeed, her tension was clearly shared by most of her teammates. Ashley, Brooke, Grace, and even team leader Cassie Henderson seemed intimidated by the competition.

And the boys weren't immune either. Toby Green, who'd also never been at a national meet before, looked like he'd throw up from sheer nerves.

There were just so many contestants. Everywhere Jess looked, she saw more and more young adults getting ready to compete, kids at peak fitness. Each of these teenage runners had looks of utter concentration on their faces, like they intended to trample Jess and the rest of the competition face-down into the running trail.

"How in the world are we gonna even place in the top ten rankings, let alone win? she wondered, as the officials assigned everyone their race bibs.

Adding to everyone's nerves were the tons of news reporters and camera crews stalking everywhere. There were camera drones overhead, and in a nearby field, helicopters waited as if there was a military operation in progress.

"Listen, boys and girls," Coach Jameson told everyone during a group huddle, "this ain't any different from any of those other competitions that you've run in. Sure, you're feeling the nerves now, but once that starter pistol goes and you start running, that's it. All of that adrenaline that's now giving the 'flight' response is automatically gonna flip its own switch into the 'fight' response. You wait and see."

"Coach, I'm just surprised there's so many people," Toby said. "We've watched this on TV more than once, but here in person, it's like an ocean of people out there, waiting to drown us all."

"Yeah, seeing so many people makes me feel like a drop in the ocean," Jess added.

"The *most significant* drop, Jess," Coach Bixby told her and her young colleagues. "Make sure you keep that in mind, you and your teammates are the most significant drops in the running waters here. Each and every one of you has the grit to do this. You all know your personal best times and they're as good and even better than those of the other contestants here. So, the only thing that's stopping you boys and girls from winning here today is your own minds, your own fears."

Coach Jameson nodded. "Yeah, like the old saying: 'we got nothing to fear . . .'" He waved a hand at the teams to indicate that they

complete the sentence themselves. "Yeah, guys, we got nothing to fear
..."

"... But fear itself," they all repeated.

"Hey, lemme hear that one more time!"

"But fear itself!"

"Okay, guys, let me have the whole thing this time. And say it like
you mean it."

"WE HAVE NOTHING TO FEAR BUT FEAR ITSELF!!!"

The head coach grinned and said: "Hahaha, yeah. Now y'all get it.
The only one who can defeat any of you here today is you yourself.
Don't forget that. No one out there is really better than any of you.
It's all in your heads and in their heads, too. Your bodies are fit and
strong, and so you've gotta be strong in your minds also."

Coach Jane Bixby nodded. "Yeah, guys, remember that: No one
out there can defeat you: You can only defeat yourself."

"Okay, now that y'all in the right frame of mind for the
competition, let's get some warmups in," the head coach told them.

***

There was still some time before the girls' race would begin.

Jess felt very sad that her father was too ill to watch her compete in
the national finals, more so because with the meet held in Charleston,
the distance he'd have had to travel to do so was just a two-hour drive,
a mere stone's throw from Bridgeport.

*But daddy's still in the hospital, and the doctors can't make up their mind if
he's getting better or worse.*

Her father's doctors seemed to change their minds weekly about his
condition. One week they'd say David Harris could be out of the
hospital by next Tuesday, and then, the Monday before that Tuesday,
they'd recant and decided they needed to run additional tests on him.

Jess knew the uncertainty was driving her mother crazy.

I'd like it to be over too.

But then she brightened up a little:

But, with all of these news people here, he's gonna get to watch the race on TV!

"Oh, heavenly father, please help me run the race of my life today. Help my team to win so I can dedicate the win to you and to my dad!"

Then she settled down again and once more tried not to worry about Chloe Zana and Tima Ziffa, who both had the fastest cross-country times this year, or about Gadsden High, who'd blown the wheels off the competition with a dazzling sweep of all five top positions in the New Mexico state championships.

And then it was time to run.

CHAPTER 100

The girls ran first.

Everyone assembled in their teams' starting boxes along the start line. There were girls, girls, and more girls as far as Jess could see, which wasn't exactly very far, seeing as she wasn't the tallest girl there.

In front of her lay the course, left and right were the long line of spectators and camera-people behind fences, and behind those, tents, cars, and the rest of the world.

But the rest of the world didn't matter at all now.

Jess looked at her arm. "I can do all things, through Christ who strengthens me," she chanted to herself under her breath.

"Lord God, help me run my best race ever today," she prayed.

As if to convince herself that she was in the right place, she looked around at her teammates, each of whom looked both determined and tense in their own way.

Jess was relieved that it wasn't a particularly windy day, which would have created its own problems for them.

"Listen, you biatches," Cassie told them all through gritted teeth, "if you forget everything else for the next twenty-five minutes, remember this one thing: that we're here today because we *damn well deserve* to be here. We earned our spot at this championship because we're as good as these other girls are!"

"And this is our chance to show that we're better than they are!" Jess found herself adding.

"Yes, we are!" her teammates agreed loudly.

A girl from Florida heard what she'd said and smirked at her. Jess shrugged back, completely unfazed now.

The starter pistol went 'Bang!' and they were on their way.

CHAPTER 101

Jess had run in large groups before, but this was crazy. Thirty-eight schools were competing in this national meet, meaning she was running against two hundred and sixty-five other girls.

Her previous comparison of feeling like a drop in an ocean really came back to haunt her now.

There's so many of us! It's like we don't even matter at all as individuals. With this number of people, some of us could vanish and no one would ever find us!

But still, unreasoning dread aside, it was supremely intimidating to be running against this number of girls.

Jess's number was 184, which clearly stated, on her chest and back, like a target for the others to shoot at, that there were 183 young adult women numbered before her, including Cassie at 180.

But there indeed was a danger of running with so many people at first because it created a misplaced sense of community, presenting the facade of one's being involved in a cooperative venture rather than a competitive one.

Oh no, Jess told herself to counter that dulling feeling: *Today it's every woman for herself . . . and for her team.*

"Let's move up," Cassie told Jess. "We need to keep up with Zana and Ziffa."

Chloe Zana and Tima Ziffa were two East African girls who held the records for fastest speeds for the past two years. The pair both attended Lincoln Mission High in Missouri, who were the defending girls' USA high school cross-country champions, and who were everyone's favorite to win this year too.

Both were currently leading the mob of runners by a distance of about fifteen meters, just a short distance behind the jeep that led the way along the race course and filmed the front runners.

Wishing she lived up in the Allegheny Mountains to get an oxygen advantage too, Jess accelerated alongside Cassie till they were running ahead of the wolf pack, behind the two black girls.

She looked back and saw that Ashley, Brooke and their other teammates were following their lead, pushing forward through the throng and staking a claim at the front of the field.

So far, so good, Jess thought. *But it's still early minutes yet.*

***

At the end of the second kilometer, Jess assessed her team's progress so far and decided everyone was running okay today.

By now, as they followed the Jeep's course alongside a river, Jess had become aware of a significant difference between home contests and this national one.

Here, even closing on halfway through their 3.1-mile run, there was almost zero separation between the runners. A few glances behind them confirmed that there seemed to be very few stragglers also.

She mentioned this to Cassie.

"That's 'cos today, we're competing against the best of the best," Cassie replied as the river part of the course ended and they started up a low hill.

The hill proved fortunate, as it enabled Jess and Cassie to gain ground on Zana and Ziffa, who appeared to be better at running on level ground.

But the hill was taking its toll on Jess, too.

It was right now, like it always happened to her, that she reached that point where running turned from being pleasant exercise to being stressful exertion. Runners affectionally called this point "The Wall."

Most other times, reaching this point in a race angered Jess, but today, she welcomed it.

She lifted her left arm. "I can do all things through Christ who strengthens me," she read off of it, and then she slipped into the same meditative zone that she entered during training.

They that wait upon the Lord shall renew their strength,
They shall mount up with wings like eagles,
They shall run and not be weary . . .

She felt her willpower overriding the strain that had begun plaguing her limbs.

The feeling of her body doing too much was still present, but now Jess felt like she'd turned it outwards as a weapon against her opponents, rather than inward at herself.

She slipped completely into her running zone. Her world contracted to herself and the runners closest to her, the Jeep up ahead that led the way, the ground—sand, mud, or grass—that her feet ran over, and the open sky above in which strangely shaped camera-equipped mechanical birds now floated.

They hit the third mile/last kilometer running hard and fast.

By now, knowing that the point of no return in this contest of hard young bodies and wills would soon be reached, at least fifteen other girls had moved up out of the throng to keep pace with Jess and Cassie.

Jess felt a nudge at the peripheral of her running 'zone.' She slipped out of her space of meditation and stared at Cassie, who nodded at her.

Jess nodded back. She understood what Cassie meant.

***

Coaches Jameson and Bixby had given the team a running plan.

"Listen carefully here. We've got one real chance to win this one," Coach Jameson had told them. "Don't let those two African girls out of your sight. Stick to them like white sticks on rice." Coach Jameson had next looked each of his female runners in the eyes, taking his time to move his gaze from each one to the next, before saying: "And now, here's the thing you gotta do: We're gonna hit 'em before they hit us."

"Huh?" Jess had asked. "What do you mean, coach?"

The head coach had laughed. "It's simple. Coach Bixby and I did some cross-checking on each of your running times, and we think that, given the right tactics, you can beat those girls."

"But to do so, you can't wait like the others for them to make their break at the end," Jane Bixby had come in saying. "We've watched their races, and they normally power up to run that final stretch at about a hundred and fifty meters from the finish line." She scowled. "So, what all of you are gonna do is go earlier than that. You make your own push at about two hundred meters out."

"That'll catch them off guard and make them panic. At the best you'll knock 'em for a loop. At the worst, you're certain to get places on the podium."

Then Coach Jameson frowned. "That goes for all of you young ladies, not just Cassie and Jess. Once you reach that point, each of you run like you've been doused in gasoline and the girls behind you are racing after you with matches to light you on fire 'cos you stole their boyfriends!"

Everyone had laughed. Jess had laughed loudest of all.

***

Yesterday, it had sounded like a fantastic plan.

Today? Jess didn't know. The fact that everyone here was the crème de la crème of high school cross-country meant that she was almost running at her best already just to keep up with them.

And it looks like Cassie is, too. So, how are we gonna get up any final burst of energy to rattle everyone else?

By now, the spectators, who'd previously been relatively sparse in number along the cross-country course, had greatly increased in number to crowd-strength. The final line was clearly coming up.

The crowds began cheering the runners on.

Cassie was certain to give the signal to break out from the pack soon.

But am I gonna have enough left to do it?

It was a question that Jess felt unable to answer, because already, on her and Cassie's right and left, some of the other runners were starting to overtake them, jostling for finishing positions in what was certain to be a very closely contested finish.

A glance back for the same bibs revealed that Brooke and Ashley, while still in sight, were visibly being swallowed up in the ocean of female bodies.

How are we gonna do this?

And then, a verse of scripture came to Jess's mind; *He maketh my feet like hinds' feet.*

That startled Jess. She knew this scripture was in the Bible, but it wasn't one of those she'd painted on herself.

He maketh my feet like hinds' feet.

The words floated in Jess's head until she accepted them as a divine message to herself.

All of a sudden Jess got it. She smiled to herself.

Yep, I got this! she thought. *God makes my feet like hinds' feet. Hinds are deer and they run pretty fast! Haha!*

A moment later, Cassie nodded to her. It was 'Go' time…time to *kick it!*

Jess hit her personal gas pedal and went all out. She ran like she'd never run before, as if she really was doused in gasoline and everyone else in the race, including her own teammates, was out to set her ablaze.

***

Chloe Zana and Tima Ziffa were taken completely by surprise. Yes, others had challenged their dominance of the cross-country course, but never from so far out.

Normally, those contenders all waited for them to make their own run before panicking and attempting to catch them, which never paid dividends.

And yet, all of a sudden, two girls were sprinting past them.

The two black girls looked at one another for a few moments and then set off after them.

After that it was a mad run for the finish line, with Zana and Ziffa now finding themselves at a disadvantage because their running plan had been upset, and Jess and Cassie (who'd gained about a 5-meter lead over their two African counterparts before Zana and Ziffa began giving chase) doing their utmost to not let those two young women catch them.

With the high quality of the competition forcing a high pace to the race, everyone was already hurting and close to their personal speed and endurance limit, but now, even the weakest teenage young woman on that cross-country course cranked up their internal gears and ran harder.

The crowd packed behind the fences was going hysterical, now, screaming like mad.

Two hundred meters to go . . . One-fifty . . . One hundred . . . Fifty . . . Thirty . . .

Jess and Cassie, Zana and Ziffa and about eight other girls who'd broken out from the wolf pack where the main contenders.

By now, Jess ran without seeing who was beside her. That was totally unimportant. She hoped that Cassie was keeping up with her but she didn't glance either sideways or behind her to confirm that she was.

Where Cassie was now didn't matter.

What *was* important and what was Jess's sole aim now, was that no one get *in front* of her.

And as she closed in on the finish line and finish gate, with the crowd screaming like mad all around her, Jess realized that no one *had* gotten in front of her.

Feet like hinds' feet! she thought as she crossed the finish line in first place. *Feet like hinds' feet!*

Jess ran herself to a standstill. And then, on realizing that she'd just run and won the race of her life, she dropped to her knees.

Exhausted beyond belief, and feeling like she was about to throw up, she began weeping and thanking God.

CHAPTER 102

Coach Bixby ran over to Jess, helped her to her feet, and handed her a bottle of Gatorade.

And then, as the main throng of the runners began arriving through the finish gate, Jess was grabbed and hugged by Cassie.

They began nervously checking the positions and times on the giant electronic scoreboard near the finishing line.

Jess had come in first.

Tima Ziffa was second.

Cassie was third.

Chloe Zana was fourth.

Then there had been a gap, and Ashley crossed the line in twentieth position. Brooke was thirty-sixth.

Along with their individual positions, the scoreboard was also aggregating each high school's finishing positions into a tally of their first five.

College High was currently first with sixty points, but needed that all-critical high-enough final position to seal their win.

The closest team to them was Crystal Mathis High School from Wyoming with 92 points. So, as long as their own fifth runner did well, they were solid contenders for the win.

And then they saw Tiffany Welsh, normally one of their slower varsity runners, charging towards the finish line, running like mad in her haste to finish.

"It looks like we're gonna do it!" Cassie told everyone excitedly.

"Come on, Tiff, just one more!" Jess yelped just as excitedly.

Once Tiffany Welsh crossed the finish line in fifty-second place, it was over.

"Ladies and Gentlemen, I'm pleased to announce to you all that with a score of one hundred and twelve points, College High School from West Virginia has won this year's AAA Female National High School Cross-Country Championships!"

The jubilations and celebrations and TV interviews began in earnest.

It turned out that Jess had also smashed the national girls cross-country record with a new time of 14 minutes 57 seconds.

"I'm dedicating this victory to my dad, David Harris, who's currently in the hospital recovering from a heart attack," Jess told the reporters. "And I thank God too for helping me win it!"

CHAPTER 103

The College High boys didn't do well in their own race. But the girls' victory was infectious enough for everyone to share in.

And yet, standing up there on the winners' podium to receive the gold medal with her teammates, Jess found her victory bittersweet.

Yes, we're the national champions, but how much better it would've been if dad were here to watch me win. But I thought mom was going to be here. I couldn't get her on the phone earlier and . . . Oh, maybe she wanted to watch the race with dad in the hospital.

It was sad to be here alone at this moment of ultimate triumph. But then the medal presentations began, and Jess allowed the sheer glory of the moment to swallow her up.

In third place, Crystal Mathis High School from Wyoming.

In second place, Deep Valley High School from Texas.

"Hahaha! It's us next," Ashley giggled in delight. "We're winners!"

"You can say that again!" Cassie agreed brightly. "Jess ran so hard today that if she wasn't a Christian, I'd test her myself for performance enhancers."

"God enhanced me!" Jess said. "Ha ha ha!"

All the girls laughed. Over on the side of the podium, head coach Jensen, ladies coach Jane Bixby, and the other assistant coaches waited to receive their own medals too.

"Hey, Jess, aren't those your parents over there?" Cassie asked suddenly.

Jess froze like someone had hit her on the head with a 2-by-4. "Huh? Where?"

Cassie pointed. "Over *there*. Beside the old couple wearing straw hats."

Jess stared, and then she too recognized the pair of familiar beloved faces in the crush of people opposite the winner's podium. She did a double-take and then another.

Visibly supported by her mother while standing, her father was nonetheless up on his feet and waving at her, as was her mother. Both had broad smiles on their faces.

What!? Mom and dad are here? YAAAAY!

Tears of happiness filled Jess's eyes and ran down her cheeks.

She began leaping up wildly and waving and yelling at her parents: "HEY, MOM, HEY, DAD!!! I DID IT, DAD, I DID IT!!!"

The officials tactfully waited until Jess had calmed down a little before awarding her team their medals.

PART FOUR:
EPILOGUE

CHAPTER 104

Jess later discovered that her father had been scheduled for discharge yesterday, but that he and her mother had kept the news from her, so that they could surprise her at the cross-country meet.

She wasn't certain which delighted her more: the fact that she and her teammates had won the national title, or the fact that her father had finally been declared healthy enough to return home to her and her mother.

CHAPTER 105

Jess returned to College High School to a heroine's welcome. All of the girls' team did, but no one could forget the screen images of Jess racing ahead of the crowd to win first place.

"We did it," she told the crowded high school assembly. "God Almighty helped me and we won!"

There were several people listening who took Jess's statement of God's help with a pinch of salt, but no one dared voice that contrary opinion.

Then Jess remembered—there was still one person to whom Jess wanted to show her championship medal. . .

***

Jess stood outside the church after the Sunday morning service, the crisp autumn air brushing against her skin. Her medal from the national championship still hung from her neck, catching sunlight with every movement. A few girls from her youth group clustered nearby, laughing and chatting. Jess smiled, but her eyes searched the parking lot for someone else.

Then she saw her.

Rose Hodder, carrying a well-worn Bible and a thermos of coffee, waved as she made her way over. Her stride wasn't fast, but it was steady—the same steady presence Jess remembered from her very first week at church.

"There's my little firecracker," Rose said with a wink. "Still running circles around the devil?"

Jess laughed. "Trying to. One lap at a time."

Rose reached out and gently touched the medal. "You've come a long way, Jess. But it's not the gold around your neck that shines the most—it's the light in your eyes. I'm proud of you."

Jess swallowed a lump in her throat. "You helped me start all this. If you hadn't been there when I first came, I don't know where I'd be."

Rose nodded thoughtfully. "That's the beauty of faith, sweetheart. Sometimes all it takes is one person to show up... and God does the rest."

She paused and opened her Bible, flipping to a marked page. "You know what I've been praying for you?"

Jess shook her head gently.

Rose smiled and read aloud:

"'But they that wait upon the Lord shall renew their strength; they shall mount up with wings as eagles; they shall run, and not be weary; and they shall walk, and not faint.'— *Isaiah 40:31* "

Jess closed her eyes. The verse didn't just sound beautiful—it was alive in her. She had carried those words onto the track, scrawled them on her arms, whispered them before races, and lived them through pain and perseverance. And now, hearing them spoken back to her, it felt like God Himself was affirming the truth she had once declared in faith.

"That's your race now, Jess," Rose said. "Not just on the track— but in life. You keep running toward God, and He'll carry you farther than your legs ever could."

They stood in silence for a moment, the weight of it all settling sweetly between them. And then, without needing to say anything more, Jess reached out and hugged her.

***

After that, Jess's life returned to normal. She continued training, differently now because the spring/summer track and field season was about to begin again, and she was about to start doing sprints again.

Realizing that she had a positive influence on her teammates, the coaches put Jess in charge of the younger athletes, who didn't yet understand how life-changing sports could be.

Jess shared her own story of faith and perseverance with these young girls and boys and helped a lot of them develop a firm foundation, both in competitive track sports and in the Christian faith.

On the track, people continued to inquire about the Bible verses that she painted on herself before races.

Jess took every opportunity to enlighten others about the love of God for lost mankind and the sacrifice of his son Jesus Christ for the world.

Jess's church participation grew even more fervent. She began regularly traveling to evangelistic outreaches with the youth group and sharing her story there also.

And yes, she did attend the summer youth retreat down in Tampa, Florida like she wanted to.

Best of all, Jess continued running. Running into the future, running into the hope she saw in each brand-new day that dawned.

And Jess kept on winning races.

CHAPTER 106

David Harris's health continued to improve.

Of course, he'd learned his lesson now and resolved never to overwork himself again.

Really, he had no choice: the doctors had insisted that he trim his workload by half if he didn't want to suffer another heart attack.

David's consulting business finally took off, but with a couple of employees handling the legwork for him.

David was grateful to God for keeping him alive.

He was even more grateful to God for turning Jess's life around as miraculously as he'd done.

Her journey. Her incredible comeback from depression to champion was wonderful to behold. Truly wonderful.

If David had one thing that truly inspired him to heed his doctor's instruction to get better, it was his desire not to miss any of the beautiful steps that Jess would be taking as she grew into the woman she would become, the young woman he was certain God wanted her to be.

"Hon, I'm truly grateful to God for getting your life back *on track*," he told Jess one evening while the family was having dinner at a restaurant.

And everyone laughed at that.

CHAPTER 107

Step by step, Willow Harris realized that she couldn't mold her daughter into a clone of herself.

One day, while driving the backroads of Dodridge County to an early evening house showing, it hit her: That what she was really doing was attempting to make a replica of herself out of Jess.

And now it also became obvious why the project was failing. She and her daughter were entirely different in nature.

Okay, I'll admit it to myself: it's not like Jess is actually doing badly in school. She's scoring about the same grades as she did before that nasty rape mess happened to her. It's just that I think she'd do even better if academics were all she had to think about, that's all.

Yes, I'm plan-driven and highly strung, and Jess is laid-back like her father. I just wish she was more in my mold of person.

The late spring countryside zipped past her car in all its bright greenery, and she thought pleasantly of David, who was now well enough to once again drop Jess off at school in the mornings and bring her home again in the evenings after her track and field training.

As Willow thought of David, tears formed in her eyes.

Thank you, heavenly father, she prayed silently. *Thank you, my Lord God for keeping my husband alive for both myself and my daughter to keep enjoying his company. I don't know what I'd have done if he'd been taken from me and I'm glad I don't need to find out.*

Willow slowed at a red light. Thinking of all that God had done for her, Willow Harris reached a decision.

"You know what, Lord?" she said aloud, while once more fiercely concentrating her gaze on the highway ahead. "I think I've been too harsh on Jess, put too much pressure on her to become my kind of person. But she's not me and she'll never be me. So, Lord God, I hand Jess over to you totally from the bottom of my heart. *You* mold her into what *you* want her to be."

Willow sighed, half a sigh of acceptance of God's sovereignty in her life; half a sigh of regret that it had taken her so long to understand the true meaning of so simple a biblical principle: "Not my will be done in this, o Lord, but thine."

The End.

ABOUT THE AUTHOR

Gary Lee Vincent was born in Clarksburg, West Virginia, and is an accomplished author, musician, actor, producer, director, and entrepreneur. To date, he has written over two dozen novels and created several mini-series.

As an actor, Gary has appeared in over seventy feature films and multiple television series, including *House of Cards*, *Mindhunter*, *The Walking Dead*, and *Stranger Things*.

As a director, Gary made his directorial debut with *A Promise to Astrid*. He has also directed the films *Desk Clerk*, *Dispatched*, the 2020 remake of John Russo's iconic horror film *Midnight*, *Godsend*, and *Strange Friends*.

Also by Gary Lee Vincent:

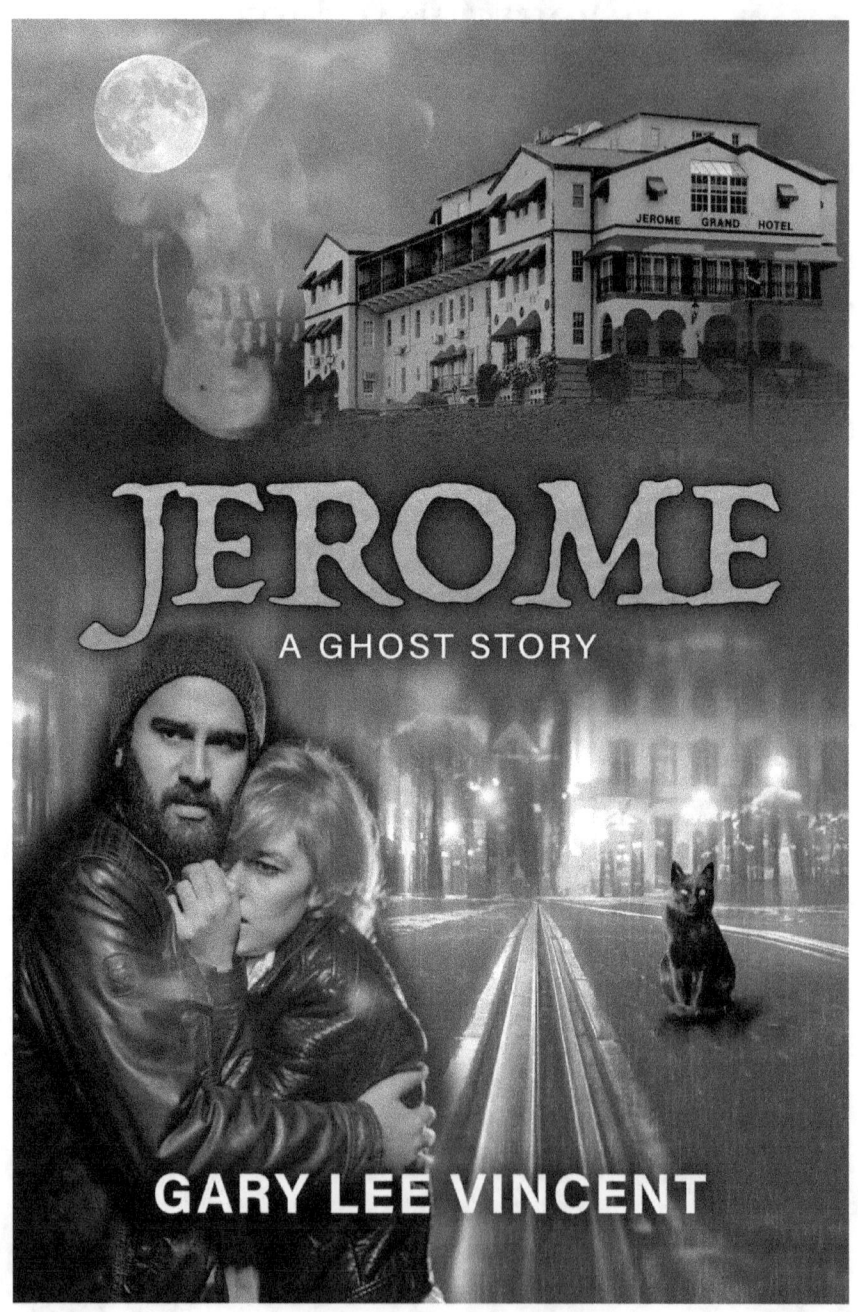

JEROME

A GHOST STORY

GARY LEE VINCENT